Champagne and a Gardener

Champagne and a Gardener

A Little Maine Murder

B. J. MORISON

Thorndike Press • Thorndike, Maine

Library of Congress Cataloging in Publication Data:

Morison, Betty Jane, 1924—
   Champagne and a gardener.

   I. Title.
PS3563.87167C5 1982   813'.54   82-16787
ISBN 0-89621-069-3
ISBN 0-89621-070-7 (pbk.)

Copyright 1982 by Betty Jane Morison. All rights reserved.

Acknowledgement: From the "Author's Note" in GAUDY NIGHT by Dorothy Sayers. Copyright, 1936, by Dorothy Leigh Sayers Fleming. Reprinted by permission of Harper & Row, Publishers, Inc.

To the three generations of Elizabeths who knew Mount Desert Island — to the still-remembered Bessie, to kind Blip, and to my own dear Liz, who helped — this little *divertissement* (as we say on M.D.I.) is affectionately dedicated.

Those who love the island also appreciate the soft Maine twang of many of its inhabitants. To reproduce it faithfully in print, however, except on occasion, has so many attendant difficulties as to cause the speakers to appear as mere bucolic caricatures of themselves. Little attempt at reproduction, therefore, is made in this narrative.

FOREWORD
TO MY FIRST READER

Dear Wendy,

Mount Desert Island indubitably exists, as you have known longer than I, and nothing I could say of it can to any degree add to or detract from its beauty and unique charm. You may not agree with some of my observations of it and its people, but the picture I give should be regarded as one person's version only — as a painting rather than a photograph.

Since we know some of the same people, and have heard some of the same stories, a few of the characters or incidents may seem familiar to you; however, (as you have known, also, longer than I) it is very hard to keep well-known characters and traits from influencing fictional characters. I do assure you that in this fantasy no character is intended as a portrait of any person who lives or has ever lived, nor is meant to bring even fleetingly to mind any such person, with the exceptions of the characters of Persis and Elizabeth Lamb, who are Emmy and Liz as they might have been in their childhood.

As Dorothy Sayers included in her foreword to her immortal *Gaudy Night:* "For, however realistic the background, the novelist's only native country is Cloud-Cuckooland, where they do but jest, poison in jest: no offence in the world."

B.J.M.
Bar Harbor, 1982

CONTENTS

THE DOCUMENTS BEFORE THE CURTAIN	13
Chapter 1 — THE BACKDROP	19
Chapter 2 — THE SET	24
Chapter 3 — PRELIMINARY REHEARSALS	29
Chapter 4 — INTERMISSION WITH EXIT LINE	38
Chapter 5 — INTERMISSION WITHOUT	42
Chapter 6 — INTERLUDE ON ANOTHER PORCH	48
Chapter 7 — ENTER THE INGENUE	56
Chapter 8 — OVER THE RIVER AND THROUGH THE WOODS	66
Chapter 9 — THE PLAYERS ASSEMBLE	72
Chapter 10 — THE BUNGALOW AT NIGHT	85
Chapter 11 — CONVERSATIONS BY CANDLELIGHT, 1	96
Chapter 12 — MAINE MORNING	103
Chapter 13 — TO THE MOUNTAIN	114
Chapter 14 — MOUNTAIN SCENERY	121

Chapter 15 —	TEA AND ATMOSPHERE	132
Chapter 16 —	DRINKS AND DIALOGUE	142
Chapter 17 —	CONVERSATIONS BY CANDLELIGHT, 2	168
Chapter 18 —	BY GUESS AND BY GOD	175
Chapter 19 —	ENTER THE INVESTIGATOR	182
Chapter 20 —	TIME AND TIDE	202
Chapter 21 —	SOLILOQUY, WITH ANSWER, BY CANDLELIGHT	216
THE DOCUMENTS AFTER THE CURTAIN		223

THE PLAYERS
(In Order of Appearance)

F. Hill Halstead—a Boston attorney, with a Philadelphia background.

Sarah Worthington Halstead—his wife. A most proper young Boston matron.

Elizabeth Elbridge Worthington—(Mrs. Otis Worthington, Jr.) a Bostonian *grande dame,* with artistic talents, mother of three children: Sarah, Peter, and Isabella.

Doreen Dorr—the cook's daughter.

Mrs. Wilson (Lettice) Parker—a magnate in rope-making; a woman of decision.

The Grafin Isabella Worthington von Lichtenfeld—a free spirit, and Mrs. Worthington's youngest child.

Emily Elbridge—the spinster sister of Elizabeth Worthington. A world traveler.

Horatio Blanchard—a strange young man, son of Frederick and Kitty Blanchard.

Capt. Frederick Blanchard—a naval personage.

Kitty Blanchard—the Captain's lady. A sweet Virginian and a dedicated mother.

Pherousa Blanchard—the Blanchards' daughter.

Junior Noyes—a caretaker, called June by his intimates.

Persis Halstead—the young daughter of Hill and Sarah. A bird-watcher.

Elizabeth Lamb—an eight-year-old gourmet and woman of the world.

Jane Lamb—her mother, a secretary.

Varner Prouty—a Native.

Augustus Worthington Halstead—Persis' older brother. A devotee of sailing and of both high and low cuisine.

Dora Dorr—a Native, a cook, and no fool.

Peyton Dorr—Dora's brother, a store-keeper and general hand.

General Lemuel Otis Alison—Mrs. Worthington's cousin. A retired Marine, a wit, and a writer of history and rhymes.

Miss Thurna Thorssen—his secretary, from Iceland via Radcliffe.

Henry Wasgatt—a Worthington cousin and a movie theatre owner.

Betsy Wasgatt—his wife.

Buzzie Higgins—a deputy sheriff.

Peter Worthington—a black sheep.

THE DOCUMENTS
BEFORE THE CURTAIN

From F. Hill Halstead to Mrs. Wheeler Knox; Secretaries Unlimited, New York, N.Y.:

June 10

Dear Dodie:
    To conclude our telephone conversation of day before yesterday, may I inform you that my mother-in-law has quite definitely decided that, of the applicants whose curriculum vitae she has received from you, Mrs. Jane Lamb will be most suitable for her needs? My delay in confirming this has been because of Mrs. Lamb's child, but if she must accompany her mother (and Mrs. Worthington's offer to pay a one hundred dollar bonus if the little girl can possibly be left in New York still stands), then so be it. We should like them to reach The Bungalow by Friday, June 22.

The salary Mrs. Lamb requests is acceptable to Mrs. Worthington, though a bit high by our cold-roast-Bostonian standards, as you will remember. I, for one, had better not complain, after the hell I have been through these past weeks helping to interview every creature in Boston who could type and who had the slightest excuse to a claim to some knowledge of art. By the time we had finished with the first dozen, my mother-in-law was treating them like kitchen-maids caught nipping at what is left of her *Nautilius* madeira, and I was treating myself to anything I could find on the sideboard. I have not seen her so quietly and so thoroughly furious and disgusted since Peter decamped, unless it was when she later learned of his marriage to that Parisienne shopgirl.

I am still congratulating myself for consulting you, though it was really Sarah who remembered you were now running an agency for secretaries. I gather you are making a success of it, but what a long way you have come from Miss Winsor's! One of these days, though, Sarah and your other Winsor schoolmates will be imploring you to persuade Wheeler to accept an offer from the Symphony, and your fortune will be made — and you can grasp from that prediction of mine how highly we all regard your husband's professional abilities.

Thanks very much indeed for all your help in this matter.

All the best,
Hill

Telegram from Secretaries Unlimited to F. Hill Halstead, Esq.:
Regret Mrs. Lamb now unable accept. Please wire second choice.
Dodie

Night letter from F. Hill Halstead to Mrs. Knox, Secretaries Unlimited:
Trying to reach you by phone all day. Mrs. Worthington determined on Lamb. Implore you persuade her. Add 20% increase to salary. Traveling expenses and your commission now paid by us. Hill

Telegram from Secretaries Unlimited to F. Hill Halstead (collect):
Mrs. Lamb agrees. Am wiring you now instead of calling tomorrow morning so can say thing is done in case she changes mind tonight. Seems ambivalant. Please write travel directions. Sorry must ask commission of four weeks salary. Dodie.

From F. Hill Halstead to Mrs. Wheeler Knox:

June 12

Dear Dodie,

I was much relieved when your wire arrived just now, and am scrawling you this note instead of writing tomorrow from the office. The urgency over, my mother-in-law has directed me to give up Western Union — not only because of the expense but because she has been annoyed with them ever since she sent a telegram to an elderly cousin of hers who has always refused to have a telephone installed, and then found that the cousin had never received the wire. When Mrs. Worthington complained about it, the company replied, sounding most aggrieved, that the telegram had not been delivered because the recipient did not have a phone it could have been called in on.

Mrs. Worthington being, as you know, such an independent person, I was greatly surprised when she dug in her heels and offered all those inducements to get your Mrs. Lamb. I suppose she felt that anyone who had studied art at the Sorbonne and in addition is as literate as you claim her to be deserves all she can get — if only because she may be able to hold her own in the evening conversation in Maine. One can read only just so long by those oil lamps, and we are finding it harder to get parts for them.

Do you remember that secretary whom Sarah had at The Bungalow a few summers ago when she was writing a book that was supposed to be the final word on everything from when to clip dew-claws to teaching the mutt how to bite selectively? And that all she ever said at the dinner table was, "It does get so very chilly at night, doesn't it?" That book sold about two hundred copies and Sarah always has blamed, probably most unfairly, poor little Miss Chilly's numbing conversation for throwing her off her form. (I, being more worldly, suspect the publisher was looking for a loss to take on his taxes.)

Well, to business. Mrs. Lamb will be met (and by me, of course; I earn my month in Maine) at the Bar Harbor Airport on Friday, June 22, at 2:10 in the afternoon. I will make the reservations and get the tickets and mail them to you. I hope to God that the child is as docile as you claim. I assume you have seen her, though the thought of your having to interview children so that their mamas can get jobs does seem a bit 1984.

You do understand, Dodie, that if the child is in any way a disturbance, the employment terminates at once, with only return fare and salary to date owing? The monographs must be delivered to the museum's publisher by September 15th, and Mrs. Worthington will need all her powers of concentration to finish them in addition to the commissions for ikons she has in hand and means to complete in Maine. And then there are, also, some small landscapes on silver plaques ordered by that not-quite-royal-personage with whom Sarah's Great-uncle Saville painted Peiping red (was that a forerunner of tints to come?) many long years ago when he was a mere underling at the Embassy and she only — oh, well. I must say that to a simple boy from Philadelphia like me, the number of fascinating exploits that some of my wife's ancestors indulged in makes me feel that a more literary type than myself would garner a lot of cash by researching and writing something called "The Improper You-Know-Whos."

Sarah requests me to tell you that we all would love to have you and Wheeler come up to The Bungalow when you get tired of loving New York in June, and you know how fond Mrs. Worthington has always been of you both. Unfortunately, I must now speak out of the other side of my mouth, with my best legal technique, and say that Sarah has persuaded her mother that entertaining in Maine this summer will be just too very difficult. Not that she isn't right — I find that my wife is always so — but one would think that Sarah was the famous, busy, and authoritative Elizabeth Worthington and that it was her work that the Fine Arts' planned to publish.

Yours very truly,
Hill Halstead

P.S. Really, Dodie, that extra week's commission! My mother-in-law says that one can tell you were born a descendant of Yankee merchant princes. However, send your bill to her at The Bungalow, Seal Cove, Mount Desert Island, Maine, if you would, and thanks again.

Chapter 1

THE BACKDROP

The "backside of Mount Desert Island" at one time meant that part of the coast facing eastward to the Atlantic Ocean, from the entrance to Somes Sound in the center of the southern coast to Bar Harbor on the east. Now it means entirely the opposite — the western region along Blue Hill Bay.

The backside is a region of small Native houses, a few boatyards, two or three fish piers, one sardine factory, one crabmeat-packing plant, one mountain of size, one ferry (to a smaller island), one lighthouse, an unspoiled National Park picnic area, one or two pretty ponds, a goodly amount of lobstering, a greater amount of integrity (a well-known local product), — and some of the most quietly beautiful vistas of shore, woods, islands, fog and sun to be seen anywhere in the world.

Most of the tourists who, since the Great Fire of 1947 destroyed so many of the old summer estates in Bar Harbor, come to the new motels in and around the town never see the "backside" at all. These prefer to wander through Bar Harbor's stores featuring colorful T-shirts, Taiwanese treasures, over-wrought, hand-wrought belts and pottery jugs, lobster-shaped pillows, and the like. Some of these come to take the ferry *Bluenose* to Nova Scotia, some come to fish, some to camp, some to motor the island roads, some to walk the lovely trails with their incredible views of sea and mountains — and some, far fewer, to climb those mountains. Not getting over to the "backside" would not cause these visitors to feel that they had missed much; considering the more spectacular features of the rest of Mount Desert, they might, perhaps — but only perhaps — be right.

The summer people of the backside, whose cottages and camps are usually not in the view of the casual motorist, are, many of them, the second and third generations of the families who first discovered the unsurpassed charm of that part of the island. They scorned Bar Harbor when the summer colony there was extravagantly wealthy and showily feudal; now that it is practically non-existent in the old sense, they think of it only for what the town itself offers them. There is an excellent old movie theatre for a rainy afternoon, an old-fashioned candy store, a good Italian restaurant, some charming shops featuring both classic clothes and amusing trinkets — these, and other attractions, are what lure the conservative backside summer resident over to the more glossy eastern shore, though only rarely.

He, or she, is quietly superior about the rustically over-groomed beauty of fashionable Northeast Harbor; its happy summer citizens, at their carefully casual cocktail parties or aboard their slightly underplayed sailing yachts, would be somewhat surprised to know how little they are envied — or even regarded. Seal Harbor is considered as heavily-and-gratefully Rockefeller, and Southwest Harbor is thought of as fine when it is not emulating towns whose summer people have more money and sophistication, if fewer university degrees.

So think the summer inhabitants of the backside, and the opinion of the year-round residents there — on Mount Desert they are not the natives but the Natives — is very similar. But they all feel a loyalty to, and a proprietary interest in, the island, the whole island, by right of appreciation and because they know that they "belong" on Mount Desert Island, even if some of them "belong" for only two months of the year.

Any four-year-old summer resident of the backside, her nurse (if she has such an expensive possession) left behind in Boston, Philadelphia, or Washington, knows all this as truly as does her forty-year-old doctor, lawyer, or broker father, or her seemingly-not-too-much-older-than-forty maternal grandmother. (That grandmother often rules the family summer roost as well as the family trust fund.)

The outstanding characteristics among the summer people of the backside are intelligence, breeding, and a sure and certain knowledge that one and one's family are almost always right. An intelligent ability to profit by these traits of the summer people, while always maintaining that vaunted integrity, of course, is the leading characteristic of the Natives who deal with them.

Of all the coves on the backside of Mount Desert, Schooner Cove was declared by many to be the prize. About a quarter-mile in length, possessed of deepwater anchorage at any tide, ringed by a bold shore of rocks of the most beautiful pink and grey granite set off by the darkness of the spruce behind them, it looked out past Dead Man's Reef at its mouth to three little green islands called the Three Follies, and then between two larger islands straight up the bay to the smoky Blue Hill at the head that gave the bay its name.

Otis Worthington, Jr. had first sailed into it in 1914, in his Bar Harbor Thirty sloop *Elizabeth,* and, with his forthcoming marriage to the seventeen-year-old Miss Elizabeth Elbridge in mind, had the next morning begun negotiations for purchase of the property with the old couple whose farmhouse was at the head of the meadow above the cove. The marriage was advanced a year because of the European war, but by the time Miss Elbridge had become Mrs. Otis Worthington, Jr., the farmhouse had disappeared. It had been superseded by a shingled, high-ceilinged structure of no particular style, topped by an enormous fieldstone chimney, which graced the rocks at the innermost point of the cove. The building, maid's room and all, had cost just one thousand dollars to have built.

The house was named The Bungalow by the widowed Mrs. Otis Worthington, Sr., for the very good reasons that she liked the title and it was her thousand dollars. Its inner walls were of pine, innocent of paint or plaster, and its furnishings were of the "camp" rather than of the "cottage" mode. "Cottages" built on Mount Desert Island in 1915 could easily cost up to thirty thousand dollars and were not for young Bostonians just starting out in life. (Young Philadelphians and Washingtonians, and most certainly the elite young from New York, were not held by their parents to such plain living any more than they had been required by them ever to do the high thinking that so naturally complements it.)

By the time the young Worthingtons had returned from their long wedding trip to a Georgian sea island plantation, upon which they had embarked the day after Otis' graduation from Harvard, it was known that one of the bedrooms would require nursery furniture and a bed for a nursemaid.

Decorating the rest of the establishment was simple: posters brought back from Europe before 1914 by returning relatives were tacked on the pine walls, and India print curtains, plaid madras pillows, Navaho rugs and odds and ends of pottery, together with paintings done by Elizabeth herself, made The Bungalow refreshingly different from Otis' mother's Mount Vernon Street house in Boston. Elizabeth Elbridge Worthington had, of course, been expected to move into that house, upon her marriage, and had complied. Young Mrs. Worthington was pleased by an aspect of her summer residence other than its uncomplicated decor: it appeared that for ten weeks a year she would be a good three hours' drive by buckboard from her mother-in-law's simple twenty-room cottage on Sargent Drive in Northeast Harbor.

Several other buildings had been added over the years by Otis and Elizabeth Worthington. A guest cottage had been built, along with a pretty rustic pump house to cover the artesian well, and a children's bunk-room, with a separate entrance, had been annexed to a windowless wall of the kitchen in the main Bungalow. There was a garage for a succession of cars which were not too often turned in for a later model, despite Otis' large inheritances and his well-rewarded efforts as a trustee for his friends' inheritances.

Last, in 1935, a studio had been erected to house the kiln and other equipment that Elizabeth Worthington had been using in The Bungalow's kitchen to produce, in her leisure time, the exquisite little enameled landscapes on copper and pewter and silver that were already beginning to be highly prized by those fortunate relatives and friends to whom they were given. Elizabeth had been taught in one of those countries to which her raffish and charming guardian uncle had been posted in the course of his diplomatic career — she would never say which country or who had taught her — a method of combining enamel with precious metals that produced an utterly unique medium.

A painting done in what was beginning to be called the "Worthington technique" was as glowing as a jewel. She learned the art of goldsmithing and began to make settings for stones that, embellished with her enamelled designs, commanded most unladylike high commissions from a famous European jeweler. She became interested in ikon-painting, and in that esoteric field the name of Worthington soon ranked just below that of the immortal Rubloff.

What the little lonesome dark-eyed girl from Boston had learned as a pastime from some unknown artisan in the Near or Far East, and perfected while her Uncle Saville was pursuing his professional and his pleasurable exploits, had developed into a most profitable means of self-expression for the young Boston matron. Not only was her husband's mother much too impressed with the large fees paid to her daughter-in-law — no true Bostonian ever loses respect for those who can make money — to intrude into her studio, either at The Bungalow or on the fourth floor of the Boston house, but also Elizabeth Worthington's known industry protected her from the innumerable lunch-parties, amateur theatricals, and charity balls that were the occupations enjoyed, or at least endured, by her contemporaries, with stalwart Bostonian grace.

Chapter 2

THE SET

On a morning in June in the late nineteen-sixties, Schooner Cove looked much the same as it had the day that Otis Worthington, Jr. had escaped from his mother for his first solitary overnight sail. Three other summer cottages had been built on the shores of the cove, but they were barely visible from The Bungalow or from the water. Their floats, at the ends of the long bridges made necessary by the rising and falling of the tides of the cove — always a few feet both higher and lower than were recorded anywhere else on the island — indicated where the houses were located. The diversity of the craft around each float or at moorings nearby gave the Worthingtons what had always been to them an amusing revelation of the differences in character and taste among the Schooner Cove summer families.

To the left of The Bungalow, almost as far into the cove as the Worthingtons, but hidden from them by a thick stand of spruce, was a plain weathered frame building, large and airy, with many healthful and frigid sleeping-porches. It was inhabited by Captain and Mrs. Frederick Blanchard, Bostonians who lived most of the year in Kittery, Maine. Although attached to the Portsmouth, New Hampshire, Naval Base (which, for some reason known only to the rarefied higher levels of naval intelligence, is so titled although it certainly appears to be in Kittery), the Captain chose to go even farther east for his holiday pleasures. He had built on the cove in the 1940's, after his return from contributing to victory in the Pacific, and with his wife, son Horatio, and daughter Pherousa, led a simple existence. The Blanchards delighted in the pleasures offered by Mount Desert Island in much the same way that its first visitors from the cities, over a hundred years before, had done.

Walking, berrying, rowing, and reading naval history occupied the Blanchards' summer days. Pherousa, sixteen, was allowed to read fiction if it had a nautical setting. Horatio, ten years older, was, in the opinion of Otis Worthinton, Jr., from the day he first saw the boy until the day Otis died, as mad as a hatter. Indeed, the last words Otis ever spoke were in relation to Horatio, one August day in 1955 just before Otis went in to take the last post-luncheon nap that his always weak heart — the "Worthington heart", as his family, not unproudly, referred to its handicap — allowed him to take. "Poor chap," Otis had said, gazing across the cove to the shore where Horatio was (with much care taken not to step on the cracks in the rocks, any more than he had ever stepped on a pavement crack) dragging up driftwood to put in his marine museum, while loudly singing the Navy hymn.

The Blanchards' fleet consisted of an ancient, six-oared rowing barge, titled *Nelson*, and two Spartan rowboats. If they could ever afford a sailboat, they said, (no Bostonian, however far transplanted from his native heath, or, rather, Common, ever minds referring to his poverty, real or imagined) they would try to find one of the good old Friendship sloops. One rowboat had a small outboard motor on the stern, and the Blanchards used it to put-put out in a slow and dignified manner to picnic on one of the beautiful little islands far out in Blue Hill Bay. The other rowboat was Horatio's, and he had painted it in a camouflage pattern in case an unfriendly submarine entered the cove when he was out rowing.

When the Blanchards had guests, the latter were marched each morning, very early, down to the float, where they embarked in ship-shape fashion and manned the oars of the *Nelson* for a long row out to the reef or around the Follies. Surprisingly to some, they had no lack of guests, for the Captain and Kitty Blanchard were kindly people, young Pherousa was mannered and charming, the young officers at the Captain's base were often lonely, and Horatio could, though admittedly with difficulty, be overlooked. It was more difficult to overlook the large blue HORATIO's which he had painted in three-feet-high letters on the large sloping rocks that bordered the path down to the Blanchards' bridge. Augustus Halstead, the Worthingtons' young grandson, had slipped over one September evening, after the Blanchards' departure for Kittery, and painted out the offending sights with dark grey paint. The next spring, Horatio relettered his banners, this time in purple. Augustus did no more.

Beyond the Blanchards, in the woods on the left at the very entrance to the cove, was the property of Mrs. Wilson Parker, of Dedham, Massachusetts. For some years a widow, and an exceedingly wealthy one thanks to the excellence of the marine cordage firm her father had founded and she had carried on, Mrs. Parker maintained her late grandmother's large cottage in Bar Harbor and stayed there in the summers because her adored only daughter preferred, not unnaturally, swimming in the Bar Harbor Club's pool and sailing and dancing with the summer boys of Bar and Northeast Harbors to the more isolated beauty of Schooner Cove.

But Mrs. Parker's husband had been a poor boy in a cold-water flat in Roxbury before he grew up to marry his employer's daughter, and he preferred the simplicity of the white-clap-boarded cottage he and his wife had built on Schooner Cove after some inventions of his had greatly increased the revenue of the cordage company and enhanced his standing there. In his memory, and because she had been happy at the cove, Mrs. Parker had the cottage opened and cleaned every summer, in case she and her maids and cook should come over from Bar Harbor for a night or two.

Each June, the mooring for the trim forty-foot yawl her husband had painfully and proudly learned to sail was put out, the bridge and float were repaired and repainted, and the deaf old man from Thomaston who had joined the Parkers years before as yacht hand came to live on the *Hesperus* and have her in readiness for the rare times Miss Parker brought her friends across the island for a sail. Everything about the Parker float was expensive but discreet. The old man, George Paine, wore khakis and a duck-billed cap — there is little gold braid to be seen nowadays, in any case, on the hired hands on Mount Desert yachts — and the yawl herself was fitted out most unostentatiously. The *Hesperus's* neat little mahogany dinghy lay on the float when old Paine was taken by the caretaker, who serviced all the Schooner Cove cottages, to Southwest Harbor to get his week's supply of groceries; otherwise she lay astern of the yawl. All summer long, Paine polished and painted the *Hesperus*. He listened, sometimes, to his radio, turned very loud, or followed in the newspapers the big-league baseball games in which his son played. And he read and re-read his son's few letters.

What the Worthingtons saw from The Bungalow of the Parker place was well-kept, lonesome, and very sad. What they could not see, the cottage itself, was the same, including the large wine cellar hewn out of the granite ledge on which the cottage was built. Mr. Parker had stocked it with the choicest wines, brandies, and whiskies that S.S. Pierce had had to offer, and on his European trips he had been guided in his purchases by expert advice. Mrs. Parker was reported to have refused some enormously large offers for some of the vintages in her husband's cellar. However, like his yawl, it was kept the way he had left it. Her guests in Maine, whether they were at the Bar Harbor house or, more rarely, at Schooner Cove, were served cold and palatable well water or a domestic sherry at $2.20 a bottle. A lesser woman would have been tempted by the small fortune she might so easily have reaped by selling her beloved husband's dozens of bottles of Napoleon brandy, and his dozens of cases of post-World-War II Puligny-Montrachets, and Mersaults, and the almost-legendary still red champagne of Bouzy — but a lesser woman than Lettice Parker would not have become so rich in her own right through her inspired commercial efforts in the manufacture of ropes.

On the right of the Worthingtons, the only house on that side of the cove, was the habitation of Dr. and Mrs. Horton Gambel. Dr. Gambel, a psychiatrist from Washington, D.C., was said, by Native report, to have behind his trees a building that was mainly of plate glass. It had redwood buttresses and roof edgings flying out at such extreme angles, the report went, that "it looks like the damn-fool thing was 'bout to skun off t'Bartlett's Island; might make it out fur's the reef, at that."

No neighboring summer resident had laid eyes on the Gambels' cottage. The Gambels, at the times of their first courtesy invitations to The Bungalow or the Blanchards' "Quarterdeck", had made it clear that they had no time for anyone incapable of sitting in their rather hard and damp conversation pit and holding technical and elevating discussions with Dr. Gambel's professional confrères from New York and Washington. These associates of Dr. Gambel's had, according to the Native grapevine, spectacles, bony knees, bad manners, and the accents of Mittel Europa.

The Gambels had a new sloop of the excellent "Controversy" class that had been designed and built on Mount Desert Island — the class so called because of the arguments its reversed-sheer design had provoked when introduced a few years before. This sloop, *Psyche*, was expertly sailed by Dr. Gambel and his numerous small sons, all of whom seemed rather hungry and bedraggled when they stole over to visit the other Schooner Cove cottages to be superior there.

Mrs. Gambel was seldom seen. She worked at her loom, report went, especially when she was pregnant, which was almost always. Occasionally she was observed climbing heavily into the Gambels' sleek power boat, of the newest, wave-skimming design, and sitting aft to read a book while the whole family piled in and headed out to sea.

No one could imagine what they did there, for they took no picnic or fishing gear. "Rendezvous with a Red sub, that's what they do," was the loudly snorted opinion of Mrs. Worthington's cousin, General Lemuel Otis Alison, whenever he was visiting The Bungalow and heard the Gambels' explosive exit from the cove.

The Bungalow itself had fewer craft around its float than when Otis Worthington still lived. After his death, his widow had given Otis' ketch *Ancestress* to a young cousin who had bought the movie theatre in Bar Harbor and taken up year-round residence there. The Bungalow nowadays was provided only with an old skiff called *Hilda*, after the servant who had presented her to the young Worthingtons as a wedding present over fifty years before, a light flat-bottomed punt in which Elizabeth Worthington rowed each day, and a small fiberglass sloop, a present to her grandson Augustus Halstead, just this year, on the occasion of his thirteenth birthday.

Chapter 3

PRELIMINARY REHEARSALS

Not only did the cove look much the same on this June morning, except for the floats and the craft near them, as it had almost six decades before, but the quality of Mount Desert Island mornings was as high as it had been over a century before when the first of the summer people, the artists, laid appreciative eyes on it. An ideal summer morning on that most ideal of islands has a soft southwest wind and a clear blue sky that causes the sea to look a deeper, more brilliant blue. There hang a few traces of clouds high above the smaller islands lying offshore, the sun rests fragrant on the spruce and pine, and above all steals a delicious salt odor to which the clam flats contribute no small part. Sometimes the touch of a foreign scent, tropical, even a little musty and rank, can be perceived in the pervading clean cold Maine air, reminding the traveller who has visited the islands of the Caribbean of the kinship of all islands.

A large open porch graced the front of The Bungalow and Hill Halstead emerged upon it, slamming the screen door behind him. He was about forty, lean, sandy and angular, and appeared to be smiling most of the time, even when upset to the limited extent his habitual sardonic good humour permitted. Mild annoyance now seemed to be his mood, although he smiled pleasantly at the three grinning Dalmatians who came to surround him, and although he held his coffee cup and saucer quite lightly, in an unclenched hand. The dogs, however, instantly retreated to a respectful distance and sat down, tongues lolling, staring intently at him.

"It's no damned use at all, Sarah, to keep at me," he said loudly over his shoulder. "The thing is settled and I certainly did not influence your mother to the slightest degree. Why the hell should I?"

Sarah Worthington Halstead followed him out on to the porch, not slamming the door. She was dressed in neat navy-blue Bermuda shorts and a prim white blouse with a little round collar piped in matching blue. Sarah was small and plump, brown-haired and brown-eyed, and possessed of a certain tightness of jaw and mouth that indicated, along with her propensity for securing for herself anything desirable that was going, why her younger brother and sister had, with a faculty for punning unusual even in Bostonian children, long ago dubbed her "Seizer."

"Really, Hill," she said, in her usual reasonable way, "I might have been consulted. Why in the world has she agreed to a child, and to that ridiculous amount of salary? Are you sure you have never met this Mrs. Lamb before? It is all most peculiar."

She paused to wave affectionately at a fat little girl who, seated in the juniper bushes some distance from the porch and staring fixedly through opera glasses at the treetops, had turned at the sound of her mother's voice.

Sarah continued, no less reasonably and a shade more quietly, "And now Persis will have to share the bunkroom with a strange child who may tip over the lamp or upset the candles or disturb her when she is writing . . ." She stopped at a loud laugh from Hill, instantly muffled so it resolved itself into an unsuccessful sneeze.

"God in heaven, Sarah," he said. "I never heard of this woman before, nor did your mother, and as for the child, even if she can't think of two things to say about the love life of the vesper sparrow, she just possibly might have quite good manners and not be a junior pyromaniac. Why do you object to your mother's selecting the person she thinks can best help her with these articles, no matter what she had to pay her? If the Worthington technique is to be at last revealed to a panting world . . ."

Sarah interrupted. "There is no need for sarcasm, Hill." She was beginning to get angry. "You always end by speaking sarcastically to me, but I have a feeling, a very, very uneasy feeling about this whole thing." She stopped, and they both turned with morning smiles as Elizabeth Worthington came around the corner of the house.

Elizabeth Worthington at seventy-two was as straight and as slim and almost as darkly beautiful as she had been when she wed Otis Worthington in 1915 at the altar of the Church of the Advent. Old Mrs. Worthington had congratulated herself that day on the probable durability of the successful candidate to replace her as Mrs. Worthington of Mount Vernon Street. She had reason for self-congratulation, for she had more or less chosen the candidate or, at least, guided her son most assiduously in his selection of that particular Elizabeth.

For there had been, by birth or marriage, an Elizabeth in every generation of the Worthington family for at least three hundred years. First daughters were born and promptly named Elizabeth. Sons in daughterless generations were led by inclination or manipulation to marry young ladies of that name. A New Hampshire magazine dedicated to New England subjects of interest — and what is more New England, and therefore more interesting, than genealogy? — had once devoted a number of its pages to an article entitled "Eleven Generations of New England Beauty." This article had thoroughly explored, while cautiously omitting photographs of the paintings of the more unsightly Elizabeths, this fascinating Worthington phenomenon.

The article had been written before the birth, and the death a week later, of the little Elizabeth born to Otis and Elizabeth Worthington in 1916, she for whom that first nursery furniture had been ordered for the Schooner Cove cottage. For many years it had then seemed that there would be no more Worthingtons, either named Elizabeth or anything else.

At the birth of Sarah, in 1930, old Mrs. Worthington had been five years in wherever it is that good and rich old Bostonian ladies go when they die. Since they have already spent the greater part of their days on earth in the only place really worthy of them, it is doubtful if they, or rather their spirits, feel the need to ascend to what is called Heaven. Most probably, they hover in the atmosphere a little above Mt. Auburn Cemetery, and on Friday afternoons drift in slightly toward Symphony Hall.

Mt. Auburn or Heaven, Mrs. Worthington was far enough away for Elizabeth Worthington to follow her desire to name her first surviving child after her own long-dead mother. The small amount of grey in her black hair appeared not at her little Elizabeth's birth and death, but at the time she summoned the courage to break the Worthington tradition of several centuries.

This morning, as she approached, Hill again thought how fervently he hoped that the old saw about taking a good look at the mother before one marries the girl was as true as some held it to be.

Mrs. Worthington spoke gently to her daughter: "Sarah, Doreen seems to have disappeared before I could speak to her. About an hour ago I heard her being very impertinent to Junior, and you know that I will not tolerate rudeness directed by one member of my household to another.

"Please remind her of this, and would you ask her to bring me some salad and cheese to the studio at one-thirty? I must go directly there and work till tea; Junior brought me another cablegram from Paris this morning inquiring about those landscapes. Why I ever engaged to undertake anything for that wretched woman . . . really, I must have been demented."

"Of course, Mother," Sarah said. "I'll attend to Doreen. But Junior sometimes seems a bit overbearing, you must admit, especially to Doreen and her mother."

"No wonder he's overbearing — June's a darned important man," offered Hill. "He was away from the island a long time, in the army and then working in Bangor, but now that he's back, he owns half of the Duck Cove Store and part of that excursion boat business. Being caretaker for the whole cove and keeping a check on those four new cottages over on Greene Point also brings him in a sizeable income, at least sizeable for the backside, and he must not be even thirty-five yet."

"Why," asked Sarah irritably, "must you always call Junior 'June'? You make it sound as if we had a feminine caretaker."

"His friends call him June and I regard myself as one of them. And, to get on with what I was saying, with his looks and money, not to mention his being a selectman and a personable guy who just might some day get elected to the State Legislature — and who knows what after that — it's a wonder Doreen casts him such a cold eye.

"I should think she might even try setting her cap for him, if cap-setting isn't outmoded now, even in Maine. Come to think of it, maybe she's tried and failed and that's the reason for the bickering. Or maybe it's just plain old envy.''

"Resentment, envy, or even frustrated love, on which your mind seems to run lately, Hill, this must stop," Elizabeth Worthington said. "Not that there is any real reason for envy. Junior works hard and it is not his fault that Dora and Doreen are not as well off as he. He did not cause Dora to leave that school to which Otis and Mrs. Parker so kindly sent her. Had she not run off to marry that scoundrel who fathered Doreen and then disappeared, she would have become a trained secretary and might now be an executive making far more money than Junior does."

"You know, Elizabeth, the boys down at the store say Doreen is actually June's daughter," Hill said idly, gazing innocently up at the bay.

"Really, Hill, you simply must stop trying to provoke mischief!" cried Sarah.

Her mother gave Hill a half-smile. "That is enough, Hill, dear. Now, will you remember that you are picking up Mrs. Lamb at the airport this afternoon?"

"Since you mention Mrs. Lamb, Mother," said Sarah, "I wanted to say; that is, I wanted to ask, or rather, I felt I should . . ."

"Elizabeth," Hill said, in a voice that sucessfully drowned Sarah's, "just let me tell you something that happened at the store yesterday. You'll love it." He turned to his wife and made a grimace of warning that sent the dogs into a frightened retreat towards the bushes.

Sarah merely looked more resolved. "Mother, you know how kind I think it is of you to have the children and me here all summer, and you know that I am never critical . . ."

Hill increased his volume. "Elizabeth, you know old Robert Prouty, or Spider, as he's called . . ."

"I cannot bear to hear one more word, let alone one more anecdote, about those miserable thieving Proutys," said Sarah, walking to the far end of the porch. "Nor can I see why we all call the caretaker and the other locals by their childish Native nicknames. Junior and Spider, indeed!"

Elizabeth Worthington lit a cigarette and sat down on the porch steps to listen, with an expectant smile.

"Well," continued Hill, finally, "when I went in yesterday, some of the regulars at the store were sitting around talking about that big buck that jumped through the post office window last winter, and somehow old Spider — all right, Sarah, old Robert — was then moved to tell, at great length and with more chuckling and spitting than I really cared for, how just last Thursday he'd shot the biggest buck he'd ever poached in his long and nefarious life.

"After about five or six minutes of this, a quiet middle-aged fellow came over and said, 'Guess you don't know who I am yet, mister. Name's Ericson, the new game warden, and I have to remind you that it's illegal to shoot deer on Mount Desert Island.'

"Well, of course everyone knew who he was, except Prouty, and they were all sitting quietly waiting for his answer. He never batted an eye. 'Guess you don't know who I am yet, warden,' he answered. 'I'm Spider Prouty, the biggest liar in Hancock County'!"

Elizabeth laughed heartily. Sarah frowned. "I've heard that story as having happened in about four other states," she said. "Mother, if we can elevate the conversation a little above the Proutys, Persis has finished several more little nature essays you might like to take along to the studio with you. Perhaps you could read them while you lunch."

"Oh, God," said Hill wearily. "Sarah, you are making an absolute ass of yourself in encouraging Persis to embark on a literary career at the age of seven. Her observing birds and animals is fine, but being told she should write about them — really, you're headed completely 'round the bend!"

"We have a literary tradition in the Worthington family," replied Sarah, reddening unbecomingly. "Almost all old Boston families do. I would not expect people from Philadelphia to be able to encourage anything but rudeness in their children, but they might refrain from criticizing what they cannot possibly understand."

"If by literary tradition, dearie, you mean those tiresome journals of European travels, or those privately printed eulogies to departed wives that necessitate the new incumbents, who always seem to be possessed of jealous natures and vicious tempers, to be pacified with charge accounts at Shreve, Crump and Low, plus those little studies of ancestors that might correctly be titled 'Adventures in Early Federalist Crookery', well, you can take your literary tradition and shove it in . . . the Frog Pond on the Common."

"Hill!" said Elizabeth, with some severity. "Sarah, Persis writes very interestingly indeed, but, and I believe I have said this before, I am certainly not going to publish her works privately. It would be comparable to poor Cousin Tom's having to hire Jordan Hall every year or so for his misguided wife's concerts."

"I," Hill said with enthusiasm, "am going to found yet another New England Society: 'The Society to Prevent Southern Ladies With A Very Little Talent From Singing In Public.' I think I'll go find Emily and get a starting contribution; she got roped in for the last concert."

"I'll subscribe, too," Elizabeth Worthington said. "Sarah, when you speak to Doreen, would you remind her to make up the other bunk in Persis' room for the little Lamb girl? And you remember that Cousin Lem is coming over tomorrow evening for drinks. Would you tell Emily and Isabella? Emily will want to be here, I know; she is so very fond of Lem. And Isabella must be reminded to postpone, until after dinner, her evening swim and, ah, communion, as she calls it."

"Is Lem bringing that smashing Swede?" Hill asked with interest.

"Do you mean his assistant?" Mrs. Worthington spoke with more stiffness than she usually showed to Hill. "I believe he has a new one, again, this summer. She is Icelandic, as I remember."

"Good," said Hill. "Maybe I'll join Isabella in her communion with the elements and persuade the Icelandic blonde to take the evening off, as well as a few clothes, and come too."

"How do you know she's a blonde?" Sarah was interested but not annoyed. She was almost unbaitable except in the matters of her family descent, her children's talents, and the virtues of Dalmatians, which she had bred commercially for some years.

"When I was in Iceland —" began Hill happily.

"But, Hill, you certainly never were —"

"I will see you both this evening," interrupted Elizabeth firmly, and walked up the path to her studio.

She was met by Doreen, who emerged from the studio still languidly flicking her dustcloth, now at empty air.

"Mis' Parker's in there waiting for you," she said. "Seems kind of upset."

Mrs. Worthington sighed, but as she opened the door, she smiled pleasantly in at her guest, who did not rise to greet her.

Mrs. Parker sat stolidly, staring disapprovingly straight in front of her at the cigarettes and ashtray on the worktable. Her short iron-grey hair was tightly set in rigid rows of curls, her nose was pug and her small eyes showed a cold, pale blue. Her round face, with deep horizontal lines on the forehead and deep vertical lines anywhere else there was room for them, turned slowly to regard Mrs. Worthington.

She shuffled her feet, clad stoutly in the type of shoes that lighter-hearted Bostonian ladies term "beetle-crunchers," gratingly on the pine floor.

"Well, Elizabeth," she said in a low, rasping voice, "I see you're still smoking."

"Good morning, Lettie. Yes, I'm afraid so."

"You'd do better to take my advice about that, and a number of other things as well."

"I did take your advice once, Lettie, and your help, also, and I'm greatly in your debt for both," Mrs. Worthington answered, still smiling graciously.

Mrs. Parker was not moved to do the same. She regarded her hostess with something like contempt.

"You'd better take it again; this time about that precious child of yours," she said harshly.

Mrs. Worthington raised her brows. "I have three children, Lettie," she said gently. "All of them are precious to me. Of which one are you speaking?"

Mrs. Parker laughed. Her laugh was most unpleasant. "You would never guess," she said, "so I'll have to tell you. You always were a bit of a fool, Elizabeth, though not such a fool as that sister of yours."

With colour rising in her cheeks, but her lips still framed in a smile, Mrs. Worthington regarded her visitor calmly. "You were speaking first of my child and now you have switched to my sister Emily?" she questioned politely.

"Shut the door, Elizabeth," Mrs. Parker ordered, waving her hand in a commanding manner. "I wish to speak most seriously to you about a number of things."

Fifteen minutes later, the ladies emerged from the studio. Elizabeth Worthington no longer smiled. Lettice Parker merely looked as unpleasant as usual, no more, no less.

"Mind you do what I tell you, Elizabeth," she said, and turned to go with no further farewell.

"Lettie," Mrs. Worthington called after her, "I told you I will deal with not only . . ." She stopped as Doreen came out of the guest cottage and ambled toward her. "I will do as you suggest, Lettie. Good-bye."

Doreen proffered her employer what would be described by some as a handful of joints and by others as a number of marijuana cigarettes.

"You said to give these to you if I found any of 'em in Isabella's room, mam," she said.

"Thank you," Mrs. Worthington said. She sighed. "I really don't know what her end will be, if she goes on as she does."

"No, mam, me neither," Doreen replied politely. But she was looking up the path, at the receding back of Mrs. Parker.

Chapter 4

INTERMISSION WITH EXIT LINE

As Elizabeth Worthington left The Bungalow porch for her studio, her second daughter and youngest child, the Grafin Isabella Worthington von Lichtenfeld, arose, in a manner that was successfully both majestic and undulating, from a juniper thicket just off the edge of the porch. She had been lying there quietly since breakfast, unnoticed by anyone but the dogs, who had snuffled at the bushes once or twice. Sarah braced herself, as always, when confronted with yet another of her sister's varied and inadequate choices of costume.

"Aren't those bushes scratchy?" she asked mildly.

The Grafin looked down with vague approval at a rather large expanse of her bare and interestingly modeled pale flesh and smiled distantly. She was fairly tall, dark-haired like her mother, and rather attractive, despite beginning to be both much too flabby and a trifle overweight.

Her face, with its little pointed chin, wide cheekbones, limpid dark eyes and tiny mouth, had once been compared with that of the young Queen Victoria; hence, over the years, she had attempted to develop a nineteenth-century manner of comportment. She had succeeded, but to her family's dismay it was of the nineteenth century of Victoria's raffish relative known as Prinny, rather than that of Her Late Majesty's succeeding and more subdued era.

Isabella had, she felt, a voluptuous and fascinating appearance. Men always turned to look at her, and she was quite convinced that they did so with desire and admiration. She had once confided to her sister that she had never slept with a man who had not been deeply in love with her. It is to Sarah's credit that, although much tempted to reply that she had heard that men usually did profess deep love at such times, she had said nothing aloud, and it would have taken larger ears than Isabella's shell-pink Victorian ones to hear Sarah's almost inaudible mutter of "vain naivety."

Hill regarded Isabella with a slight frown. It was, indeed, difficult for him to look anywhere but at her, since Isabella invariably moved to the nearest male and loosely draped her considerable figure around him.

He spoke quietly, and, for Hill, slowly. "I thought, Isabella, that you promised your mother to dress properly the whole time you are up here, except when you are swimming, naturally. H'm, that's rather good, you know, 'naturally,' since I don't suppose you own a bathing suit."

He paused for Isabella to smile at his wit, but she merely breathed deeply and clung a little tighter, while parting her lips in what she had been told was a fetching moue.

Hill shook himself a little to loosen her hold and went on, "And you'd do well to be a bit more discreet in that area, as when a visiting boat is anchored in the cove, for instance, or when Junior is required to do some of his work near you."

"Hill, sweetest," said Isabella, pressing her unconfined bosom against him, "Ma*ma*" — she gave it the Victorian pronounciation, of course, with the accent on the second syllable — "is not bourgeois, though you try your level best to make her appear so. She brought me up as a lady, and she respects my judgment."

She finished with a burst of bubbling laughter, a pleasant sound to a new acquaintance until said acquaintance learned that Isabella ended most of her utterances thusly. Worse still, she often interrupted herself with that bubbling sound, in her first youth charming, but less so now that she was thirty.

Sarah abruptly crossed the porch and stepped down to the crushed clamshell path that descended steeply through large granite boulders to the bridge and float off the shore line fifty feet below. She turned to look thoughtfully at Isabella, then sighed and started down to the shore. Her older child, Augustus, had appeared around the point in his new Bullseye *Coacher* and was making for the float.

"Listen, Isabella," Hill lowered his voice and looked over his shoulder into the living room of the main Bungalow where Doreen could now be seen and heard languidly dusting and humming. She paused often to bare her teeth at her reflection in a pine-framed mirror and to turn her head slowly from side to side in an unnerving manner. "Must be a Sophia Loren movie in Bar Harbor," thought Hill. He reached around the screen door to shut the inner door.

"Listen," he said again, and then paused. He lit a cigarette and, gazing far out past the reef at the entrance to the cove, went carefully on. "I know about that party you had here last September after you thought everyone on the cove had left. Mrs. Parker was over at her place and took pictures of some of those charming scenes on the rocks. It appears that she has a camera with a telescopic lens. She showed them to me, and she promised that she'll show them to Elizabeth unless you absolutely swear that you'll never put on an orgy like that here again — and don't snicker — what would anyone call it but an orgy? I couldn't believe my eyes, if I may coin a phrase.

"How could you possibly have done it here — here in this place your mother loves! Why can't you confine that sort of filth to your apartment in New York, or save it for your trips abroad? And where in the name of God did you find those people — and I use the word loosely. They all looked like the sort your late unlamented husband cultivated, but I thought his friends were all dead or locked up. It would kill Elizabeth to see those photographs — well, no, perhaps it wouldn't, since she has a great deal more real toughness than you have. The whole thing was such a desecration, though, that she could never feel the same about The Bungalow again. Nor about you, either."

Isabella was rigid. "Pictures — you mean that dirty old woman took pictures of *me?* How dare she spy and snoop, the nasty old bitch! What was she doing here, anyway — she always stays in Bar Harbor! I always hated her; now I could kill her! She had better not interfere with me — who else has she shown her precious little pictures to?"

"Be quiet," said Hill. "Be quiet and listen. She hasn't shown them to anyone but me, and she won't, unless you act the damned fool again. She'll be watching for more of your little soirees on the shore.

"Oh, yes, and you are to stop sun-bathing au naturel, too. She intends to spend more time over here and to have guests here now that her daughter is engaged and she doesn't need to see her through the social swim every summer. She has every right to stay here, as you know perfectly well. We don't own the whole cove."

Isabella stared blankly out at the reef, now almost completely revealed by the low tide. Gus had left the Bullseye at the float and was rowing with his mother out to the reef in the ancient skiff, with clam hod and rake. With one of her quick changes of mood, Isabella turned to Hill and flashed a few fleeting Victorian dimples.

"Don't worry, darling Hill, I'll be good; I will be good!"

Hill relaxed. "Well, then, friend, let's run over to Southwest and get some beer to go with those clams that Sarah and Gus are so nobly digging, and we'll drink to your continued goodness. You are going to change out of that, ah . . . dishtowel, or whatever it is you're wearing?"

Isabella smiled tolerantly and leaned to pat Hill's cheek. The dishtowel slid dangerously. "Yes, sweetest, anything you say. But," she was slipping round the corner of the porch that led to the guest cottage she was occupying, "it's more than your little friend had on that night I ran into you in Cannes. Aren't you ever going to tell your dear wife and the rest of us what you were doing there?"

Chapter 5

INTERMISSION WITHOUT

Emily Elbridge, Elizabeth Worthington's sister, came out on to the porch as her niece left it. At sixty, Miss Elbridge possessed her sister's happy faculty for looking young, but not her dark beauty. She did have a handsome carriage and a majestic Roman profile. Her grey hair was long and braided neatly around her head; her voice was low and clipped in a manner more British than Bostonian; her whole demeanor was calm, and suggestive of a lifetime of great self-control. She looked as the mother of the Gracchi might have looked if attired in a Liberty print shirtwaist dress.

Emily was laughing. She had a pleasant laugh. "Hill, dear, the most amusing thing — this morning I woke early and thought I would just see what Dora was doing in the kitchen. You know how she crashes about so, and then there are those frightening periods of utter silence?

"Well, I crept to the knothole in the wall of my room that backs on to the kitchen, and put my eye to it. And there was a cold blue eye facing me in the knothole! Dora had decided to investigate the strange noises that, evidently, I make!"

Hill liked his aunt-by-marriage. "Why don't you move out of the main house and into the other bedroom in the guest cottage? I suppose Isabella has her unmentionables spread all around it — if she owns any — but I'll pitch them out for you. What with Dora's morning breakages, Gus' nightly trips to the ice-box, Persis' sleep-talking out in the bunkroom, not to mention Sarah's and my disputes about Boston vs. Philadelphia — well, I think Elizabeth was wise to have had her own quarters added to the studio last year."

"No, dear," said Emily. "I like to see a little life. Nyack's rather dull people are my lot all winter, although, of course, we are not very far from the fleshpots of New York City."

"Why did you ever leave Boston, Emily? I don't mean originally, but after so many years abroad I should have thought, if you preferred not to move in with Elizabeth, that you'd have looked for some little apartment in Cambridge or perhaps a house on West Cedar Street? I mean, why in the world Nyack, where everyone seems to be either the minority of ultra-conservative, invitation-repaying, Episcopalian upper-middle-class-who-think-they-are-upper-class, or else they are the half-baked-liberal majority who, no doubt, indulge in wife-swapping."

"Really, Hill, your one visit to me there cannot possibly have given you such a broad and perceptive view of the population. But you were asking why I chose Nyack? Well, I admit it is a trifle dispiriting to spend ten months of the year amongst people who pronounce words like 'aquamarine' with a broad 'a' to show how cultured they are; however, I believe I said some years ago that one can't go home again. I believe it was even before the phrase occurred to young Mr. Wolfe."

"Why did you stay in Europe so many years, Emily? I seem to be nothing but questions this morning, but no one has ever told me. Not a dark Bostonian scandal, surely? And don't tell me that you were the family's black sheep and sent to live in Switzerland on a remittance?"

Emily was amused. "There have been many black sheep in Boston families, although I question the writer who said there had never been a First Family spendthrift. I have known a good many, among them Peter. But, no, my uncle would not have paid me to practise my sins in Europe and, really, Hill, I have led a most blameless life. Unless, of course, one counts the sins of omission as outweighing the sins of commission."

She looked across the cove at the *Hesperus*, on which old George had appeared to scrub the deck, and her lips tightened.

But she spoke gently. "There were reasons why I went to Europe so young and stayed so long, not important now."

Hill followed her glance and laughed. "Now, Emily, had you formed a misalliance with George Paine? I thought he had never ventured west of Thomaston."

Emily's voice was still gentle, but her tone became a trifle cold. Hill had unconsciously used that patronizing manner that is so easily assumed by those in their forties towards those in their sixties when life and love are the matters under discussion. (It is more pronounced, of course, when the twenties are talking to the forties.)

"No, Hill, not quite a misalliance, and not with George Paine. Elizabeth was about to announce my engagement when the young man asked me to release him. He had his way to make in the world and, also, my Uncle Saville was never really very welcoming to him. Saville was a bit of a snob, you know, as we all are, I suppose."

She paused painfully. "My friend married very shortly afterward, and very well, one might say. The girl was his employer's only child. He, my friend, met her here, at a party Elizabeth and Otis gave for us. He rose quickly in his father-in-law's cordage company. He was very able."

She looked again at the *Hesperus*. "I was the first person to invite him to Maine, to The Bungalow," she said sadly. "It was the first time he had ever seen Maine. Elizabeth and Otis were charmed with his appreciation. He fell in love with Maine. He said over and over that it was so clean, so blue and white and clean.

"Well, it was years ago, and, besides, he is long dead."

Hill's seniors in his firm valued him for his perspicuity that amounted sometimes to a seeming clairvoyance, a very useful talent in a lawyer, even in Boston. He also looked across to the Parkers' part of the cove. "My God, Emily, are you telling me —"

"No, Hill, I'm really telling nothing at all, nothing of any importance any more. I came out to ask you if Junior were here. One of the catches on the window in my room is loose, and the whole window rattles at night when the wind blows."

"I think he's over at 'Quarterdeck' now. Want to row over with me? We can tell him to stop by later, and also ask the Blanchards over for tomorrow night, to have drinks with Lem. I like to set the

Marine Corps against the Navy, not that Lem stands a chance when Captain Blanchard raises his voice and brings up his big artillery. If Elizabeth would agree to our having a telephone put in, these little social niceties like asking people to cocktails would be so very much easier. We breakfasted shamefully late this morning, so the Blanchards will be sure to be back from their row."

"Lemuel's coming over? Oh, yes, do let's go across and invite them. We'll have to take the punt, since I see Sarah and Gus haven't brought the *Hilda* in yet."

They proceeded sedately down the path to the float, Emily stopping just at the start of the bridge to look with affection at two hollows in one of the huge granite boulders that sloped down to the shore.

"There are Peter's and Sarah's bathing pools," she said. "Poor Peter almost drowned in his when he was quite small. I was back from Europe for a few weeks for Cousin Tom's wedding, his real wedding, as we call it now. I wish you could have known Amelia, Hill. She was so very beautiful and good, and now Tom's dreadful second wife is telling all of Boston that Tom's first marriage wasn't a real, live, true romantic one like theirs is —," Emily's voice shrilled into a parody of an affectedly girlish Baltimore accent, "— and all Amelia's old friends must listen to her."

"Well, Emily, they really don't have to, do they?"

"No, I suppose not, but it is strange how well-bred people so often feel that their breeding compels them to overlook the horrors of taste perpetrated by dreadful people. They seem to feel guilty about being nicer! And then, too, the dead lose our loyalty so quickly. No matter how much we loved them, their claims on us are so frail, simply because they are dead and we are alive. I often ponder on this, and it saddens me."

"No more deep thinking on a morning like this, Aunt Emily. Tell me about Peter's drowning, or near-drowning."

"Well, you've heard how Sarah bullied Peter, but she was also very protective of him. So it was the more strange when she — this was when she was not quite four and Peter only two — wandered up from these rocks one morning and the nurse, a most careless girl, one of the Proutys, I think, asked where Peter was. 'Sitting in his pool with his head down in the water, blowing bubbles,' said Sarah. Peter was like the drawing of a child in a story-book, chubby and with a large round head, so large he couldn't lift it out of the water!"

Hill smiled at this thoroughly aunt-like and rather insipid anecdote, and waved to the occupants of the *Hilda*, now rowing laden for home. "Where was Peter when last heard from? Sarah says she knows nothing at all, and I don't like to ask Elizabeth.'.'

Emily stepped carefully into the flat-bottomed boat and sighed. "I really don't know. I am sure Elizabeth hears from him from time to time, but she never tells me. The whole thing was so unnecessary, I felt. Why Peter was ever persuaded, allowed, or however one may put it, to work in Cousin Ralph's bank when all his life he had treated money so lightly, I have never understood. And whatever happened, even if discreditable to him, as it must have been, I always felt was not entirely his fault."

"I suppose that after the time he'd had in Korea, everyone thought not only that he might have become more sober and altered, but that he deserved to be treated as if he were now above any sort of weakness, if I may put it that way, that he might have shown in the past. I didn't know Peter very well. I had barely married Sarah when he left Boston, but I must say that he was always very decent to me."

"Yes, he liked you, and thought you were just what Sarah needed."

"After Gus was born, we got a magnificent silver cup sent from Peru and inscribed, 'May you never be thirsty, Gus — Uncle Peter.' When Persis arrived, the same sort of cup, but from the Paris Cartier's. I always wondered how he knew the kids' names. As you say, Elizabeth must correspond with him. Unless he still receives the Social Register. Poor Peter did so dote on the Social Register. He used to win bets from his tough friends all the time, Sarah says, as to whether he was in it or not. I can just see him sitting on the Left Bank and reading the latest edition Elizabeth probably sent him from Boston, with his feet in the water and a bottle of vin ordinaire beside him!"

"I'm quite sure Elizabeth is somehow in touch with him. I remember a cable arriving from somewhere or other just when we women of the family were trying to decide if we should go back to tradition in the matter of naming little Persis. Elizabeth read it, murmuring something like 'officious but timely,' and announced that the baby's name was to be Persis, after our great-aunt.

"Peter was always terribly bossy, you know, when Sarah allowed him to be, when they were children. He did so love to put names to all their toys and dogs. Do you suppose he really named your daughter? Sarah was extremely annoyed, since she was insisting on

'Elizabeth Worthington Halstead,' but her mother laughed and said it was too dignified for such a lovable little girl. And since Elizabeth was paying the hospital bill, Sarah gave in."

Emily leaned on her oar for a second; she and Hill were rowing tandem, and went on. "I do know that the money was all paid back to Cousin Ralph, and I fear Elizabeth had to do it. I do wish Peter would come home soon. He was the jolliest little boy, fat, curly-haired, and loud — oh, so loud. He had the dark good looks, as Elizabeth has, of our connections the Batchedlers. The 'black Batchedlers' as they were called in New Hampshire."

They were nearing the Blanchards' float. A peculiar chuckling sound arose from the shoreward side of it. As they tied up the punt and stepped off her, a brown crew-cut head appeared over the farther side and the chuckling stopped.

The head spoke, in formal, affected tones, heightened by a rather ghastly lisp. "Good morning. Are you friend or enemy?"

"Good morning, Horatio." Emily was brisk. "I'm sure you remember us. Are your parents at home?"

"Dead, I fear. All dead." The head emerged further. Horatio appeared to be submerged to the shoulders in the water, holding on to the float, but completely clothed. His face was pointed and elfin. His eyes were close-set slits, and his mouth, like the dogs Ogden Nash wrote about, went sideways. Hill was always reminded, when looking at Horatio Blanchard, of a once-seen portrait of a prince of the Middle Ages, the face, under a velvet beret, completely unscrupulous, charming, cunning — and quite mad.

Emily, however, subscribed to the more widely-held and much less frightening verdict of "Poor Horatio." She attempted to pat his head. He ducked. "Well," she said reassuringly, "we'll just go up and see if we can help. They may not be quite dead. Aren't you cold, Horatio?"

"No. I have on my skin-diving suit. They took away my helmet because that horrible old Parker woman said that if I swam under old Paine's dinghy and upset him again, she'd have him sue my father. I hate that old woman; I really hate her. I'd like to kill her dead, just like my poor parents are."

Emily started up the ladder, shaking her head. Hill paused to look at Horatio. "You have on a shirt and trousers, Horatio," he said, "and they'll shrink from that cold water."

Horatio merely smiled.

Chapter 6

INTERLUDE ON ANOTHER PORCH

The Blanchards were, for once, guestless; however, they appeared to be preparing to remedy their lorn situation. They sat side by side on a dilapidated porch glider, retrieved for fifty cents, they boasted, from the Morgan Memorial. They were making lists. From time to time they consulted official-looking records that probably indicated the degree of talent of various naval personnel as to rowing, berrying, and so forth, and, after short, civil altercations with each other, did much crossing-out and rearranging of names.

They rose in unison as Miss Elbridge and Hill came up the path. The Captain was short and powerfully-built; his wife, tall, ash-blonde and wraith-like, a gentle Virginian lady whose quiet charm had completely captivated her many brisk Bostonian in-laws.

"Emily, dear, and Hill. How nice," said Kitty Blanchard warmly.

The Captain was just as warm. "Sun's over the yard-arm; how about it?" he said, and without waiting for a reply whipped into the house, emerging almost instantly with two healthy-looking tumblers of what appeared to be straight dark rum.

His daughter Pherousa followed shyly, carrying two more, and whispered, in a soft, almost-undistinguishable slur, "Goodmorningeveryone." She then moved gracefully away around a corner of the cottage, her long fair hair drifting airily behind her.

"That child reminds me of a mermaid," said Hill. "She's very lovely," he added hastily, but he need not have troubled. The Captain was enchanted at the comparison.

"Does, doesn't she? Though more a sea-nymph, maybe?" He took a noisy swig of his rum and his dark-red face deepened to a pleasing mahogany. "Ahhh. Now, that's the only thing the Navy lacks."

"Sea-nymphs?" asked Emily, bewildered.

"Rum!" shouted the Captain. "Drink up, drink up!"

"Well, we will, Fred, but we want you to come over to The Bungalow tomorrow evening around six-thirty and drink up with us. Lemuel's coming over from Northeast Harbor and Elizabeth's new secretary will have arrived. We want you both to meet her. She'll be here all summer."

"Lem, hey? Hear he's got another of those assistants. Know he gets a new one out of Radcliffe every year — don't know why the Marines pay for such goings-on. When is he going to finish that history of the Corps? Not that I'd expect him to hurry himself any. Hey?"

Emily felt it in order to show a little family feeling. "Lem has a great need for these young ladies —"

"Bet he has," rumbled the Captain.

"— and it is very necessary and stimulating to him to have their services."

"Hmm," said the Captain.

"As you know," went on Emily, "the Corps agreed to provide him with research workers and a secretary, and these girls just out of college are very eager to please and anxious to spend a year with Lem learning his methods —"

"Aha!"

"Lem doesn't choose them, you know, Fred. I believe they are procured for him by General Stanley, and I do wish you wouldn't be so worldly about it!"

The Captain subsided, but let loose one last small salvo. "Procured, hey? Worse even than I thought," he confided to his glass."

"Freddy," said Kitty Blanchard, "please behave. Where is Horatio, do you know?"

The Captain perceptibly saddened. "It's all right, dear. He's down on the float."

"But I don't see him. Would you go down and see that he's all right?"

Sighing, but obedient to his superior's orders, the Captain rose, efficiently downing his rum as he did so. His burly figure went down the path, loudly crunching the shells underfoot.

"Of course, we want Pherousa and Horatio to come over, too," Emily said quickly.

"Thank you, Emily. I really think they would enjoy it. Horatio is much better this summer, don't you think so?"

Hill thought a change of conversation might be beneficial to his aunt's New England conscience. "Your clamshell paths are much wider and handsomer than ours. And you don't really need them."

"Well, we did copy yours. They are so pretty, winding amongst your juniper and blueberry bushes. But why do you say we don't need them?"

Hill was surprised. "Otis and Elizabeth put them in so that one could walk about safely at night. They show up in the dark even without a flashlight, and Otis would never consent to having electric lights on the place. But you have electricity."

"Why, I declare," said Kitty. "And all this time we thought yours were only ornamental. Freddy, did you hear that?"

The Captain had returned, towing a dripping, smiling Horatio, "Yes, dear, yes. Now, son, go and change and then find Junior. He might let you help him paint the boat."

Horatio stopped smiling and became stubborn. Hill was fascinated. "Like a Borgia mule," he thought.

"I will not go near that evil man," proclaimed Horatio. "He is evil, evil, evil! He kisses persons of the female sex he is not married to."

Kitty's pretty, faded face crumpled. "Darling, if you will do as your father says, I will let you have your helmet this afternoon."

"Very well, Muvver, dear. But you promised the old lady, you know. They tell me all the time at school to keep my promises."

Captain Blanchard led Horatio into the house and returned, rubbing his short, iron-grey hair. "Well," he said heartily, "the boy wants to be honest, hey, Kitty? Now, let's have another." He wrested their still fairly full glasses from his guests.

"Is Horatio at school now?" Emily asked politely.

"The most marvelous school, dear. It is in Canada. They have great hopes of Horatio, have they not, Freddy? I am sorry I held him so long at home, but I wanted so badly to help him myself."

"I have often noticed," Hill observed musingly, "that it is the children one keeps nearest one and does the most for that one cares for the most. I don't mean this, of course, personally," he added hastily, "but I have seen that children who are handed over as soon and as often as possible to servants and schools are so much less valued than the ones whose cribs the parents themselves hung over.

"I suppose," he concluded, thinking the sooner he ended, the better, "it is the old case of which came first — the disinterest leading to the handing-over, or vice versa."

"I was brought up entirely by servants and governesses," said Miss Elbridge, never one to let a subject drop. "Elizabeth was the lucky one. My uncle fancied her and took her to every diplomatic post he had, after our parents were killed. And then, when I grew up, he never really cared for me. I think you're quite right, Hill."

"I don't quite agree," Kitty said, "that one cares more for the children one spends more time with. What about the Proutys? They have hordes of children always about but they don't stay awake nights, I am sure, concerned if one of them is in jail or is having a baby at fifteen."

"But the Proutys are Natives," cried Emily, and then blushed, as Junior Noyes, the caretaker of the cottages on the cove, came up to the porch of "Quarterdeck."

Hill could quite see that the stories his friends the Proutys told about Junior might possibly have some truth in them. According to the not-very-reliable Proutys, he was a devil with the ladies, not excepting some of the summer ladies of the backside who were left alone for anything from a week at a time to half the summer, their lords being busy adding to the family assets in Boston, Philadelphia, or points west and south.

Junior was tall and lank, his sun-bleached blonde hair contrasting nicely with deep blue eyes and very tanned skin. His smile was tentative and shy, but his general bearing most self-assured. "A very intriguing contrast," Hill had always thought, and wondered, not for the first time, how Junior diverted himself in the winter. The Proutys, of course, had assured him that it was in much the same fashion, though a little harder to arrange, the Maine climate being what it is, and the Native husbands being, by and large, no fools.

The minute Junior spoke, however, his utter lack of guile was revealed, in every gesture and intonation, and it was quite obvious that the rascally Proutys spoke from jealousy, jealousy of a sober young man who was hard-working and much-valued, and valued not without reason. Any child, even, of the families for which he worked, who needed advice or whose possessions needed fixing had only to speak to Junior. He knew a great many things, and he could do almost anything, and he knew how to arrange efficiently to have done the few things he could not do.

He had this day been up since before five, had checked the pumps for the artesian wells at the cottages in his care, manually starting Mrs. Worthington's gasoline pump, had repaired Mrs. Gambel's loom, adjusted the motor of the Gambel's Boston Whaler which had, as usual, been put out of commission by one of their superior offspring, taken old George Paine to Southwest Harbor, had there collected mail, dry-cleaned clothes, and various groceries for the cove cottages, brought back the ice for The Bungalow — Sarah had as yet had no luck in the matter of the bottled gas refrigerator she weekly urged upon her mother —, put several new planks in the Blanchards' float and was now preparing to paint one of their boats. It was now just a little after noon.

Junior was paid $1.50 an hour by his cottagers in the summer and twenty dollars a month for the nine or ten months a year that they were not in Maine. The Gambels paid him ten dollars a month; they believed in the equality of man and thought it embarrassing to the recipient of wages if he were paid enough to indicate he was a servant and not a friend who just obliged. (A policy that did not work at all, for them in Washington, in the winter.) They insisted, or tried to insist, that Junior call them "Horton" and "Minerva." Junior addressed them as "Dr. Gambel" and "Ma'am" and was preparing to inform them that his friendship would not be strained by his charging them thirty dollars a month during the winter.

"Good morning, Mrs. Blanchard, Miss Elbridge, Captain, Hill," he said. "Cove's flat's a millpond this morning, isn't it? Mrs. Parker asked me to bring you this, ma'am."

He held out an envelope to Kitty, who regarded it with distaste.

"Thank you, Junior," she said, taking it by one corner. "Would you mind very, very much taking Horatio down to help you paint?" she asked winningly, walking with the note to the far end of the porch.

Behind the Captain's back, Hill made a grimace to Junior

denoting sympathy. "Could you come over to us for a few minutes, later?" he asked.

Junior remained polite and inscrutable. "Of course, Mrs. Blanchard," he said, firmly grasping Horatio's sleeve. Horatio had suddenly appeared in their midst with closed eyes and out-stretched arms, pretending to be sleep-walking. "I'll be over soon, Hill."

Junior and Horatio took the path through the woods to the shed, Junior talking pleasantly to Horatio, who was now rolling his eyes wildly and singing.

The three watching them turned at an exclamation from Kitty. Her face was flushed with anger and her hand violently crumpled the letter. She seemed to have aged ten years in as many seconds. Her voice was hoarse: "This is not to be borne! I will not endure any further persecution from that dreadful woman. Excuse me, please, Emily." She fled into the house.

The Captain followed, anxiety and apology mixed in the look he gave Hill and Emily.

Before they reached their boat, they were hailed by Captain Blanchard, who lumbered unsteadily down the path to them, his usually ruddy face quite pale.

"Awfully sorry," he said, leaning heavily against the railing of the bridge to the float. "Kitty's not, not herself. Don't know what to do, either." He turned away from them and rubbed his hand roughly across his eyes. "Damned old woman!" he burst out.

"What's the matter?" asked Emily. "Are you all right, Fred?"

Hill's legal training brought him quickly to the point. "Who?" he asked.

"That Parker creature," Captain Blanchard answered, with a look of hate directed at the left shore of the cove. "She's written Kitty that she's taking steps to have Horatio placed in a State home. Says my poor boy's a danger to himself and his neighbors and that she's not about to have her daughter and son-in-law exposed to him."

"Oh, Fred," Emily said, "she hasn't the right to do that, or the power. Hill, has she?"

"Well," Hill answered slowly, "she might be able to do something. She's got a lot of influence, as any woman as rich as she is has, and she retains an impressive battery of lawyers for Parker Cordage. She may know of some loop-hole."

"I won't stand for it," said Captain Blanchard. His voice was unusually low and cold. "I won't have Kitty worried any more. That bitch . . .

"I apologize for worrying you with our problems. I've got to go back to Kitty now."

Hill and Emily rowed silently back across the cove. Isabella, in a bright yellow bikini, was gathering mussels from the rocks by the float, reaching down into the cold water with a pained Victorian expression.

"Why in the world did you wait until the tide started coming in to do that?" called Hill.

"Because I have to make Moules Mariniere for lunch, *stupide!* You've spent so much time boozing at 'Quarterdeck' that there's no time to go to Southwest Harbor for beer to go with the clams, and I refuse to eat clams without beer. We shall have my moules and a good white wine with them to fortify you for your drive to Trenton.

"I think I'll go along with you, to protect my dear sister's interests. I don't trust you with secretaries, sweetest. You know what the sea air does to you, in Maine or on the Riviera, yes?"

Hill went up to The Bungalow looking as though his brotherly restraint might not hold much longer. Emily lingered. "You are getting them now from just where the waste pipes go down into the cove, dear."

"That's where they're the fattest, Em. It's nothing less than a crime the way the Natives turn up their noses at mussels. In New York we pay four-fifty an entree and here they are thought of as paupers' food. Maine women are as ignorant of good food as they are of everything else!"

"I wish you wouldn't be so intolerant, Isabella. Maine women don't have very easy lives, you know. The income, low as it usually is, is largely in the hands of their husbands, and it is not so easy to acquire good taste when there is no money to help it along. Dora tells me that the reason so many of the women on the backside work at sardine packing, even the ones with small children, is just to have some money of their own."

"But that hair, dear Auntie! That frizzy Maine look! Every time I overtake a car on this island going twenty miles an hour I know it is going to have Maine plates and a woman driver with frizzy hair and a nasty expression."

Emily laughed. "Well, Issa, every time *I* get behind a car going twenty miles an hour, it has Massachusetts or Pennsylvania plates and a woman driver with the hair and facial expression you describe. I believe it is the fog that works on the hair and our daring to want to pass them that causes these maddeningly-slow drivers to look so outraged. They cause more accidents than the fast drivers, I'm convinced."

"That's why you are my favourite aunt as well as my only one, Emily; you aren't reactionary."

"I don't know that I'm not, Issa. Except in the matter of driving, I am pretty cautious and set in my ways, as they say up here. I'd never be able to learn to row standing up, for instance."

They watched Junior rowing across the cove to their float, standing in the local fashion, facing forward and pushing at his oars instead of pulling.

Isabella put her bucket into her aunt's hand. "If you put Dora to scrubbing these, darling, I'll be up in just a minute. There does happen to be one thing that Native women have that I don't, you know."

"And what," asked Emily, "could that possibly be? An inferiority complex?"

"They have a year-long chance at the Native men. And I've seldom seen one who wasn't *most* attractive."

Emily left her to it.

Chapter 7

ENTER THE INGENUE

A delegation of three from The Bungalow awaited the arrival of Mrs. Worthington's secretary at the Bar Harbor Airport, which is, for the necessary area of flat landing space, actually not even on Mount Desert Island, much less in Bar Harbor, but on the mainland in a sort of limbo between the island and Ellsworth called the Trenton Flats.

Isabella was not one of the delegation. She had stamped into The Bungalow's kitchen in a healthy rage, prepared her mussels most deliciously, eaten and drunk heartily, and said little, except to murmur over her coffee that some idiots didn't know a good thing when it was offered them. This confused her family, all except Emily, but they hastened to assure her that they did, indeed, appreciate her Moules Mariniere.

Their expressions of gratitude were received with regal grace, and then Isabella announced that she was going to begin to paint again. Her family received this news with calm approval, and helped her locate her supplies, which had been tossed into a cupboard in the woodshed the summer before.

Her gear having been ascertained to be in usable condition, she had driven off in her car with an unwilling Gus for company, his blonde hair sticking up in defiance and his blue eyes rolling back for a last look at his beloved boat. Only the promise of unlimited ice-cream at the Southwest Harbor drug store had secured his attention, which was riveted on *Coacher* only when it was not concentrated on his palate. Even so, poor Gus knew it to be quite possible that his untrustworthy aunt might persuade him to by-pass the drug store with promises of tracking a brand of ice-cream known only in Hancock County and its environs and much loved by him above all others — and then just never be able, somehow, to find a place that sold it.

Since Gus rather suspected this would happen, and since he had observed that Isabella's painting equipment, which he was to carry up hill and down dale for her, was unreasonably heavy and cumbersome, he looked forward to a desolate afternoon.

Sarah had remained at the cove to see to the enormous amount of housekeeping that a well-run Mount Desert summer camp seems to require, even with some Native help, the more so when the owner demands that life be plain and ungarnished, as Mrs. Worthington did.

"To live simply up here in the summer takes more time, money and servants than most people can afford," Sarah had said in a moment of unusual perspicuity. "No wonder you love Maine so much, Mother; it is the rest of us who have to exert a complication of skills to insure that your life here shall be uncomplicated."

Mrs. Worthington had smilingly disagreed. She had then asked Sarah to find Junior, wherever about the cove he might be, and to give him a telegram to be telephoned in from his house, then to put the sinkable garbage in the skiff for Gus to row out beyond the reef at high tide, to write a note for Dora to remind her of the drip-pan under the ice-box, which had a tendency to overflow just at the moment when dinner was announced, to tell Persis to clean and trim the wicks of the oil lamps, and to be sure that Doreen did not forget that night the pitcher of spring water still served twice a week at dinner, in place of wine, as Otis Worthington had decreed; the spring was in the woods a quarter-mile away.

Persis, Miss Elbridge, and Hill stood behind the steel mesh fence looking up at the grey cotton wool that is frequently the summer cover of the Trenton Flats. A plane was most distinctly overhead, but invisible to them. Persis was wearing a starched smocked lavender dress with a little white collar, clean new red sneakers, and a worried expression. "Daddy?" she whispered. "Daddy? What shall I say to the little girl?"

Before Hill could speak, Emily was firm. "You just say 'How-do-you-do' to her, and smile. And you must be very sweet, very kind to her all summer. Remember, she is a little girl who has probably never been out of New York City and hasn't had the things you have had, dogs and boats and toys. If she doesn't speak the way we do, or behave nicely at table, you must pretend not to notice."

"Will she chase the birds, Aunt Emily? There are hermit thrushes nesting under the big beech tree."

"If she does, we must teach her not to. And you must both be as quiet as you can so that her mother can help your grandmother to write her articles. Otherwise, she will have to leave, and her mother too, and your father will have to find Grandmother a new secretary."

"God deliver me," said Hill loudly and prayerfully, unsuccessfully avoiding the quizzical eye of one of the Episcopal rectors of the island, who, in a striking ensemble of cut-off blue jeans with a piece of rope for a belt, topped by a black clerical blouse with white collar, was waiting next to him, looking glum.

"Good afternoon, Rev; why the dog collar?" asked Hill.

"Mary's mother. Unexpected. Moment's notice. Couldn't finish changing," answered the priest, a man of few words except when in the pulpit.

"You'd never get away with that outfit if you had Jack's parish," Hill observed.

"From that, God has delivered *me,*" answered the reverend gentleman, turning with an unfilial expression of Christian fortitude to the DC-3 that had suddenly appeared on the ground and taxied to a stop. After the usual interlude, passengers began to appear, with the stunned and/or exalted expression common to disembarking air travellers.

"Late as usual," a man standing near Hill announced. He sounded proud rather than annoyed. "Always know I have time for one more stinger before racing up here to meet our guests."

"Often late, but always safe," answered Hill. "Haven't had a fatality yet, I believe."

"Two weeks ago," informed his acquaintance, "I was going down to Baltimore for a few days. We were just taking off when this fellow rushed up, wife panting behind with his bags, and began to holler.

Pretty soon the guy here who seems to run the whole shebang signalled us to stop and take him on. He told us in flight that since he'd never known them to take off on time before, he was mentally unprepared to get here at take-off time. Sounded like a psychologist of some sort. Said he'd demanded that therefore they let him on, and they did. Good old Northeast!"

"It's what I call a good airline," answered Hill, as he became aware of a certain rigidity in his women-folk. He followed their stares to the top of the low landing-ramp. A girl-child of about eight stood there, calmly surveying the motley crowd of thin, tanned summer people and paler, plumper Maine citizens.

She was the most striking child Hill had ever seen. Thick hair of a silver gilt color hung to her shoulders and just cleared, in a heavy bang, her dark brows. Her features were delicate and regular, with the promise of even greater beauty. Her eyes were enormous and, Hill discovered later, of a true, deep green. She wore a straight-cut dress of heavy scarlet linen, hand-stitched in white, with circular cut-outs under the arms that revealed her body to be the same golden tan as her slim, bare arms and legs. She had red patent-leather slippers with silver buckles on her feet, and she carried an Air France flight bag and a red lizard dressing case.

"Isn't she beautiful!" gasped round little Persis. "Who is she, Daddy?"

The child descended the steps and walked through the gate to stop before Hill. "I am sure you are Mr. Halstead," she said graciously, extending a small hand in a spotless white cotton glove. "I am Elizabeth Lamb, and this is my mother."

The dazed Halsteads and Miss Elbridge fixed their eyes on a slight, disheveled young woman who had followed in the wake of the vision. She had the same silver hair, tarnished here and there to a pewter color, and worn short and tousled. She had the same dark brows and green eyes, but they were faded and ineffective compared to her daughter's. She also wore linen, a pale pink suit that was sadly crumpled. Her skirt zipper had shifted to a place where it was not designed to be, and she clutched a single, soiled glove in one hand and with the other worried at the straps of a black crocodile handbag that had obviously suffered that treatment before.

"How do you do?" she whispered, swallowing several times first.

Hill recovered. "Emily, Mrs. Lamb, Miss Lamb. Mrs. Lamb, my wife's aunt, Miss Elbridge. My daughter Persis."

Emily greeted the Lambs. Persis remained silent, her eyes and mouth wide.

"I'll see about the luggage, Mummy," said Miss Lamb, and entered the airport building. Hill followed. He emerged two minutes later, carrying four large Vuitton cases. What had evidently been an innocent bystander had been pressed by Miss Lamb into service to walk beside her and carry two more. Emily and Persis fell into line, and Mrs. Lamb came quietly behind them.

Hill stacked the bags in the back of his station wagon. "I'm afraid the floor is rather dirty," he began, looking at the Lambs' worn but still impressive baggage. Elizabeth Lamb, however, was very reassuring.

"They've been in worse places," she said kindly. "We flew back from Jamaica last month and our bags sat in a downpour there at the airport for four hours. They've only just dried out."

Hill directed his passengers to seats and finished loading. He observed myriad Compagnie Generale Transatlantique labels, or their remains, several dozen airline stickers, half torn off, of course, and many hotel tags, likewise carefully partially obliterated. He wistfully observed a label from the one discreet and prohibitively expensive hotel in London at which he had always wanted to stay but had never dared.

It occurred to him that he might relate a story about his great-aunt, who was so socially secure that she always left all of the stickers in toto on her suitcases and let those who chose think she was showing-off. He decided against it. Emily would not see any point to it, since she had the same theory as his great-aunt, and Mrs. Lamb might.

The car headed out for the main road, no one speaking. Mrs. Lamb, sitting in the back seat beside Emily, looked straight ahead. Hill drove stolidly. Miss Elbridge attempted to think of something to say suitable to this most unsecretarial pair.

Persis gulped several draughts of the air near Elizabeth Lamb. "You smell so good," she said timidly.

"Thank you." Elizabeth Lamb was again gracious. "I am too young to use scent, but today is my eighth birthday, so Mummy allowed me to open my bottle."

Mrs. Lamb smiled nervously. "She'd had it for years. Her father had given it to her," she mumbled, looking out her side window.

"I won't be eight until next week," offered Persis. Her chin quivered sadly.

Emily overlooked a father who would buy *Replique* for an infant daughter. "Your birthday today! How nice for you to be here for it, and not in New York City, where it is so hot. We must have a cake."

"Yes, thank you," replied the child, "but I really do not enjoy fancy cakes. I prefer plain *gâteau sec*. We were going to be in Paris today, but instead Mummy decided we couldn't refuse to come to Mrs. Worthington. M. Vondel can jolly well wait."

"Yes," said Emily. "Well, how nice. Do you travel much in your work, Mrs. Lamb?"

Mrs. Lamb's answer was inaudible. Her daughter seemed to be accustomed to replying for her. "We'll travel only in the summer, after next year, Miss Elbridge. I shall have to settle down to one school by then."

"And where will that be?" asked Emily.

"Probably somewhere near Boston. My grandfather came from Lynn."

"Lynn. Yes. Well, Lynn can be very nice. What was his name?"

"It was my father," whispered Mrs. Lamb. "We went to live in Europe when I was very small, and seldom came back. He painted." Overcome by this torrent of not-too-enlightening speech, she subsided back against her seat, blushing.

The car left the airport grounds, passed a few roadside stands, and swung round a curve. Elizabeth Lamb gasped. Far ahead of them to the southeast, across the whole horizon, above a fringe of spruce and a sign announcing "Sightseeing Flights, $2.50", was a long, impressive range of low humped mountains, looking like nothing so much as a giant's circus procession of mastodons, noses to tails.

"*Voilà, chère Maman! Regardez les éléphants de Mont Desert!*" exclaimed Elizabeth Lamb showily.

Mrs. Lamb was still quiet but not timid. She gave her child a stiff rap on the shoulder and distinctly admonished, "That will quite do, Elizabeth Lamb."

Elizabeth dropped her eyes and said meekly, "Yes, Mummy."

The others were astounded. It was like the proverbial worm-turn. Immediately, Mrs. Lamb went back into her shell, or her hole, if we are to stick to the metaphor, and whispered, "I do not like Elizabeth Lamb to use French as much as she does."

"I do understand," Emily replied quickly. "She could appear quite *outré*" — and then laughed at herself as Hill snorted gleefully.

"But how clever of you, Elizabeth," she went on, "to realize that the mountains appear to be elephants. Mrs. Worthington's children, when they were small, always waited for that spot, where they could see their 'elephants,' and know that the summer had really begun for them."

"I knew that they were called the elephants before I saw them, Miss Elbridge," said Elizabeth politely.

"She reads in advance about every place we go," her mother explained.

Emily was surprised. "Really? There have been very few things written about Mount Desert Island, at least in recent years, since the demise of the 'Bar Harbor novels,' and I didn't know anything had ever referred to 'our' elephants. Of course, the resemblance must have occurred to many people. How sad it is to realize one's thoughts are not unique, especially one's witty or playful thoughts. Those always seem so very personal."

A pall of depressed silence settled on the car, since no one could think of an answer to Miss Elbridge that would not sound either flippant or labored. "Oh, lord," thought Hill, "she's a great old girl but she certainly has a gift for dampening a conversation!"

He drove across a short bridge and on to a small island, where there were a cluster of out-of-state cars in front of a little white building offering information about Mount Desert. Persis was disdainful. "Tourists," she told Elizabeth, wrinkling up her short nose.

"We are all tourists somewhere," she was answered. Hill laughed, and Elizabeth was offended. "Well, we are! My mummy said so, to a fat lady in Martinique. She didn't think we could understand French, and she was saying she didn't like tourists."

"We are not tourists." Persis' voice trembled indignantly.

"Well, what are you then? I thought you lived near Boston."

"*We* are summer people." Persis was firm.

Elizabeth Lamb had no answer. She looked thoughtful.

"Persis," said her father, "we are only visitors, you know. We visit your grandmother, who is a summer resident. We are visiting, just as Elizabeth is doing. And look, with all this talk, you've missed telling her when she actually arrived on Mount Desert Island."

By this time, they had indeed driven across another short bridge, leaving Thompson's Island's information center to the mercy of its inquisitors, and were on the soil of what the more enthusiastic of Mount Desert's residents and visitors call "The Most Beautiful Island In The World." Hill disdained the left fork in the road, leading to Bar

Harbor, and drove straight ahead.

Persis had been thinking her own thoughts. "Where were you born?" she asked Elizabeth Lamb.

"In Cape Town."

"Where's that?"

"It's a very long ways away. You have to take the Pacific and Orient to get back to England, or else fly."

"What's the Pacific and Orient?"

"It's a steamship company, though I don't know if there is real steam any more. Oh, you know, like Cunard or the French Line."

Persis was bewildered.

Elizabeth tried again. "You must know; it's the one they got 'posh' from. You know, 'port out, starboard home.' P.O.S.H. *Posh.*"

Persis gave up. She settled back, nodding ingratiatingly and sniffing the rarefied and expensive air about this fascinating creature who knew everything.

"When we sail, we don't have to change sides to come back to The Bungalow," she ventured. "We just come about. But I guess your way is *much* better."

Hill turned to smile at his little girl, who smiled confidingly back.

"They just might be very good for each other," he thought, "in spite of the fact that this kid is probably really a midget and the Paris correspondent of *The New Yorker* to boot!" Then: "But if Sarah ever hears them talking together — I'll bet this one knows everything there is to know, and she doesn't appear to have a trace of reticence."

He was about to come out with, "Elizabeth, do you know the Facts of Life?" when a meek sneeze from Jane Lamb reminded him of the existence of the two ladies in the back seat. He switched quickly to, "Elizabeth, do you know — the Follies Bergère?"

Hill was aware of a disapproving sniff from Emily.

"What did you say, Mr. Halstead?" asked Elizabeth Lamb, not unreasonably, phrase-switching in mid-sentence not being conducive to controlled articulation.

Feeling more than a little foolish, Hill repeated his question, while at the back of his mind was the happy thought that Sarah would be pleased that the child did not say, "Pardon?"

"Oh, yes," the child answered. "I've been twice, and I've been backstage. It was very informative — how they change their sets and get their effects, I mean. I know," she said clearly, leaning forward to look across Persis at what she could see of Hill's face, "a great many things older people know, but I'm not supposed to tell unless I'm asked. My mother says never to tell a direct lie."

Miss Elbridge sniffed louder.

"You reassure me," said Hill. "I have a feeling you will know what I'm saying even when I'm not."

Elizabeth Lamb nodded kindly. "That's all right," she said, inscrutably.

"What nonsense are you talking to the child, Hill?" cried Emily. "And do slow down. Here is Somesville and you know very well you can't do more than twenty-five."

Out of perversity, Hill was about to speed up to well over the forty-five he was driving, when, as usual, he saw in the distance the Somesville summer traffic policeman, whose dour and cold down-wagging of the hands could subdue even the most dedicated speed demon. Indeed, there had been, once, for several years, a policeman on duty in Somesville who fiendishly had stopped speeders, inquired their destination, and then ordered them from their cars to sit on the curb for exactly the number of minutes he calculated it would have taken them to get there at the legal speed.

Hill subsided gracefully down to twenty-five.

"What a beautiful little village!" Jane Lamb exclaimed softly.

"Oh, it is," Emily agreed. "But because it is so perfect and because most of the people are always out of sight when I drive through, I have always maintained that the whole thing is a stage set and not real at all! One sees a few people outside the two stores, and of course the policeman is in clear view except during his dinner hour — when, I suspect, crime runs rampant — but there just do not seem to be people enough for all the beautiful houses. And there is no litter and no noise — it is just unreal!"

Mrs. Lamb turned to look back yearningly at the pretty village street, the church that had graced a magazine cover, and a brook falling charmingly into a placid pool. She sighed. "I would love to have a little house in a town like this, and just become a quiet old lady in it," she said.

Emily regarded her more kindly than she had before. "You have many years to go before you can become an old lady, my dear."

Persis turned around to Mrs. Lamb. "Why do you call your little girl by her last name?"

Jane looked alarmed. Her daughter spoke for her. "Oh, she doesn't, really. It was my dreadful daddy. He —"

"All right, Elizabeth," said her mother. "I see what you mean, Persis. It was a habit I got into years ago, when Elizabeth's father engaged a Southern nurse who called Elizabeth 'Elizabeth, lamb' and me 'Jane, honey.'"

"We couldn't afford her. In fact, we couldn't even pay her, which is different, and worse," went on Elizabeth Lamb, "and she wanted to leave and go back to New Orleans anyway, and then my mummy and daddy, they —"

"Where is your daddy?" interrupted Persis.

Elizabeth gesticulated grandly up at the sky over the Somesville woods. "He went up there," she answered vaguely. "High time, too."

No one asked why.

Chapter 8

OVER THE RIVER
AND THROUGH THE WOODS

Hill drove down the slope towards the intersection at Center, announcing to his silent passengers the name of this point of backside interest. Jane Lamb became articulate enough to wonder aloud, in a modest tone of voice, as to why it was so called, since there appeared only to be a marsh filled with cattails and wild iris and a crossroads with an enormous assortment of rural mailboxes in the two righthand corners. At one of these boxes, a thin, dark, harassed-looking woman was struggling to untie a large package hooked on to it. Her companion, fair, calm, and florid of face, sat at the wheel of their car, gazing peacefully at the iris and utterly ignoring her.

"Teddy, please —" she was squeaking as Hill passed her. Hill and Emily waved, and she waved back, dropping the package with an ominous crunch. Teddy, after waving in a leisurely fashion, shifted his attention up to a small, high-flying cloud.

"Poor Cousin Cordelia," observed Emily. "Now she, Mrs. Lamb, actually did spend a winter once in a rented house in Somesville, at a low point in her fortune. I believe it was then she formed the habit of talking to herself, because practically no one in town spoke to her. Cordelia was in the store once, and she heard someone ask, 'Who's that?' Another person answered, 'That's a summer lady.' The questioner laughed and said, 'But it's December,' and was answered, 'Oh, she's a summer lady who stays all winter'!"

"If only that worthless Ted would ever stir himself to do something, anything!" said Hill. "I wouldn't put the blame for Cordelia's talking to herself completely on Somesville, Emily. It must be frustrating for her that all Ted does is spend her capital, now that she's finally come into some money."

"Spend her capital!" echoed Persis, in horror. She may not have had the exotic worldly thrills that Elizabeth Lamb had experienced, but almost eight years of life spent in the vicinity of Boston had taught her what was the unforgiveable worldly sin.

Hill went on, "But you were asking, Jane, why that corner is named 'Center.' Years ago there were several churches there, and it was the center of religious activity on the west side of the island, and for that reason came to be called Center."

Elizabeth Lamb was looking back at the distraught figure at the cross-roads, now scrabbling around in the roadside trying to put the package together. "Is that lady everybody's cousin?"

Hill laughed. "Well, no. Actually her father and Mrs. Worthington were the children of first cousins. Mrs. Woodhue is only my wife's third cousin, but in Boston they cling to their cousins. Everybody must have something."

He turned off to the right and went along a narrow gravelled road. The road became, briefly, a wooden plank bridge that crossed a little stream. "Jordan River," said Hill. "No, really, that's its name."

Across the Jordan there was a small old cemetery on the right side of the road and, a little farther on, a two-story clapboard house that had once been painted white and green. Several dusty, half-clad children looked up from their play with small trucks in a puddle of mud and water to wave joyfully at the travellers. A handsome brown cow chewed on the roadside grass, and rabbits and ducks were scattered about the door-yard, which was screened by an enormous lilac bush, garnished with a brilliant half-circle of nasturtiums and petunias, and filled to the brim with every sort of rusty, junked article imaginable.

"I see Varner put his new stove in the kitchen, right along with his old one," Hill observed over his shoulder to Emily.

"How do you know? I didn't think you'd had a chance to go down to visit him yet."

"I haven't, but the old stove isn't outside, and he was saying at the store that he'd put a new one in for Minnie. I suppose they'll leave the old one in the kitchen and just walk around it." He braked sharply on a rise as a short, stalwart figure, its dark face adorned with several days' growth of beard, appeared on the crest brandishing a hatchet. Jane gave a low shriek and leaned forward to clutch her daughter by both shoulders.

"Hey, deah!" shouted the apparition.

"Hey, Varner!" answered Hill. "Why ain't you down to the factory?"

"Got awful jagged last night, deah. Woke up so late Minnie said 'twasn't no use to go. Said I'd best get more firewood for her. She's putting up a mess of wild strawberry jam for to sell at that Exchange place down to the Harbor."

"Would she hold out for me as many jars as she can, Varner?" Emily asked. "As long as it lasts, Minnie's jam brightens my breakfast every winter morning down in New York."

"Yes, ma'm, Miss Elbridge. Minnie says she'd like for you to stop by sometime and see the baby. She named him Peter, says he looks just like Peter. She always liked Peter, says some day he'll be appreciated."

"Why, that's nice, Varner." Emily sounded faintly taken-aback. "I'll tell Mrs. Worthington, and I'll come by in a few days."

"Bye, son. Behave yourself, now," said Hill.

As the car started past him, Varner swept off his decrepit old felt hat and made an exaggerated bow to the two little girls in the front seat. Straightening up, he gave Jane a raffish wink.

Persis giggled, but Elizabeth Lamb was uneasy. "He's awfully dirty," she said. "What was it he called you, Mr. Halstead?"

"He was calling me 'dear'. The old-timers call both men and women 'dear.' They call their men-friends 'son,' too. Varner Prouty isn't any older than I am, but he's learned a lot of the old ways from his father and his uncles. The Proutys have been on the island or over on Bartlett's Island for more than two hundred years. They aren't exactly typical of the Natives here, but you do meet some like them. They drink heavily and fight and — ah — do other things that aren't well looked upon, but they are good friends.

"Varner was decorated for bravery in the field on Guadalcanal, Jane. I think of him, you know, as a Renaissance man out of his time."

Jane was too much interested to be shy. "Good heavens, why? He doesn't look to be a well-rounded, inquiring mind, open to new ideas?"

"Lord, no, I'm afraid he's a rank bigot, and he feels, rather than thinks, but he's just so darned versatile. He can castrate a pig or slaughter it and smoke the hams and bacon, shoe a horse or vet it, take a truck apart and put it together again, drop a deer with one shot, build a house or a boat or a lobster trap, sail, cook, ride, grow any flower or vegetable, and steal anything you ask him to or that he fancies himself. He even writes verse, makes it up, that is.

"And, except for when he was in the Marines, he's never been farther away from the island than Bangor."

Elizabeth was more interested in Mr. Prouty's vocabulary than his talents. "He didn't call Miss Elbridge 'dear,' " she said.

"No, there are a few people he'll give a title to, the people he admires as well as likes. The people he doesn't like, he speaks to most disrespectfully. All the Proutys are the same; you can't force respect out of them."

"Anyway," Hill went on, to an attentive audience, "almost all the Maine people call you what they called you when you were a child. If you were called Lemmy or Nelson when you came up in the summer at the age of five, you can grow up and become a general, like Mrs. Worthington's cousin General Alison, whom you'll meet tomorrow, or a governor, like Mr. Rockefeller, but when you're here in the summers, the old-timers will still address you as Lemmy or Nelson."

The road grew more rough, and narrowed. Overhead, the tamaracks and tall pines almost met in the middle, high above. A coolness could be felt that was not that of the forest.

"Almost there," said Hill. "I must tell you one thing about Varner, Jane. If he appears, as he will, at The Bungalow, and you happen to be the one to receive him, it's fatal to offer him a drink, no matter how hard he hints. He'd stay all night, hinting for more. I usually give him a quarter of a bottle or so to take home and share with Minnie."

Miss Elbridge laughed. "Just be sure it's the right bottle."

"That was pretty funny. Last year I gave him a bottle of whiskey, not very full, but as he was leaving by the kitchen door he spied what he thought was an almost full bottle of rum, and since the kitchen has only a wall gas lamp, it was dark enough for him to switch bottles without my seeing.

"Well, what he got was a bottle of household cleaner. The company was putting it out for a time in handsome purple or amber bottles with a ship design on them and no label. Minnie said Varner had two big drinks out of it before she could convince him he'd made a bad trade. Didn't hurt him, either."

Hill swung off the road and followed a narrow, grassy track. After a drive of about a mile, he stopped in a clearing. A large weathered grey garage was in front of them, its left side leaning into the dark pines and Miss Elbridge's little Swedish car showing through its open door. A rail fence hung with lobster buoys of varying shapes and degrees of decrepitude extended across the clearing from the right-hand wall of the garage.

Beyond the fence, the green-black woods rising up on the far sides, was a great sunny meadow ringed with gnarled old apple trees. Blueberry and juniper bushes were scattered amongst the daisies and meadow flowers, and a crushed clamshell path wound down to three grey buildings beyond and below which the beautiful deep blue of Schooner Cove shone brightly in the afternoon sun.

"Oh, lovely!" said Jane softly. Her daughter leaped out of the car beside a high bush of fragrant deep red blooms growing beside the fence. "What are they?" she asked. "They smell better than my perfume."

"They don't, either!" said the smitten Persis. "They're wild roses. Sometimes they are gone by now, but sometimes they last till August, out on Tinker's or Bar Island, where we go to picnic."

"The blessing of the landscape of Maine," added Hill. "Just as alder bushes are the curse, although I'm beginning to think that beer cans are the real curse."

He began to put the luggage in a brightly-painted wheelbarrow that stood handily beside the garage. Persis ran to open the gate in the fence. As they started down the path, a pick-up truck pulled up behind their car, and Junior jumped out and came up beside Hill to take over the wheelbarrow.

"Never knew you to make an entrance that wasn't timed to perfection," said Hill to him. "Jane, this is Junior Noyes, who looks after the place. Here are Mrs. Lamb and her daughter, Elizabeth Lamb, June."

Elizabeth Lamb seemed to be, for the first time since her arrival, impressed. "Are you the gardener?" she asked, almost shyly.

"Well, no, not exactly." Junior's blue eyes crinkled pleasantly. "General factotum and bottle-washer, you might say."

"I would like to meet an American gardener. My mother loves gardens, but we never have had one of our own. We just have some plants in pots on our window-sill in Paris. When I'm rich, she'll have a garden, and a gardener to do the work, because she'll be too old.

"And we'll have champagne every evening when she's tired and her head aches. I'm planning, you know, to marry into a great deal of money so she can have what she wants — champagne and a gardener!"

Chapter 9

THE PLAYERS ASSEMBLE

Promptly at six, as she had been requested by Sarah, Jane timidly entered the living room of The Bungalow, from the porch door. No one else, despite Sarah's announcement that all the family congregated there at six, was as yet in evidence.

When she first arrived at The Bungalow, she and her bags had been deposited by Junior at the outer door of her room in the studio building, where Sarah and Doreen had awaited her, Sarah, as Mrs. Worthington's deputy, to welcome her, and Doreen to help her unpack. The help had consisted mainly of such wholehearted admiration of a pair of bright green silk Italian trousers that Jane had finally presented them to her. Doreen had then immediately departed to the kitchen to inform her mother, in rather carrying tones, that the secretary was not much to look at, but good-hearted.

Jane had then unpacked in peace, not much regretting the loss of the trousers. They had never fitted properly, and one glance at Sarah's demure shirt and shorts had reminded her that this was not Positano, but the sovereign State of Maine. As she unpacked, she had wondered with some foreboding what her daughter was divulging to the flatteringly attentive ears of little Persis, who had disappeared with Elizabeth Lamb into the bunkroom built on the main Bungalow, which room they were to share.

"I hope," she had murmured to herself, recalling Sarah's antiseptic appearance, "she's not announcing that sometimes I'm too tired to wash out my stockings at night and so wear them two days in a row unwashed."

At six, the sun was still high over Bartlett's Island; a sailing chart of Blue Hill Bay, framed and hanging on the wall beside the huge fieldstone chimney breast, had informed her of the island's name. The fire was already lighted against the evening's coming chill; andirons in the shape of Hessian soldiers held three large logs.

As she faced the porch, the fireplace with the kitchen beyond it was at her back. The door in that wall was shut, but such delicious odors wafting through it, combined with a mumble of disputing voices and an occasional crash, made it certain that nothing but the kitchen could lie behind it.

To her left, an enormous divan was built into the entire length of the wall, with a window above it through which a corner of the guest cottage, some yards away, could be seen. The studio was out of sight behind the guest cottage, farther along the path back to the garage. To her right, a ceiling-high bookcase acted as a screen to shut off the dining area.

The living room was large, shabby, and pleasant. The furniture was mostly peel chairs, wooden rocking-chairs, and hassocks. Yellow-painted tables held the oil lamps, and ancient hooked and braided rugs were scattered over the dark wood floor. The windows were framed by soft blue cotton curtains. There were bright plaid and printed pillows on the red divan. The unpainted pine walls had darkened with time and wood-smoke and were covered with framed water-colors of Maine scenes, some signed with artists' names Jane recognized.

All about her were the evidences of a travelled and cultured family — the brass vases someone had brought from Greece, the pieces of Spanish pottery, a flute lying on the mantelpiece, a novel in French open on a table, a bouquet of wildflowers and ferns arranged by somebody who had learned how.

Jane sighed and moved to look more closely at an oil on the south wall, beside the window above the divan. It might have been an Utrillo but was not; it was signed "Isabella." It showed a small, colorful room, obviously a woman's room. There was the corner of a narrow bed, straight chairs strewn with clothes and books, and an open window with thin, blowing curtains that opened on to a grassy, flower-covered slope, with white mountains behind it. Somehow, it was a very appealing painting.

"That place nearly killed me," said a voice behind Jane. "Every day for two hours we had to crawl about on the damned Alps searching for something — I never learned what I was supposed to be looking for, some damned berry — with our heads lower than our knees. It was called the exercise period. I think the school made gin out of the berries and sold it for a huge profit.

"If you didn't speak French, you got no dinner. I had a German room-mate who wouldn't speak French if she starved to death, so we left after a year twenty pounds thinner and unable to hold our necks up straight. I married her brother before I got my senses back."

"You must be Isabella," said Jane nervously, following Sarah's instructions about first names. "I am Jane Lamb."

Isabella raised her eyebrows. "How informal the world has become," she said gently, managing to sound more thoughtful than offensive. "Good evening. If you wish to change for dinner, you may."

Jane looked despairingly down at her unimpressive pale blue cashmere sweater and matching flannel skirt, and did not announce that she had already changed. The Grafin was wearing a low-cut violet jersey blouse and a pink and violet tweed floor-length skirt.

"I will tomorrow," she answered. "You look most terribly chic, Isabella."

Isabella raised her eyebrows again, a little higher this time. "Personal compliments are so hard to give graciously, I think."

"Good evening, Jane," said Hill, entering from the kitchen with a tray of drinks. "Shut up, Issa. You look God-awful, I must say. Like an ad for what the nouveau riche wear at home in the evenings in the Hamptons. Have you got your b.v.d.'s on?"

Isabella reached for an old-fashioned from the tray, pouring more whiskey into it as soon as she had taken a large swallow.

"I needed that," she said. "After I got back from painting, I took a touch of Valium to brace myself to go over to that wretched old biddy's place to give her a piece of my mind. The trip took a lot out of me, and tranquilizers always make me sleepy and confused in the day-time."

74

"To Mrs. Parker's?" Hill was surprised. "I thought I told you to be discreet." He looked uneasily at Jane, who had turned politely away to examine the books on the shelves.

"I didn't get a chance to be anything. She wasn't there, but just the sight of that mausoleum gives me a creepy feeling. She's probably over in Bar Harbor this weekend, giving her daughter a hellish time, as usual.

"Funny, though; I thought I heard a man shouting when I got near the house, but no one answered my knock."

"Shouting?" asked Hill. "No one would dare shout at Mrs. Parker. Have you been taking too many of your expensive and varied medications? They don't combine well with liquor, you know."

"I heard, very distinctly, a sort of martial voice yelling — reminded me of Lem's voice, somehow, or maybe Fred Blanchard's."

She added, thoughtfully, "And also of an army drill sergeant I used to know; maybe that's why I call it martial."

"I can't believe you'd ever bother with such small fry as a sergeant, unless he had large and redeeming, ah, features. And you wouldn't be making up this whole tale to prove that you've had one walk this summer and can be excused tomorrow from the annual Sargent Mountain climb? The mention of an army sergeant seems to my legal mind to be a kind of Freudian slip."

Isabella poured more whiskey. "You are so nouveau gauche, dear, though I'm sure my wit escapes you," she answered. "Don't your compadrés at the Somerset Club feel you should grow up a little and stop being such a self-conscious liberal? There is nothing worse than a snob who is also a bleeding-heart."

Hill's face reddened. Before he could answer, there was a giggle from the hallway behind the dining area, and a voice with an adolescent break in it declaimed loudly:

> "Aunt Issa wed a dinge with dough,
> One liberal Sarah didn't *know*,
> And Hill says no one's *ever* met
> The fellow at the Somerset."

"Gus!" shouted Hill. "You are not to repeat your Cousin Lem's damned limericks. I'll deal with you later!"

There was the sound of a scuffle in the region of the versifier, and Sarah and Emily emerged from the dining room, Emily smiling and

Sarah looking defensive.

"I have sent Gus back to his room," Sarah said, "but, Hill, Lem doesn't write limericks. A limerick has five lines."

"Damn Lem and his non-limericks!" Hill turned to hand a drink to Jane, who was looking more frightened than usual at Hill's explosive speech. "What," she whispered, "is a dinge?"

"A person of colour, Jane," answered Emily. "My Uncle Saville used the term; he had what he considered humourous euphemisms for almost everything and everybody, including himself and his own class. Of course, no one dares use the term 'class' nowadays. Everything must be universal, solemn, and dignified.

"My cousin General Alison is a hold-out, though, and he has a naughty habit of composing these four-line verses about anything that strikes his fancy, particularly the foibles of his own relatives or himself. We call them 'Bungalow Rhymes,' because he came up with many of them here. They're really supposed to have a calamitous ending. That one about Isabella and Hill is the only one that doesn't."

"Like the old Victorian 'Ruthless Rhymes for Happy Homes,' " said Jane. "I always loved those."

"The girl really is literate," murmured Isabella to her glass.

Sarah was drinking a martini and appearing to be perplexed. "I have never seen the point of that one about Issa and Hill," she said. "It implies that I know only white liberals, which is not at all true, and that Hill is stuffy, which he isn't, and that Issa would marry a Negro for his money, which would be redundant. She'd marry anybody at all for any reason whatever — or none!" She took another sip and looked pink and triumphant and quite pretty.

"Oh, lord," said Isabella. "It was only that Lem had had a few drinks and was trying to find a rhyme for 'Somerset,' which isn't easy, you must admit. Artistic fervour, and all that. I think most of his childish efforts do hit the spot, though. What about:

> General A. one summer day,
> Was scuttled in the Western Way.
> Said Cousin Liz, 'At least I will
> Not have to pay his funeral bill.'

Ma*ma* has paid off a few of his debts, you know."

"If only Lem had been successful in his Antarctic expedition,"

Sarah remarked. "He wouldn't mind so much being poor if he'd been able to carry through the one great desire of his life. Probably that new mountain range would have been named after him, too. It was so much salt in the wound, also, to have the Navy get there first."

"My cousin," Emily explained to Jane, "some years ago conceived the idea of an exploration of a certain region near the South Pole, but his financial backing was held up just long enough for a government expedition to get there first, and make many discoveries. All of them have not been divulged even yet, for reasons of our national interest, or so Lem's friends in the service have told him."

"It was Mrs. Parker, our charming neighbor across the cove, who wrecked it all for Lem," Isabella said bitterly. "Her father and husband were arranging the financing, but she convinced them at the last moment that the expedition would be futile and a waste of money. By the time Lem got what he needed from other sources, it was too late in the year to go.

"When the weather was right again, the Navy had taken over. Just the sight of old Nosy Parker gives Lem apoplexy."

"Well," sighed Emily, "it was a great disappointment, but he's over it, I hope. This history of the Marine Corps that he's writing gives him an income, in addition to his pension, and also the hope of some fame, although perhaps recognition would be a better word."

"No, Emily," said Hill, "I think he believes General Stanley got him the commission to do the history out of charity and old comradeship, and that must be very hard to take. But he looks far younger than his years, and he does have some other diversions besides his rhyming." He winked at Isabella, who grinned.

Emily frowned at them. "We are boring Jane with our family discussion, I fear. Issa, where did you go to paint this afternoon?"

"To the marsh near McKinley, Aunt Em. By the road, where one gets that aspect of Western Mountain that they call the 'Sleeping Elephant.' I did it quickly in a pointilist manner and made rather a hash of it. I'll show you later.

"Cordelia and Ted were there, poor Cordelia churning about with a butterfly net, wet to the ankles, while Ted sat on a shooting stick reading and vaguely directing her hither and yon. She made so many wild rushes near me that she finally knocked the canvas-board off my easel, which didn't improve my composition any. I thought Teddy was the one who collected butterflies."

"He does, the ass," said Hill, "but she does all the work in their enterprises, in addition to paying all the bills. What about Lem's rhyme about them:

> Whilst dining gaily at the Ritz
> Cordelia died of choking fits
> And then, to make his sorrow greater,
> Just Ted was left to tip the waiter."

There was a general laugh, and a general movement towards the tray of drinks.

"Aren't they going to change McKinley's name to Bass Harbor?" asked Sarah, as Hill refilled their glasses. "Or have they already? I don't know the reason for the change, though."

"Because they think it'll attract more tourists," came a shout from the kitchen, the door to which had mysteriously managed to open itself some time before. "Guess they think it has more style, like Bar Harbor or Northeast. Who wants to say they've spent their vacation in a town called McKinley? But I say it's all foolishness; that's what I say."

"Shut the door, please, Dora," said Mrs. Worthington, coming quietly in from the porch. "I always liked the name McKinley, too. Well, you all look very happy."

She stood smiling with her usual grace, wearing white linen with a brilliant pink rebozo of rough wool around her shoulders. Other well-bred old ladies wore navy cable-knit cardigan sweaters or fluffy angora throws in the evening to keep warm, but Elizabeth Worthington, thought Hill, would have style even on her death-bed.

Beside her, Emily and Sarah in their pastel silk Best and Company shirt-dresses looked nondescript. As Mrs. Worthington spoke, Jane's glass halted mid-way to her lips. She spilled her drink down her sweater front, looked nervously at Isabella to see if she had noticed, and then smiled appealingly at her employer.

"Jane, I am glad to see you looking more rested," Elizabeth Worthington said. "Where is your little girl? I haven't yet met her, you know."

"Oh, God," mumbled Hill, and, quickly, in an aside to his mother-in-law, who turned away from the company to face him: "Elizabeth, I'm rather afraid you may be in for a disappointment.

Mrs. Lamb is not at all what I expected nor what that wretched Dodie led us to believe. She is very timid and ill-at-ease, and as for the daughter —"

"Why, what can you mean, Hill? Jane and I had tea together in the studio after my row and I find her perfectly charming. She knows several of my acquaintances in Paris and Rome, and her father owned a Rubloff ikon. Imagine that! But it had to be sold, unfortunately. He left her and her mother very badly off, or so I understand, and until Jane trained as a secretary, she and her mother had to take any work they could get.

"I gather, too, that her marriage was not very successful, poor child, but she seems a perfectly competent person. We started an outline of the points to be covered in my monographs after tea, and I never saw anyone so knowing about her work, nor so understanding of mine, as she is."

"She is? I can hardly believe it. She goes into spasms of shyness if one so much as speaks to her — you saw her jump when you came in just now — and the daughter —"

"Why," demanded Mrs. Worthington, "do you keep repeating 'the daughter' in that peculiar fashion? What is the matter with the child?"

As Hill struggled for words that would be both fair and succinct, the door from the kitchen was opened again, visibly, this time, by a large red hand, to permit the entrance of two little figures, each clutching a dish of nuts and crackers. They wore similar printed lawn dresses, with little white collars and smocked bodices, and wreaths of daisies crowned their shining, well-brushed heads.

Elizabeth Lamb's dress was a little short and loose for her, and Sarah, who was drinking her second martini, looked at it with fuzzy recognition. The two children bobbed identical curtsies at Mrs. Worthington, who was charmed.

"Good evening, Persis. And this is Elizabeth? I hope you will have a pleasant summer with us. Several little Elizabeths have visited The Bungalow during my years here, and they have all grown up to be my special friends. I am sure you will, too. I am so very glad to meet you; Mr. Halstead," she glanced severely at the stunned Hill, "was just speaking of you."

Elizabeth Lamb was demure. "Yes, ma'am, thank you," she said, dropping her eyes winningly. "It is nice here and Persis is my friend and she is going to teach me to row."

"She's doing her ingenue turn," thought Hill. "Next, she'll be darting around tinkling a bell and imploring us all to believe in fairies." He was then immediately ashamed of himself.

Isabella moved forward. After three large cocktails, she was pleased to be majestically gracious. "I am the Grafin von Lichtenfeld," she announced. "You may call me Aunt Isabella, as Persis does."

"Yes, Aunt Isabella," said Elizabeth Lamb, who pronounced the second word with a long "a."

Isabella's laugh bubbled. "I don't have antennae, you know, child."

Mrs. Worthington flashed an angry look at Isabella. Elizabeth Lamb's green eyes flashed a similar spark of anger for just a second, before she lowered her lids and answered quietly. "I thought," she said, "pronounciation was never corrected by nice people, especially nice people from Boston."

She looked straight up at Isabella, who had nothing to say, but shrugged her shoulders and moved away to the fire, to lean fetchingly on the mantelpiece. Jane made a pathetic little sound of distress, and everyone else began to talk at once. Elizabeth Worthington stood looking thoughtfully at her young guest, who returned her regard.

"I hear today is your birthday," she said to the child, "and your mother tells me you do not eat cake, so we shall have a special dessert. Now, come, dinner should be ready."

She led them around the bookcase and seated them at the long scrubbed pine table on Mexican chairs of red and blue. A subdued Gus joined them and was introduced to the Lambs. Hill lighted the candelabra on the table and Doreen, wearing the new green pants and a tight white sweater, attended to those on the wall.

The assemblage sat in silence, drinking their goblets of spring water and awaiting the arrival of the source of the tantalizingly good smell that permeated The Bungalow. A short, plump figure, with a shiny round face and frizzy, greying blonde hair, wearing a pale pink uniform which she had enlivened by the addition of an orange and lavender printed cotton apron, came out of the darkness. She carried an enormous old ironstone tureen, which was forcefully plunked on the table in front of Mrs. Worthington, who began to ladle its contents into deep green and white bowls of Chinese ballast china.

"Not's good's it might be," said the pink uniform, addressing her mistress but thoroughly examining Jane and her daughter with her pale, rather protuberant eyes. "I'd say that Junior passed off some harbor pollock on us. You don't," she went on darkly, "always know what you're gettin' out of that store of his'n Peyton's. I've told you and told you, Sarah, you had ought to go in there yourself and look at what you get."

Her scrutiny of the new arrivals completed, and Sarah's ire successfully aroused, she left for the kitchen, pushing her daughter before her with an ungentle hand.

"It's divine, Dora," called Emily, who had been served first. "Jane, have you ever had a Maine fish chowder before? It's just fish and salt pork, onions, potatoes and milk and butter, but it is Cordon Bleu fare, to my way of thinking. Especially when eaten with pilot bread the way Dora fixes it."

"She just butters the crackers and heats them in the oven, Emily," said Hill. "It's no great secret. Would you pass me some, please?

"I think," he went on, "this chowder is made from haddock, so why that crack about harbor pollock? Reminds me of when I was trying to make conversation with a dour old party, one day on the fish wharf in Southwest. I asked him if harbor pollock were any good for making chowder.

"He looked at me coldly and said, 'Best fish they is — if you ain't got nawthin' else'!'"

The chowder was succeeded by a platter of crisp brown clam fritters and a large bowl of leafy green lettuce lightly coated with an olive oil and vinegar dressing. These were proffered by Doreen, who was humming to herself in an absent manner despite Mrs. Worthington's frown.

"Funny," said Hill, "how Boston lettuce is called 'native lettuce' around Boston and 'Boston lettuce' everywhere else. I don't think it originated there. This, though, Jane, is from our own 'gaadin,' as they call it up here. June always starts some early, under glass, for us, since it is still a struggle to get anything but iceberg lettuce on Mount Desert except at the height of the tourist season."

"All leaf lettuce isn't Boston lettuce," began Elizabeth Lamb, knowledgeably, until a frown from her mother silenced her. Dora appeared with a basket of rolls and put them on the table as far from Gus as possible. "Them," she proclaimed, eyeing him coolly, "are for people who appreciate my yeast rolls, not boys who can swaller fourteen to a time and not taste a one of 'em."

Jane had been too shy, of course, to speak during the meal. Sarah, too, had been silent, and a trifle tipsy, Isabella sulky, Mrs. Worthington thoughtful, Gus dedicated to eating and staying out of his father's notice, and Elizabeth Lamb the model of a quiet, well-bred child in whose mouth butter would not melt.

Hill and Emily had carried on most of the conversation, and now Persis seemed to feel it was time someone gave them a hand. She struggled, her little rounded brow creased with thought, and finally came up with an offering. "Help," she announced gravely, when Dora was safely out of the room, "is not what it was!"

In the ensuing merriment the table was cleared, all hands assisting, and a tray of stemmed glasses clustered about a magnum of champagne was put before Hill.

"Hey," he said, examining the label, "living it up, aren't we, Elizabeth? This bubbly is almost too good for the likes of us. I don't see the Maine State Liquor Authority seal; did you bring this up with you? What are we celebrating, by the way?"

"When Junior and Peyton go to Boston in the spring to order their fancier groceries for the summer trade," said Mrs. Worthington, "they pick up a few bottles of the better wines and whiskies in Massachusetts or New Hampshire, where there is so much more variety than we have here. They say they do it as a favour for their customers who may want something special for a party; a favour, I must say, for which the charge runs rather high," she added dryly. "However, they deserve to be paid for the risk they are running; it amounts to bootlegging, I suppose.

"They told me, very discreetly, of course, what they had this year and I asked Junior for a bottle of this the other day. My theory, as my family knows, Jane, is always to have something especially festive on hand to eat or drink and sooner or later a festive occasion will come along and find you all prepared for it. And what could be a better excuse than Miss Elizabeth Lamb's eighth birthday?"

The glasses were passed. Mrs. Worthington lifted her glass to Elizabeth Lamb. "To the birthday girl!" she said. The recipient of the toast looked flushed and pleased.

"To the birthday girl and absent friends!" Miss Elbridge toasted. "My Uncle Saville always drank to 'absent friends,'" she explained to Jane, who had an expression of puzzled fright superimposed atop her usual one of frightened diffidence.

"To the birthday girl!" Isabella toasted. "May she get what she deserves!"

Elizabeth Lamb rose with great composure as the rest of the company drank to her. Looking at Isabella, she lifted her glass. "May we all get what we deserve," she responded gravely. She reached across the table to clink glasses with Persis, and they drank deeply, between giggles.

"It looks like ginger ale, but the bubbles tickle nicer," announced Persis. "Could I have some more? I like it."

"Not a chance," replied her father. "This is for your elders and betters. And, now, what's this?"

A large glass bowl had appeared, half full of rich yellow vanilla ice cream, with eight large peeled peaches on top. Mrs. Worthington poured a pitcher of crushed raspberries over it and spooned it into eight flat soup plates, sprinkling each plate with slivered green almonds from a little silver dish.

"The full treatment," said Isabella. "Now don't tell me Dora just whipped that up in case we felt like celebrating."

"Wasn't no trouble," Dora said. "Doreen turned the freezer crank for me. Junior brought the cream and the peaches from Ellswuth — had to go there this afternoon on an errand for the Blanchards, anyway. Raspberries I had in the freezer down to home, put them up last July."

"But the almonds," said Emily. "You don't just go out and buy green almonds any place."

"I brought some from Boston," her sister answered. "One never knows when there will be a crying need for green almonds!"

"I don't know what we'd do around here without June's know-how and your foresight, Elizabeth," observed Hill. "Although to me, his main value — spell that adjective either with or without an 'e' on the end — is that he keeps me from losing my mind amongst all you females."

Elizabeth Lamb was ecstatic. "Pêche melba," she whispered. "My very favourite of all!"

Isabella, having returned from the McKinley marsh late in the afternoon and taken her walk even later than that, had heard nothing about the Lambs that had not been known before they arrived.

"I suppose," she asked with some sarcasm, "that the last time you had it was at Maxim's? I do hope that this is up to your standards."

"Yes, it was at Maxim's," answered Elizabeth Lamb, "but I really think it wasn't as good as this is."

"Sometime, Issa," Hill advised, "you must get young Elizabeth

Lamb to tell you the story of her life to date, and then you won't keep leading with your right."

"Oh, I will," promised Elizabeth Lamb, "but right now let's eat this all up, every bit."

And they did.

There was a general sigh of contentment. Elizabeth Lamb, flown with champagne and victuals, insisted on her birthday perogative of blowing out the candles, and spattered candle grease on the walls with a forceful breath.

Isabella was lofty: "You must put your hand behind the candelabra, my dear. But it's quite all right; I realize you don't know these niceties."

"I know that one now," Elizabeth Lamb calmly replied, "and I never forget a thing."

Mrs. Worthington smiled at her, and left the table for the kitchen, where her gentle voice could be heard giving admonishment to Doreen, before she left by the back door.

Replete with food and drink, the rest of the company wandered back into the living room.

Chapter 10

THE BUNGALOW AT NIGHT

The oil lamps in the living room had been lighted during dinner and they cast bright circles of gold on the yellow tables. The night was finally dark. Miss Elbridge glanced out the glass-paned door to the porch. "It's so sad," she sighed, "to know that in a day or two the days will be getting shorter."

"But just think, Miss Elbridge," Jane offered timidly, "how nice it is in late December to think that, in deepest winter, they're actually getting longer."

"Why, of course, that is so. I never thought of that. You are very sensitive, Jane. When is your birthday?"

Jane looked distraught.

"Good heavens, Mummy. It's March thirteenth, Miss Elbridge."

"Ah," said Emily, nodding approvingly.

Jane looked perplexed.

The rest of the company looked apprehensive, fearing Miss Elbridge would now launch into one of her homilies on the subject of astrology, in which she had lately become interested. These homilies were infuriating to non-believers and equally infuriating to believers, since they were usually long and full of sweeping, inaccurate statements.

"Here's coffee," Hill said quickly, as Dora put the tray down in front of Sarah.

"I'll be here tomorrow in good time, Sarah," she said, "to do up them dishes. Junior's going to give me and Doreen a ride to Bar Harbor in a few minutes. Henry's got a good movie tonight."

Persis went to open the porch door for Junior, who carried in an armload of logs. He looked very tired, but spoke, as usual, cheerfully: "Thought I might as well bring these along from the shed. Fog's coming in and it's getting colder."

Hill moved to the window and pulled the curtain aside. "Coming in fast," he said. "Well, look at that. Lights showing through Mrs. Parker's trees. I didn't know she was over here, June."

Junior came up behind him. "She drove over alone yesterday for the weekend. Her daughter's intended is visiting in Bar Harbor and she told me she thought she'd leave the young people alone for a few days."

"I wouldn't have credited her with that much sensitivity," Isabella observed sarcastically, "but perhaps she realizes a surfeit of her company might frighten the prospect off."

"Now, that's funny," Hill said. "There's a light shining where I've never seen one before, down low and off to the left."

"That must be the window in the wine-cellar." Junior was puzzled: "I've never known Mrs. Parker to go down those steep stairs before."

"Maybe she's taking to drink in her old age," said Isabella. "It can only improve her. But who ever heard of a window in a wine-cellar?"

"Mr. Parker was advised to put one in. Some expert, a French feller, told him wine gets bored at the same temperature, and there should be a little variation. There's three thicknesses of glass in that window, specially tempered to keep extreme heat and cold out. We had a time setting them in just right, I remember, though I was just a kid helping my dad when 'twas done."

He spoke worriedly. "I wonder if she's all right, though, with the maids not there, and all. We're getting some rough customers on the island, nowadays. Maybe I'd best go over."

"I would say she can take care of herself," Hill answered. "She's absolutely the toughest old party I ever heard of, and a dead shot with that revolver she's carried around ever since her husband died.

"She makes a fetish of self-reliance, they say; handles every problem at Back Bay Cordage without any advice, except legal, from anyone. We could go over if you're really worried, but my bet is that she'd just be furious with both of us."

Elizabeth Worthington came in hurriedly, brushing drops of fog from her hair.

"Oh, Junior, I'm so glad I caught you. Could you possibly, possibly drive to Boston tonight? I have been so stupid; I came up last week without thoroughly checking over the supplies I brought with me, and now I find I am completely out of several colours of enamel. I simply must have that order for Paris in the post Monday morning if it is to reach the client as promised. And then she will still have to send it over to England for her husband's illustrious relative's birthday. I fear it has already missed the official celebration."

"Gorry, I guess I could, Mrs. Worthington," said Junior. "It can't wait until tomorrow morning?"

"It really is necessary for you to go tonight. Mr. Sheldon, my supplier — you know how to get to him — is open only until eleven on Saturday mornings, and I really would prefer that you be there as soon as he gets to the laboratory, at eight-thirty. The sooner you can get back with the enamels, the sooner I can finish the plaques."

"It can't wait, mam?" Junior's long day showed in his exhausted tone, though his manner remained obliging and polite.

"No, Junior, it can't."

"Well, then, need's must. Shall I go to your house straight off, like I did that other time I went down?"

"Yes, Katie is still there, and I know she'll have a room ready. You know I am very sorry to have to ask this of you."

"Look, Junior, you're all in," said Hill. "Instead of your taking your truck, I'll drive you to Ellsworth and we'll rent a car there. Our cars will be needed here tomorrow, and a rental car will be much easier driving than your pick-up. And I'll drop the girls off at Peyton's — he'll take his sister and niece over to the movies, surely?"

"Him and Dottie was going tonight," called Dora from the kitchen. "Spending some of all that bate of money he's been making down to the store. If you hurry, we'll catch them before they start. Second show's a little after nine."

"Call Henry from Peyton's house and tell him I said to hold the second show," Mrs. Worthington said confidently.

"Oh, Mother," cried Sarah. "He won't do that. You know what Henry is like. Why, he even makes me pay for admission when I take the children over to the movies. He surely won't hold up a show for anyone, certainly not for Dora."

"Oh, yes, he will," came over a series of crashes from the kitchen, where Dora was conducting a grand finale. "He can oblige an old friend. We cut a few capers together, in the summers, in our young days."

"And no reason, either, Sarah, why he should let you or anybody else in free. I don't notice you giving any pups away for nothing."

"What a pair of steam-rollers you and Dora would make, Elizabeth," said Hill. "Come on, June, I'll grab a pair of my pajamas for you. Let's go!"

There was a hurried exodus, the tail end of which was the tight green rear of Doreen, who was rolling up her hair in pink plastic curlers as she waggled out.

When the four arrived at Hill's car, there was a small scene caused by Dora's refusing to permit Doreen to sit in the back seat with Junior. Indeed, Doreen had herself planted her feet firmly on the ground as Junior courteously attempted to usher her into the car.

"But it's polite, Dora," Junior explained, "to let older ladies sit in front. Get in, now, Doreen."

"Older ladies my foot," Dora replied. "Since when was you so stuck on politeness? You sit yourself in front with Hill; then we'll know where your hands are — or aren't."

Junior conceded, with a sad shake of his head. Hill drove cautiously through the fog along the grassy way that led to the side road where the tracks from all the Schooner Cove cottages joined forces.

As he turned on to it, his headlights picked up a large tan cat marching along beside a short, chubby form. The form turned a flashlight into Hill's eyes, and he braked to a stop.

"Well," said the form, peering into the car, "going night-clubbing? I should think you women would be tired after an honest day's work." It shifted its cold regard to Junior, "And you, too, assuming you've done one."

"Good evening, Mrs. Parker," Hill said calmly. "Isn't it risky to be walking in this thick fog? No, no night-clubbing for us. I'm taking Dora and Doreen to Peyton's so they can get a ride to the movies and I'm driving Junior to Ellsworth."

"Really!" said Mrs. Parker. "What a lot of gallivanting you rich working people do. And as for you, Hill, a little work would be good for you and would help out your kind mother-in-law a bit."

"Look here," Hill began angrily, but stopped at a touch on his arm from Junior.

"It's helping Mrs. Worthington we're going out for to do, mam. I've got to go to Boston for her, on business."

"Really!" Mrs. Parker said again. "Just make sure you get back soon. We've got a lot of things to get at and get done. Getting done is half the fun, as I think the saying goes."

"Yes, Mrs. Parker," Junior answered politely. "I'll be back tomorrow."

Hill let the clutch out quickly and drove on, not bidding Mrs. Parker a farewell.

"In a word, 'nasty' is how I'd describe her," he said. "Does she often walk around at night with that cat? I damned near ran over it."

Junior did not answer. His eyes were closed and his head rested against the seat back.

"Hey, June, wake up!" said Hill. "You've got a lot of driving to do tonight."

"Then you had ought to let me get in a wink or two now," Junior answered, with his slow smile. "But I was just resting my eyes. Yes, she takes that crittur a mile's walk every night when she's over here. Don't know if she does in Bar Harbor."

"She seemed annoyed at all of us. What've you been neglecting at her place?"

"Gorry, Hill, I was trying to think. Only thing is, I've got an awful feeling that I didn't get the right feller over to fix her bathroom sink. There's one plumber she hates, and one she purely dotes on, and I bet I asked for the wrong one."

He sighed. "Oh, well, when I get back, I'll lay myself down right out straight on the floor and let her jump up and down on me, in a manner of speaking, and she'll come round. She always does. Her bark's just a little worse'n her bite."

"Then I wouldn't even want to hear her bite!" Dora declared from the back seat.

"And I wouldn't want to be the plumber she dotes on!" rejoined Hill, and the party drove on, laughing.

As the ladies back at The Bungalow chose books and magazines to read, Isabella quietly left them.

"Here is some coffee, Mother." Sarah was finally pouring. "Really, Dora is becoming much too outspoken. She was practically saying I am too stingy to buy a movie ticket. It is simply that I think Henry has no family feeling.

"And I wish you hadn't had to send Junior to Boston. He suddenly looked quite green with exhaustion."

"I give Junior a Christmas present of five hundred dollars," said Mrs. Worthington calmly. "I have no qualms about asking for a little extra consideration from him. Lettie Parker, who is worth five times what I am, sends him a Christmas box from S.S. Pierce. The seven-dollar-and fifty cent one, I should imagine.

"And, Sarah, I rather think that *your* family feeling would encourage you to spend your money, of which you have an ample supply, I feel, to support your Cousin Henry's business exertions."

"Really, Mother! Would you like sugar, Jane? Why, what is it?"

Jane had cried out as a white shape slid past the window, the curtain of which was still pulled back. It was a blurred, bulbous form without a head. Slowly and majestically it drifted away and disappeared into the fog.

"It's all right. It's only Aunt Isabella." Persis was frowning in her earnestness. "She takes off her clothes and walks around at night to let her body merge into the Elmers. She wears a black sou'-wester to keep her hair dry, when it's rainy or foggy. A lady in a book she read did it."

"Merge into the Elmers! Persis," said her grandmother, "I think, and hope, you must mean the elements. Yes, from childhood till now she has taken off her clothes at any opportunity.

"I rather wonder," she went on, essaying a mild joke to relieve Sarah's stern expression and Jane's bewildered one, "if the book were by D. H. Lawrence. We will trust it was not."

Jane laughed feebly, more at the thought that Mrs. Worthington evidently thought that Mr. Lawrence's works were the latest thing in salacious writing than at her trenchant wit. Someone, she remembered, possibly Dodie Wheeler at the agency, had told her that Mrs. Worthington's sense of humour was grave rather than light.

"I was really quite startled," she replied. "She looked so very ghostly."

"There are no ghosts here that I know of," Mrs. Worthington

said. "Of course, there is the schooner from which the cove gets its name." She sipped coffee while Jane's eyes widened. "There is supposed to be a phantom schooner that glides out of this cove whenever anyone from the Cape is lost at sea. It hasn't been seen for some years, not since young Bubba Prouty's PT boat went down in the Pacific."

"The Cape?" asked Jane, as Sarah murmured, "His name was George, Mother, his proper name."

Gus answered Jane. He had been sitting quietly at one of the lamp-lit tables since dinner, absorbed in a length of rope and a manual of knots.

"That's what this section of the backside is called, don't know why; the coastline doesn't bulge out like a real cape, not very much. A little farther down, it's called the Algireen Coast, don't know why that is, either. Dad thinks maybe somebody who'd sailed along the coast of Algeria and then came back here thought they looked alike. Can't see how they could have, myself.

"Well, good-night, Grandma, and everybody. I'm going to listen to the radio in my room."

He left through the door into the kitchen, his favourite aperture, as his aunt had once observed. After a stealthy pause during which the ice-box door opened and shut quietly, he was heard to thump along the porch than ran around three sides of the building and enter his room with a crash.

The ladies sat silently, for a very long time, drinking their coffee and glancing through magazines. The fog dripped mournfully off the pines on to the roof. A spark shot out of the fire and startled the three Dalmatians, who lay companionably nestled before it. Once Sarah looked up from her reading and said, apropos of nothing, seemingly, "I don't think Isabella has ever read a book, Mother. In fact, I really doubt if she can read."

"If she can't, then your father and I wasted a good deal of money on tutors," Mrs. Worthington replied, lighting a cigarette.

Persis and Elizabeth Lamb made themselves small in a corner, hoping that no one would notice the lateness of the hour, and hoping for more interesting adult conversation than they had heard so far.

The dogs lifted their heads. After a minute or two, a crunching sound was heard on the clamshell path, and a tattoo of knocks at the back door followed. "Anybody to home?" came a deep voice.

"Oh, dear, it's Varner," sighed Sarah. "Here we are, Varner," she managed to call hospitably.

Varner Prouty came in through the kitchen doorway, his short burly form looming large in the lamp-lit room. He pushed his old hat to the back of his head and smiled genially around at the company.

"Brought a present for the young lady," he said bashfully, extending towards Jane a brown paper parcel that was undoubtedly dripping blood. Jane sat frozen, staring at it, pressing her hand against her face.

"Why, that's very kind of you, Varner," said Mrs. Worthington. "Won't you go put it down on the sink? Ah — what is it?"

"Deer's liver from a buck I shot yestiddy at sun-up. Thought the young lady might relish it. Put some meat on her bones."

Jane summoned her manners and whispered, "Thank you." Her daughter stirred out of the shadows. "Why did you shoot him?" she asked.

"Been eating up my gaadin for a week," said Varner. "It's legal to shoot a deer what's doing that." He was now addressing Mrs. Worthington, who regarded him with a quizzical smile.

"I know it is," she said, "but I wouldn't want you to have to go to court and swear that's what he was doing when you shot him."

"Now, Mrs. Worthington," said Varner, sitting down easily and looking thirstily around him, "maybe he was just a-drinking up my well-water, wouldn't quarrel with you there none. But he was a sassy bugger what needed shooting, and I done it.

"Now, you have Dora fry up that liver nice in a spider with a little butter and the young lady will be the better for it. She can have it for her breakfast."

"A spider?" echoed Elizabeth Lamb.

"That's an iron skillet," said Sarah. "Well, it's certainly very generous of you, Varner. Maybe Mrs. Lamb will let us all have some. It's a great delicacy, you know," she added, turning to Jane, "and I hope, Varner, that Minnie won't light into you for giving it away."

"What Minnie don't know won't hurt her," replied Varner, managing to sound so parched that his very voice took on a gravelly tone. "That path is some old long, Sarah, dries up the mouth just walking down here. I don't suppose you have a little — ah, you know —." He measured an inch or so of air with thumb and forefinger and winked hopefully up at the ceiling.

Sarah left the room and came back with a tumbler half full of a fluid barely darker than water. Her mother raised a reproachful eyebrow at her but Varner rose and kissed the hand that proffered the tumbler.

"Hill has hisself a jewel," he announced happily, downing half of the whisky. "I said it before and I'll say it again." He swallowed the rest at a draught.

At a firm nod from her mother, Sarah carried the glass to the kitchen again. This time the liquid was even lighter. Mrs. Worthington shook her head at the economical Sarah, and Varner looked disappointed but resigned.

"Well," he said, taking a moderate sip, "them dogs look good, Sarah. One of 'em, Hobby, I think 'twas, went along of me all morning while I was cutting wood. Right at the place where I found them other three, he reared back, wouldn't come in to the clearing."

"Yes," said Sarah, "well —" She stared into the fire. "That was a very terrible affair. It has set my kennels back a good deal. I paid more than I could afford for those three; that's why I brought them here with me, to give them special attention from the beginning. It was foolish. They should have gone straight to my assistant in Dedham. It will take me a long time now to be able to get another stud and two bitches of their quality."

"What happened?" whispered Elizabeth Lamb to Persis. "Why is your mother saying that word I'm not allowed to?"

"It just means girl dogs," answered Persis. "She bought three Dalmatians in Canada last summer. They cost an awful lot and then somebody poisoned them. Varner found them in the woods."

Varner was sighing in contentment and very slowly drinking a third potion, of a healthy colour. Mrs. Worthington had got it for him, and the courteous firmness with which she had handed it over, along with its unwonted and very pleasant potency, had informed him that the pipers he was hearing would be the last of the evening.

"Do you think Mrs. Parker done it, Sarah?" he asked. "She was complaining a lot about what she called yelping. Don't know why it bothered her. She was only here a night or two that week."

"I don't know, Varner," said Sarah grimly, "and I hope I never find out for sure. I just might shoot her with her own gun. They were beautiful animals, and anyone who would poison a dog doesn't deserve to live." Her jaw trembled, and she reached for a cigarette and bit down upon it.

"Sarah, Sarah," murmured Miss Elbridge. "Bitterness harms only oneself."

Varner was feeling the whisky. His face was flushed. "That old woman is pure poison herself. I come down here tonight to see if mebbe Hill could tell me what to do, but I seen the car gone. Know what she said to Minnie yesterday — she stopped down to home on her way into the Cape?

"Bold as brass, she said she was figgering on having our house tore down, said it was an eyesore and she didn't want her new in-laws to hev to see it when they druv by coming in to her place — if they ever do come in, is what I say. Eyesore! Minnie like to hev died. That house is on Mrs. Parker's property, no denying it, but when her husband bought the land from Minnie's father, he promised any and all of us could live there long's we had a mind to."

"Oh, Varner," cried Mrs. Worthington, "that is too bad. Hill will do what he can, we all will, but if there is nothing in writing, well, I just don't know."

"Minnie took on all night. It set the kids off, too. I just don't know what to do. I'll hev to hev a talk with the old devil, hev to brace myself with a few beers first. She riles me up so I just forget what to say. That woman is a disgrace to the hull female sex."

"You talk to her first, Varner," said Miss Elbridge, "then we'll try to figure out something. And what are these children doing up so late, if I may ask?"

Persis and Elizabeth Lamb were sitting stiffly, their little bodies holding each other upright in the corner by the fire. They rested their elbows on their knees and propped their eyelids open with fat little forefingers. As Emily spoke, they jumped guiltily and unsteadily to their feet.

"Good-night, dears," said Mrs. Worthington. "I will leave it to you, Persis, to see that Elizabeth finds all that she needs."

The children staggered through the kitchen, in which Dora had left the wall gas lamp burning above the black iron sink, overflowing with the dinner dishes. Persis took Elizabeth Lamb's hand and they made for the bunkroom, whose candle-lit doorway was at the side end of the back porch.

"Goodnight, kids," called Hill's voice. He came in sleepily. "Hello, Varner. God, what a night! We could barely see the road — it took us forever to get to Ellsworth. I don't envy June his drive to Boston, though maybe he'll run out of the fog below Portland. I'm going to bed; I'm absolutely beat. Sarah, I'll put the dogs in the woodshed. Goodnight, ladies.

"Varner," he went on, "I'll light you up to your truck. Minnie was sitting out on your doorstep when I came by. She said you wanted to talk to me. What's the trouble? She looked white as a sheet and scared to death."

Varner rose frowning. "I'll tell you whiles we walk, Hill." He turned to smile engagingly at the ladies. "I'll come see you all again soon. I promise, now."

Hill's flashlight disappeared up the path. Mrs. Worthington and Miss Elbridge rose, Emily patting Jane's hand. "Goodnight, my dear Jane. I am glad you are here."

Sarah got up briskly. "There are extra blankets on the closet shelf in your room, Jane. It's going to be a typical Bungalow June night — around fifty-eight degrees, I fear. Breakfast will be at eight tomorrow."

Mrs. Worthington and Jane left for the studio through the kitchen door. As they crossed the back porch, a subdued giggling and murmuring emanated from the bunkroom.

"No stars tonight," observed Mrs. Worthington. "Sometimes in August, you know, we can see the Northern Lights."

"I haven't ever seen them," Jane answered. She spoke easily; she seemed less nervous with her employer than with the rest of the family. "You know, it's been a long time since I've seen a rainbow, I was thinking just the other day. I used to see them when I was a child. And butterflies — they were everywhere. I don't see them anymore, either."

Mrs. Worthington smiled. "I remember thinking just that when I was thirty or so. Then I began to see them again. No doubt it is a phase we all go through: in childhood we are observant because the world is so new, and as middle age approaches, we are observant because the world is so fleeting, but in the years between, our life is more occupied with action than with objects.

"I promise you though, Jane, at least one rainbow this summer. The air is so clear up here that we often see them. I understand Sarah and Hill plan to climb Sargent Mountain tomorrow. You'll see butterflies on Sargent."

They were in the studio now. Long candles in heavy Spanish holders burned on Mrs. Worthington's worktable. "Goodnight, Jane. I will be busy with the landscapes tomorrow so you and I will not start work until Sunday afternoon, at the earliest. Sleep well."

Chapter 11

CONVERSATIONS BY CANDLELIGHT, 1

Jane entered her room with the same sense of pleasant familiarity she had first experienced that afternoon. The walls were of the darkened pine common throughout the camp. There were two plump beds, the frames of dark carved wood, the covers of red and white toile. The windows, framed in wood carvings of leafy vines, had short, full curtains of the same toile.

There were straight chairs of pine with rush seats, and a hanging shelf with funny little pink curtains. A very old poster of the Bernese Oberland was on one wall, and a walker's map of the Black Forest on another. On the chest of drawers, where a candle burned in a flowered china holder, there was a Meissen pitcher and washbowl, more ornamental, now, than useful. More candles burned on a red-painted writing table, beside Jane's typewriter.

"The Hansel and Gretel room," murmured Jane absently. "Now, why should I say that?" she thought to herself. "Has anyone told me that's its name? Oh, well, a folk memory, perhaps."

She crossed to the latticed window and pulled aside the curtain. The cove was black and flat. The fog was lifting, and a haze of pearl hung above Bartlett's. A small light moved slowly across the cove.

"One of the Proutys robbing lobster traps," thought Jane, who, like most shy persons, effortlessly absorbed the local colour in an unfamiliar atmosphere, being more able to deal with physical features in a setting than the human factors in it.

Jane smiled out at the cove, and then undressed quickly. In a shabby printed Viyella wrapper, she wandered about the room for a while, thinking about many things. She took paper from her writing case and headed a sheet "The Bungalow, Mount Desert Island, Maine", and then put it back again. She took a candle from the writing table and picked up her toilet kit.

As she entered the lavatory from the vestibule on to which her and Mrs. Worthington's rooms opened, the door of the latter was pulled back and Mrs. Worthington came out. She wore a camelhair dressing gown, with her black hair hanging down her back, and she was biting into an apple. She looked surprisingly young.

"Oh!" exclaimed Jane. "You look so like — I thought you were someone else — Isabella, I thought."

Mrs. Worthington smiled. "We might be mistaken for each other, in a very poor light. There is fruit in the studio if you are hungry. Good night, again."

Jane, brushing her teeth, heard voices. She listened shamelessly. Someone asked, "What do you think of her?"

"What do you?" Mrs. Worthington asked in turn.

There was a pause. The first voice, Isabella's, was slow and puzzled. "I think she reminds me of somebody, or perhaps it is of some thing. Something unpleasant."

"You are very observant. But did you say 'unpleasant'? Who?"

"Really, Ma*ma*, if I knew, I'd say. I said 'somebody' or 'some thing.'"

"No, I mean who is the 'she' who is reminding you?"

"Why, your secretary, of course. The meek little Lamb."

"Oh," said Mrs. Worthington. "Well, do put on some warm clothes and get into bed. You'll have a long day tomorrow."

"Bon-soir, Ma*ma*."

"Bon-soir."

There was the shutting of a window, through which the pair had apparently been talking, and then Mrs. Worthington laughed. It was a gay, pretty laugh, but, in the dark and silence of the studio, an unnerving sound to Jane. She heard Mrs. Worthington blow out the candles and go back to her room. Jane stood frowning into the bathroom mirror for quite a long time.

Elizabeth Lamb and Persis had revived slightly in the chill air that came through the open window of the bunkroom. They struggled out of their clothes and into the flannel pajamas hanging handily on pegs above their beds. Persis put her sneakers on a shelf between the two beds.

"A dretful chill gets into your feet if you leave your shoes on the floor at night here," she advised. "It is as bad as when you are cruising and leave them on the deck."

Elizabeth Lamb yawned mightily. "I'm not going to brush my teeth," she announced. "If I don't, they'll fall out, and we can't afford new ones, but I'm tired. I like this place. It's what home must be like. It isn't at all like a strange place, but it is rather cold. Perhaps Europe has thinned my blood."

"I don't like any place except my house and here," Persis decreed. "I've never been abroad and I don't want to go. My friend went abroad, and her mother made her drink wine all the time, because it was cheaper than water. I've never tasted wine; I don't like it. You wouldn't, either."

Elizabeth Lamb was too sleepy for crusading or correcting. She yawned again. "Twelve o'clock," she whispered, "and all is well —"

"That's nice," murmured Persis.

"— and those who ain't, can go to hell. My father was fond of saying that."

There was no response from the other bunk. But as Persis fell asleep, her lips moved. She was memorizing something.

Gus moved carefully down the porch toward the kitchen. He saw the two little recumbent figures in the bunkroom, and went in to pull up the blankets around their shoulders and to blow out the candle.

He found his great-aunt in the kitchen, warming a pan of milk on the large old black iron woodstove, in which a fire burned, if carefully stoked beforehand by Dora, almost through the night. Miss Elbridge obligingly poured Gus a glassful of milk from the carton she was holding.

"Thanks, Aunt Em," he said, reaching for Dora's doughnut crock. "Gosh, I hate those boxes of milk. It used to be great when milk came in bottles and you could pour the top milk off for cereal.

Now it's all these boxes and that homogenized stuff."

"Does it really matter?"

"Well, I read it's all a put-on. Everybody thinks they're getting some great service and all the milk people are doing is pushing off old stale milk on us. Keeps longer if homogenized." He blushed. "I think a lot about food. Not just how it tastes, but I think it's a very important part of life and affects people more than they know."

Gus looked very earnest. Emily realized how little anyone really talked to Gus.

"It is," she answered. "Not that I mean the currently popular fad of so-called 'gourmet cooking,' which is assuming ridiculous proportions. It is even funnier when people add wine to some dish and announce it is 'gourmet.'

"But in Europe, Gus, it is the common thing to get good food well prepared and at reasonable prices, because restaurant owners know their customers will not pay for anything but good food.

"Here, it is almost impossible, unless the restauranteur is a European uncorrupted by the ignorance, or the polite American diffidence, of most of his clients. But the ridiculous prices they charge here for a bottle of wine! The whole practice discourages the patronage of any person of moderate means who knows food and drink."

Gus nodded, gulping his milk. "You like milk better hot, Aunt Emily?"

"I became used to drinking it on shipboard before going to bed. I used to travel a great deal by ship, you know. Hot milk always reminds me of travel.

"I was thinking just now how every passenger on a ship thinks the voyage is exciting and unique, and just as thrilling to the crew as to him. I'll never forget the disillusionment of a young acquaintance of mine on the *France* who noticed her captain of waiters was wearing a celluloid collar on his dress shirt, and suddenly realized that the voyage, so wonderful to her, was just a job to the crew, a way of making a living that must be very difficult at times, and the trip just another repetition of an old story."

"Yeah, that's just like life; everybody thinks every thing that happens to him is all new and different from what happens to other people. You know what I mean?"

"I know what you mean. Well, goodnight, dear. You climb Sargent tomorrow, I hear."

"Yeah." Gus sighed. "Well, there'll be tea afterward. Goodnight."

Sarah was sitting up in bed. She addressed the lean form in the other bed:

"Hill? Do you think Mrs. Lamb is attractive? Hill? Don't you think the little girl is a bit much? Fairly well-mannered, I admit, but her clothes are much too showy for what their income must be. I just happened to notice them hanging in the bunkroom. And she is not at all unspoiled, like Persis."

There was no answer from Hill.

"Hill? Don't you think that women who stay in bed in the morning until they wake up themselves keep their looks?"

Hill took the pillow off his head and turned to look at her. "Good God, Sarah, what brings that on? As long as a woman is of a proper family and has money, who needs looks?"

"I think you are trying to be funny again. Cousin Tom's wife stays in bed until she wakens and then she just rings for a tray. She says the most charming women in Baltimore do."

"That's a contradiction in terms. I have never met a charming woman from Baltimore. But, on the other hand, I've never been to Baltimore. Perhaps they export all the bitches.

"Wasn't it a Marquand character who asked why people from Baltimore always seem to be of a certain type? And she wasn't meaning to be complimentary."

"I don't know what you're talking about. And don't say bitches so loudly. Do you think Jane is pretty, I asked you?"

There was no sound from the other bed. Hill's pillow was again atop his head, and his long day was over.

The lights had long been out at "Quarterdeck." In her bed, Pherousa breathed lightly, as graceful in sleep as she was awake. In his room across the hall, Horatio lay on the floor under his bed, on his side, with knees drawn up to his chin. Junior's ax was clutched in his arms. His eyes were closed and he may have slept.

Most certainly his father did. Her head pressed into her pillow in an unsuccessful attempt to muffle the sound of the Captain's snores, Kitty Blanchard stared into the darkness and practiced, in whispers, a long and forceful speech.

At Mrs. Parker's cottage, a light still burned. Firmly, with a quick and competent hand, Mrs. Parker looked over lists and added up columns of figures. She had found that most of her mathematical work went more quickly at night. She examined letters and inventories to assist her always remarkable memory. This was her usual nightly procedure when she had a problem, and the cordage business presented her with a problem most nights.

Her round face, with the deep-cut lines running down from the corners of the mouth, was set in her customary determined expression. At the end of her night's work, she had, as always, a clear and unwavering picture of the matter she had been concentrating on, and her course of action was all planned out in her mind. All her courses of action seemed to terminate in profit and not loss; Mrs. Parker detested loss and would not suffer it, as her competitors had found.

She had been working in her usual neat costume of dark wool skirt and white blouse. Quickly she changed this for a pair of heavy silk pajamas that had belonged to her husband and, after stamping a letter and swallowing her usual nightly two glasses of water and numerous vitamin pills, threw open the window wide and, not bothering to lock her cottage doors, went to bed. She did not turn off the light. From childhood, Lettice Parker had been afraid of only one thing: the dark.

The Gambels were still awake. Dr. Gambel, a thin little man of middle age, with a heavy grey mustache and a high domed forehead on which his tortoise-shell spectacles were rakishly perched, puffed on his pipe and made notes from a thick text in German. His flowered satin dressing gown made a splash of colour in the bedroom, the decor of which was composed mainly of mud-colored burlap and brown imitation leather.

Mrs. Gambel sat up in the large bed and knitted. She wore a man's warm plaid woolen shirt as a bed-jacket and her heavy auburn hair was twisted in a no-nonsense fashion on the top of her head. Her face was pudgy and devoid of expression. Subdued rustlings from the room next to hers, where the five little boys slept in sibling companionship, roused her, and she raised her brows and snapped her fingers. Dr. Gambel at first paid her no attention. He was staring out at the cove, whether at the light still showing in the Parker cottage, at the light moving stealthily across the water, or at something he saw only in his own thoughts, he alone knew.

Finally he rose obediently and switched out the lights. "Now, children, mach schnell," he said quietly, using the double-language form in which the superior little Gambels were usually addressed, and got into bed beside his wife's bulky form.

The solitary rower had evidently accomplished his nocturnal purpose to his satisfaction. His light disappeared around the point, and the cove slept.

Chapter 12

MAINE MORNING

The Bungalow awoke around seven-thirty to a resounding salvo of breakages from the kitchen: Dora was in full operation. Doreen was heard to mumble placations. Suddenly "Taxation without representation" was very clearly heard. There was another mumble from Doreen. Then there was one final horrendous crash and a distinct: "Rich people, my eyeball! There ain't so many rich summer people no more.

"Here, Miss Smarty, you take this tray up to Mrs. Worthington, and on the way, you tell them kids to hop to and set the breakfast table. I'm not serving breakfast practically at dinner time, like yesterday. Food goes on that table in ten minutes, come hell or high water, dishes on it or not; tell 'em so!"

Persis and Elizabeth Lamb met the deadline and were sitting quietly, hands folded, at the table on the porch of the main Bungalow overlooking the cove, as the rest of the company, except for Isabella and her mother, wandered along to breakfast. Polite but brief morning salutations were exchanged.

Miss Elbridge was attired in her usual neat shirtwaist dress, and

Hill and Gus wore faded blue oxford-cloth shirts and khaki trousers. Elizabeth Lamb was chic in spotless white shorts, Greek sandals, and a pink mohair sweater. At the sight of her, Sarah sighed before patting Persis' curly little head.

Persis wore the usual Bostonian combination of a pair of jeans from W. T. Grant and a hand-knitted, obviously expensive navy-blue sweater patterned with sailboats, that had belonged to Gus in his younger and smaller days. Sarah herself, as Hill noted with one raised eyebrow, wore a most becoming pink shirt, instead of her customary white blouse, and — unheard of for Sarah before the cocktail hour — a discreet amount of pretty pink lipstick.

As Emily seated herself, Dora burst through the screened doorway, just inside which she had been lurking, and thrust a huge platter of ham and eggs at her. She then rushed back into the kitchen, from whence emitted a forceful monotone having to do with undesirable characters who left messy and illegal deer livers on the sinks in the care of respectable, hard-working women and the resulting blood all over creation which said hard-working women would be forced to clean up, because of their own lofty principles, before they left the premises for good and all, which they would do in a minute if it were not for the regard in which they held poor Mrs. Worthington, who knew how to behave even if there were others who did not.

Doreen, humming as usual, wandered in and out between the tirade in the kitchen and the silent company on the porch, oblivious, as she poured coffee and passed cornbread, to both the speech and the silence.

Jane looked around shyly. "I didn't know what to wear to climb this mountain. Is a skirt all right?" She looked down at herself rather proudly, oblivious of a cigarette burn and a faint coffee stain on her fashionable ensemble.

"Better put on shorts," advised Sarah, sighing again as she considered Jane's beautifully-tailored white pleated pongee skirt and silk Pucci shirt. "To a real climber, Sargent is just a little hill, but to most of us it is quite an expedition. It's the second highest mountain on Mount Desert, but I've walked to the top of the highest, Cadillac, in a third of the time it takes to go up Sargent, and with a third of the effort."

"You hear people in shops," Hill said, "greeting their friends and asking where so-and-so is. 'She's climbing Sargent today,' they are answered, in hushed and awed tones, as if she were climbing

Everest or walking on the moon. I suppose we'll all be walking on the moon pretty soon, though."

"I still admire the people who call the mountains by their old names," observed Emily, "though I get mixed up trying to remember them. Lemuel is quite a fanatic about it. He says Mr. Dorr did a great deal of good in getting so much of the island turned into a national park, but he should have insisted that the park leave the names as they were.

" 'Cadillac' is so showy; 'Green' was much prettier. 'St. Saveur' is plain silly, and half the people can't pronounce it; 'Dog' for the dog that got lost on it made more sense. And as for renaming 'The Bubbies' 'The Bubbles' so as not to offend old ladies like me — well!"

"Why would it?" asked Elizabeth Lamb.

"Never mind, just now," Hill answered. "You have to see them from the water, anyway, to really grasp the reference made in their original name, which, by the way, was given them by sailors and fishermen, and not the young man credited for it. And no matter what the mountains' names are, today's climb is a total of about three hours up and then down to the carriage road near the Jordan Pond House, and then a fast twenty-five minute walk to tea, so you kids had better eat a hearty breakfast now."

"Yes, do," said Sarah. "Luncheon will be peanut butter sandwiches and milk, since Dora is off until the guests come tonight. What time shall we set off for Sargent, Hill?"

Hill was standing to observe a yawl under full sail passing the mouth of the cove. Several figures in orange foul-weather gear moved about her deck. Blonde heads turned to observe the waving hands of Hill and Persis and Elizabeth Lamb. The heads turned away and no hands were lifted in reply.

"Damned Northeast Harbor snobs," murmured Hill, reaching for the binoculars that hung on the porch wall. "Yep, told you so; she's from Northeast. When they get over here to the west side, they consider it slumming and won't lift a civil finger. And why do they all have blonde hair? Must be the inbreeding that makes them so snotty."

"What does that mean?" asked Elizabeth Lamb.

"It's biology," said her mother calmly. "Never mind just now." Elizabeth Lamb sighed.

"Fools think they have to wear that Swedish stuff to show they can sail," muttered Gus through a mouthful of cornbread. "It's like a uniform. All they need is a sweatshirt and a pair of pants but they dress as if they were crewing in the Newport-Bermuda Race. Makes me tired."

"They must have anchored down by Bobby Dow's old place for the night," Hill said. "I'll say this for them: they had to get up before breakfast to get under way so early."

Gus looked puzzled at his father's wit but philosophically reached for the platter of ham and eggs while he considered it.

"It's especially sad when they won't wave to a Native in a motorboat," said Emily. " 'Sail doesn't recognize motor,' as Lemuel observed to me, quite insufferably, when I civilly nodded to a very pleasant young couple in a nice little outboard, off Sutton's Island last summer when he was giving me a day's sail."

Jane spoke timidly. "I understand there are many more tourists now than summer residents. What do the Natives think of the tourists?" she asked, and blanched as Dora came out again to the porch.

"The ones that make their living from 'em mostly think well of 'em," said Dora. "Usually, they're right likeable people, with a few bad apples, a'course, but the rest of us just wish they wouldn't clutter up the roads. You'll notice, Mis' Lamb, none of them are able to pull over to the side to read a map. No, they have to wait till they come to a crossroads and then they stop dead in the middle of it. Do it every blessed time!"

Emily frowned. "Would you make me a piece of very dry toast, Dora, please?"

The readiness with which Dora disappeared and then plummeted back with a piece of exceedingly dry and cold toast revealed to Jane that Miss Elbridge had used that ploy before to discourage Dora's conversation and that Dora was one up on her.

Dora went on, "But there's people that lives on the island year-round, not us born here but people like Mrs. Worthington's relative Henry, who not only enjoy cheering up the tourists — some of 'em do act like lost souls; 'course, I guess that's so of travellers in strange places anywhere — but get some fun, also, out of acting humble and meek to the uppity ones in the summer cottage crowd. I guess," she added thoughtfully and rather surprisingly, "it's what you call tongue-in-cheek."

Gus chimed in: "You ought to see Sam — that's Henry's son — serving the summer kids at the movie candy counter. He's top of his form at school, captain of varsity soccer, going to win the Thayer Drama Award for sure next year and already accepted at Harvard. Well, you ought to see him play the polite, dumb hick when one of those jerks in oilskins and Topsiders talks to him in a put-on Maine accent, asking for 'More buttah, theah, on this heah popcorn, son' and stuff like that. *He* gets a kick out of it, though *they* don't get more butter.''

Jane was flattered that Gus had favoured her with such a long and earnest speech. "Where does Sam go to school?" she asked.

"Oh, St. Paul's," Gus answered. He blushed. "It's a pretty good school. I go there, too."

"St. Paul's? And those summer kids can't tell? There's a certain patina Paulies have — I used to know a — a few —" Jane's voice trailed off uncertainly, as usual, after she made any definite pronouncement.

"Well, as you heard, Sam is a pretty accomplished actor," Hill answered. "And the really nasty young summer complaints, as the Natives call them, go, mostly, to schools labelled things like Rockabye Country Day, so they wouldn't know. Ah, Sister Issa, welcome to what's left of breakfast."

"Greetings, everyone. Dora, just some toast and an orange, please. Little Liz, how pretty and well-dressed you are. And, Persis, how pretty. Oh, and Dora, some more hot coffee, if you would."

Sarah frowned. Elizabeth Lamb frowned in miniature and said, politely, "Thank you."

"Her name's not Liz, Aunt Isabella," said Persis. "She doesn't like it. Her name's Elizabeth Lamb; that's what her mother calls her and we should, too."

" 'Her' is a cat, Persis," admonished Isabella, "or so they informed me in the nursery. Your mother and I were taught how to speak, when we were your age. And when not to speak, too." She dropped into a chair and added, sotto voce, "Only a kitten at the moment, but a cat before very long." She then dimpled prettily, pleased at her humour, though it could not have been offered to the whole table.

This time both Elizabeth Lamb and her mother, who were both possessed of sharp ears, frowned.

"Got no oranges, and there's no toast this morning; johnnycake," firmly announced Dora, who had been regarding Isabella with displeasure. "I'll go heat up this coffee, agin, Isabella, and please to remember I have the day off. Doreen's clearing the table straightaway, soon's you drink your coffee."

Isabella made a charming moue. "A lovely morning," she proclaimed regally, as she crumbled cornbread daintily. "I met Varner last night after you left him, Hill. We had a short ride in his truck in the moonlight. I think I may have cheered him up a little." She grimaced complacently and her laugh bubbled.

"There was fog last night," replied Hill coldly, "as you must have noticed, and it's quite dangerous to ride around in the fog. Quite dangerous, Isabella."

He grasped his son's arm as Gus began to sidle off the porch. "Gus, you are not to go out in *Coacher* this morning. June's not here and there's a lot of work to do."

Sarah rose to help Doreen stack dishes on a tray. "Let's all be back here at noon, ready to have lunch and go. Isabella, stay a bit. I think Mother would want me to speak to you."

The company took its dismissal in good grace, wandering off in varying directions as Sarah, with a modicum of sighs and headshakings, began to talk earnestly to Isabella. Jane's good hearing noticed phrases like "bad form," "poor Minnie," and "Mother would be outraged."

A few hours later the members reassembled, the Lambs looking rather sunburned and Jane now attired in pale blue silk shorts. She and her daughter each carried one of the later novels of Dorothy Sayers and Elizabeth Lamb was heatedly disputing her mother's quiet explanation that, toward the last, Miss Sayers had fallen in love with her fictional detective.

"That is enough, Elizabeth Lamb," Jane said finally, with unwonted firmness. "Alexander Woolcott said she did." Elizabeth Lamb was silenced, not knowing who or what Mr. Woolcott was or had done.

Everyone sat down at the porch table to peanut butter and bread, and milk that Sarah poured from an enormous old white ironstone pitcher.

"A proper cold-roast-Bostonian lunch," approved Miss Elbridge.

"I'd much rather have paté on toast with perhaps a light Bordeaux," Isabella complained. "And a really good pear with some Pont-l'Évêque, I think. Sarah, why are you so uninspired about food, even here, where you don't have to count the cost?"

Sarah reddened. "Got no paté and there's no toast this noon; raw

Pepperidge Farm," mimicked Gus, in Maine tones thickly overlaid with peanut butter.

"Ouefs en gelée, paté and wine are being served in my corner of the compound." Jane spoke in a breathless, little-girl voice with a convincing Farmington accent. The adults laughed appreciatively, Hill applauded and Jane blushed.

"Indeed a dreadful woman," pronounced Emily. "But I believe, at last, she has found her proper milieu. She can have her jellied eggs and paté on gold plates whilst skimming over the Aegean, if one skims in steam yachts. Oh, for the lost, never-real days of her 'Camelot.' "

"That fat girl who was up helping Cousin Lem with his book last summer made jellied eggs all the time," offered Gus. "Last time we were there, I hid mine under some rocks by the terrace. Grossest things I ever tasted, they were."

"I can't imagine your turning down anything half-edible, even gross rocks," murmured his father, rubbing his thin brown arm with a somewhat blistered left hand. "God, I don't see how June ever gets all these cottages attended to. Just starting the pump and watering the vegetable patch took my whole morning. He is certainly indispensable and not overpaid. Let's just hope he doesn't realize it.

"You know," Hill went on, "I'm beginning to believe what Archie tells me: that most caretakers do demand kick-backs from the local contractors for work they place with them. Probably they think the money they get is no more than their due, although it does end up costing the summer people more, of course."

"Who's Archie?" asked Elizabeth Lamb.

"Friend of mine, a carpenter; you'll probably never meet him," answered Hill, absently, while Jane, at the same time, answered just as absently, "Never mind, just now; you'll probably never meet him."

Sarah was shocked at Hill's disclosure. "Oh, Junior wouldn't do that. I really can't believe any of the Natives would do that, to us, at least. I'm sure their feeling for us is quite feudal. Hill, don't snicker like that.

"Why, you know how Mother and I always ask about all the members of their families, and even take an interest in what they think politically. When President Nixon was elected last year, I asked everyone if they had voted for him, although I hadn't, of course; I liked Senator McGovern because he seemed to be a gentleman —

Hill, there is nothing funny about that, especially since you voted as I did. Well, as I was trying to say, they're so shy that they wouldn't tell me, but I know they were flattered by my interest. Hill, please stop looking like that. Gus, surely you are not still hungry?"

"Gus ate two whole rows of radishes while he was helping you, Daddy," informed Persis. "Ow, you stop that, Gus."

"Je préfère des radis avec beurre," Elizabeth Lamb announced, consuming peanut butter neck and neck with Gus.

"Regional differences in food preferences are quite interesting," Emily said, with not much pertinence, "but the same food titled differently in various regions interests me more. That reminds me of a story of Lem's, from the Second World War."

Hill sighed and prepared to be depressed, especially since now that his right arm was able to cope with spreading peanut butter, the jar was empty.

Emily went on, "Just at the last stages of the battle for Guadalcanal, Lem and some other Marine field officers were invited aboard a Navy ship for breakfast. They were looking forward to hot food done up in style, and all of them had a special desire for fresh eggs, but the young coloured mess attendant said that although he could provide any amount of bacon or ham or sausage, there just were no more eggs.

"Lem remarked to the man seated next to him how disappointed he was, because he had dreamed of dropped eggs on toast for four nights running — or days, or whenever it was he got a chance to sleep. And, imagine, when the food was served, four beautiful poached eggs were put before Lem by the attendant, who muttered in Lem's ear, 'Here you are, sir. It's a long way from Scollay Square and us Bostonians has got to stick together.' "

"Hey," said Hill, delighted that at last Miss Elbridge had recounted an anecdote that had some wit, not to say point to it, "that must have been the fellow who now owns a dry-cleaning plant in Roxbury and with whom Lem dines several times a year. I met them once coming out of Locke-Ober's, looking very well-fed and congenial, and Lem introduced him as an old friend first met at Guadalcanal."

"Yes, of course," replied Emily. "The young man — well, I suppose not so young now — takes Lem to Locke-Ober's and Lem takes him to his club. Lem is quite an expert on dry-cleaning by now, can do his own in a pinch although Uncle Roger brought him up to believe that all a gentleman's clothes should ever need was a daily brushing and occasional airing. Once in a while, he goes over and helps his friend out, when he's short-handed.

"And the young man has developed a great knowledge of Marine Corps history. They talk war and politics and disagree violently and have a grand time."

"Oh, Emily, surely Lem doesn't take him to his club," Sarah said. "I don't think that, even nowadays, it would be allowed."

"I am surprised at you, Sarah," answered her aunt coldly. "Where one goes, one's friends go. And, most especially, where Lem goes, his friends go."

"Or else," agreed Hill. "Now, are we all ready?"

"Oh, Hill, just sit for a bit," said Isabella. "You really should try to rise above your upbringing and cultivate the gentlemanly art of appreciation of leisure."

Hill ignored her, and rose. "Dad," said Gus, who was observing a lobster boat just a few yards offshore as he got reluctantly up from the table, "looks like Buster Griffin's not getting any haul at all out of the cove today."

"'As if', boy, 'as if.' What is St. Paul's coming to? Even your Uncle Peter left it with some sense of grammar."

"Really, Isabella, you need not jump on Gus. He is on holiday," said Sarah, defending her young.

"Cultivating the gentlemanly art of appreciation of leisure," Jane murmured, to a haughty stare from Isabella.

She pacifically added, "But I do so dislike the use of 'like' as a conjunction. Wasn't it Nero Wolfe who said, when his assistant observed that 'like' was in the dictionary as a conjunction, 'Like is not a conjunction in this house'? I loved that."

"And who may Nero Wolfe be, pray?" Isabella was her most regal.

"A foreigner, at least by some accounts." Hill was now in good humour. "At least, he isn't a Bostonian. And yet, imagine, he's literate."

He turned to Gus. "Buster's not only late this morning, but it looks as though his trap lines may have been cut. The Proutys, perhaps?"

"Late?" asked Elizabeth Lamb, who was now quickly filling up on the cream cheese and bread supplied by Sarah to alleviate the total consumption of the peanut butter. "It's only a little after noon."

"Water's calmer in the morning, easier to pull traps. Wind makes up right after one or two in the afternoon. Belay the bread, Mlle. Lamb. You'll get fat," said Gus, reaching for some himself.

"I do believe that the pendulum will soon swing the other way, and fat women will be in vogue," said Hill, with a kindly look at Elizabeth Lamb. "Eat all you want, young lady."

"Then the majority of Mount Desert ladies will lead the fashion world," responded Isabella. "They work hard; is it the baked beans that broadens them? Their hips, that is, not their minds, by any manner of means."

"Baked beans are nourishing and cheap," informed Emily, as usual stating rather boring truisms with an air of profundity. "Strange, how they are still a Saturday night staple here and in many New England areas although the reason for that has long since faded from memory. In Puritan days, they could, you know, be eaten on Sunday, still warm in the beanpot, and so eliminate cooking on the Sabbath."

"Ladies, we have really got to start," said Hill.

"Would you have liked to be a Puritan, Hill?" asked Isabella, stirring from her seat reluctantly. "I can just see you now, striding along through a cold grey Massachusetts twilight with your rod erect; did Puritans have rods? Well, you know what I mean, dear, I am sure. Perhaps you came to Massachusetts straight from Cannes."

As Sarah regarded her with perplexity and Hill with disdain, she added, "Now, I would love to have been a lavish courtesan in Alexandria in something-or-other B.C., all stiff black lacquered hair and Byzantine jewels and rolls of fat. I'm sure I should have been very successful. What would you like to have been, Jane?

"No, don't tell me; I'm sure you're far too lady-like. I know! A young miss in muslins, of Jane Austen's period, looking for a husband and complaining daintily about the dirty roads you encountered each day on your walks as companion to a crusty old lady."

Jane blushed, and cleared her throat. "No," she said, in a low but distinct voice. "I always wanted to be a wealthy young upper-class Englishman, strolling down Bond Street in the '20's on a May morning — the air fresh, and the pavements damp but drying in the clear sunshine, and the flowers dewy in the shop-windows, and I not afraid of anything and all things possible to me."

Her voice quavered a little at the end, but she got up and stood quite straight, her fists pushed down into the pockets of her shorts to hide their trembling, and regarded the others unwaveringly. They stared back in surprise. Finally Miss Elbridge nodded in approval. "Very well put," she said.

"Please, now, let's go, for heaven's sake," said Hill, "and it's really none too soon."

Chapter 13

TO THE MOUNTAIN

 As they started down the path to the car, a series of flashes of light showed through the trees across the cove, from the Blanchards' property.

"Horatio on the roof signalling with a mirror again," Hill said to Sarah. "God knows who he thinks is the recipient of his messages. The Martian Navy, perhaps."

Sarah sighed, a common reaction when Horatio Blanchard was mentioned. "Do you know what Junior let out, oh, very discreetly, of course? Horatio insists that a huge box be sent up every summer, by Railway Express at great expense, and returned to him in Kittery in the fall. And can you guess what's in it?"

Nobody could, although Persis wistfully suggested licorice jellybeans, of which she was inordinately fond.

"Coathangers! Dozens and dozens of wire coathangers, such as the dry cleaner returns clothes on. They are all neatly packed by Horatio, and he keeps them in his room, undisturbed all summer, and just ships them back and forth, back and forth."

"My God," said Hill in awe. "He's worse than I thought. Completely looney. I think he might be dangerous, or could get to be."

"Oh, no," Emily demurred gently. "The poor boy just wants something of his own, his own property. I've seen the same thing in quite normal people."

"Now, Hill, I shall meet you all at the Jordan Pond House at four-fifteen or so. You should be at the start of the Giant Slide Trail by one-fifteen, and you plan to get up and down in just over three hours, is that right? That's awfully fast for these little girls. I really feel you'll be longer. I'm afraid it will be a squeeze after tea, all of us going back in my car to where you'll leave yours, but we'll manage. I do hope you are not very late in getting down, because Elizabeth wants us back here at six."

Packed more or less comfortably into the station wagon, with Isabella, at least, wondering how much worse it would be in Emily's little Swedish car, they waved good-bye to Emily and drove out through the woods. On the narrow side road, they were met by a large black Cadillac that occupied the middle of the way and showed no signs of moving. Hill pulled over, almost into the ditch, and stopped.

"Well," said the driver of the Cadillac, pausing to lean out her window and regard Hill and his passengers with contempt, "at it again?"

"Hello, Mrs. Parker," Hill greeted her stiffly. "We're going out to climb Sargent. Elizabeth no longer feels up to it, but she likes us to carry on the annual climb her husband loved."

Mrs. Parker nodded a grudging approval. "Elizabeth has the proper feelings," she admitted. "Shame everyone else around here isn't as responsible. When you get back, tell Emily I want to talk to her. She can come over for tea at four-thirty. Tell her to be on time."

"I'm afraid that's impossible," Hill said cheerfully. "She's joining us for tea after the climb."

Mrs. Parker's pudgy face became quite mauve with anger. She drove on, casting Isabella a contemptuous glance as she passed.

Isabella made a furious sound in her throat, but said nothing.

Indicating a pile of old rock foundation beside the road as he drove on, Hill spoke. "There's what's left of the old 'tea-house.' How long did Varner's Aunt Sally run it, anyway?"

"Oh, I think for years and years during Prohibition and well into the forties," Sarah answered. "Father was the only one who ever called her bluff. We all dressed in our finest one day, when Peter and Isabella and I were very small, and walked up here. Father said in a firm voice to old Sally, 'My family and I would like tea.'

"She was absolutely confounded and said, 'Tea, Mr. Worthington?' 'Why, yes,' said Father. 'Your sign says you have teas.' So, after a great deal of subdued commotion behind what was obviously a bar, we were served a saucepan of weak tea and a collection of cups and mugs, along with a plate of pretzels. But Sally had the last word. The bill was seven dollars."

"If she charged on the same scale for liquor, no wonder the Proutys drank a lot of vanilla," Hill observed. "The stores over here could barely keep it in stock, so I've been told."

"I can see why bootleggers used to be rampant on Mount Desert Island, since there used to be only one liquor store on the island, the Bar Harbor one," offered Isabella. "I remember Varner's taking a weekly trip over there. He called it his 'green-front run' or, sometimes, when he was feeling witty, he'd say he was going over to 'see old Doc Green' for what ailed him." Isabella turned her head away as they passed by Varner's house where a raw-boned red-haired woman was pegging out clothes on a worn line. A little farther along, Sarah pointed out a house. "That was built in Massachusetts," she informed Jane Lamb and her daughter.

"And brought here?" asked Elizabeth Lamb. "It must have been very hard to do."

"Not at all," said Isabella. "Maine used to be part of Massachusetts and that house was built before it became an independent state."

"Something else for me to remember. I do thank you for the trouble you are taking with me, Aunt Isabella," Elizabeth Lamb said sweetly, stressing the broad "a" in "aunt."

Persis giggled and Jane Lamb said, in low but firm tones, "Quite enough, Elizabeth Lamb."

Upon reaching the main road, Hill turned right, towards Southwest Harbor. "Dora asked me to pick up some olives and cocktail biscuits at the A. and P. and nowhere else," he explained. "She said 'the red-front is cheaper than most of those other places' and directed me not to go to June's and Peyton's store on Duck Cove. 'Couple of pirates' she called them. She's really taken a scunner against them lately. I wouldn't dare disobey her if I intend to eat without indigestion."

"More than the usual indigestion we all get from her temper and those all-too-frequently cindered meals?" Isabella asked, with regal disdain.

They drove along happily, noticing a number of out-of-state cars stopped at dangerous spots, the occupants consulting road maps, just as Dora had described.

"Sometimes," Sarah said, "I almost wish we were back in the early days, when the summer residents had an ordinance passed prohibiting cars on the island. That lasted, I think, till someone died because the doctor's horse was too slow."

"Truly?" asked Elizabeth Lamb. "That's something like Bermuda now. Visitors can't rent cars, but I loved the motorbikes anyway."

"We know all about Bermuda, child," murmured Isabella. "You have somewhat of a tendency, as the Natives would say, to teach your grandmother to suck eggs."

Persis put her arm comfortingly around Elizabeth Lamb, who looked downcast, and Gus muttered angrily under his breath, but Jane seemed amused.

They presently came to a neat little white-painted emporium labelled "Duck Cove Store, Fair Dealing." A mild-looking, middle-aged, light-haired man, who resembled Dora except around his mouth, whose corners turned up whereas hers turned down, nodded affably to them as he carried out a box of groceries to a waiting car.

"Look, it's that lady again, that Cordelia cousin who had fits at the Ritz," cried Elizabeth Lamb excitedly, turning around to watch, once again in her usual spirits.

Following in Peyton's wake came the distraught Cordelia, gesticulating towards his stolid back with one hand and with the other clutching a paper bag of groceries that was disintegrating with her nervous movements. Dumping the shredded bag into the seat beside Teddie, who was impassively reading *Playboy* at the wheel, she was shaking her finger furiously at Peyton as she faded from view.

"Damn," Hill said suddenly. "I'd better go back and speak to Peyton, though it will make us even later than we are."

He began to reverse recklessly along the verge, passing the Woodhues' car, which Teddie was calmly driving at a slow, steady rate, eyes fixed on the far distance. His wife talked to him rapidly as he drove, and was so occupied with waving her hands in the air that she missed the sight of the Bungalow party.

Hill stopped by the storekeeper, who was regarding the getaway of Cordelia and Teddie with a wry smile.

"Summer complaint, with bells on," he muttered to Hill. "No offense, Hill, but her carrying on every time she comes into the store about the 2¢ more I charge for catfood than the chain stores do sure gets me bent out of shape. Oh, well, only ten weeks till Labor Day."

"Boston thrift, Peyton," Hill replied. "Look, Mrs. Worthington wants me to ask you if you could stay tonight, after you bring her groceries, and serve drinks, around six-thirty or so? Usual rate; she won't try to get you to knock 2¢ off."

"Gorry, Hill, I dunno. I don't think so, with Junior gone. We get right out straight here on Saturday nights. Tell you what; I'll talk it over with Dottie, let you know when I bring your order up."

With that Hill had to be satisfied, and they proceeded, well over the speed limit, to Southwest Harbor. When they reached it, he dashed quickly into the store, and his family and the Lambs regarded the passers-by, who at the moment consisted mainly of pleasant-faced old ladies who smiled at them.

"So unlike Bar Harbor, where the meanest-looking old hags in the hemisphere congregate," asserted Isabella. "When our cousin Henry and his wife Betsy first moved there, Betsy made it a point to smile unmistakeably at every nasty-faced old lady, tourist, summer resident, or Native she saw. Henry called it her 'idiot look' and said the Natives would regard her as not quite right in the head. Or having only one oar in the water, as they'd put it."

Hill emerged from the store with a small package, looking amused. "Woman in there with a God-awful Brooklyn accent complaining because the eggs are brown. The clerk was trying to tell her that there's no difference at all, inside, between brown and white eggs, but she was quite stubborn. Then she wanted to know where there was a delicatessen. So a customer who'd had enough of her directed her to Bar Harbor."

Isabella laughed sardonically. "She isn't going to find quite what she expects, and then she'll make a scene over there."

"Of course; that's why he did it."

As they sped by the automatic laundry, Sarah made mention of the many vans and other camping-type vehicles tightly parked around it.

"There are more and more people who come up here to camp," she said. "Mother feels it is something of a pity, because many of them contribute very little to the economy of the island while enjoying its beauties and free facilities, of which there are more than what the National Park supplies. I think camping a good idea for families with children, but some of the campers are unkempt-looking and not at all concerned with preserving the wilderness they come to see. For the couple of dollars they spend for a night's campsite in the park, some of them act as if they've bought the whole island!"

"Henry likes them, poor dolt," Isabella said. "Maybe it's because they come to the movies when it rains."

"Well, some of them can't get the idea they're supporting the whole island from the amount of groceries they buy," put in Hill. "Peyton and June say a lot of them bring all their supplies with them, except milk and ice. But they do a lot of laundry; I'll say that for them. A cousin of Dora's was incensed to hear a camper in the laundromat saying that it should be reserved for campers because the summer residents can afford to buy their own machines and the Natives can wait till fall! She swears that's what the woman said."

His passengers debated the pros and cons of campers and the causes of the friction, real or alleged, between the Natives and tourists and the east and west sides of the island. Since none of them were really well acquainted with their subjects, the discussion tapered off to a calm appreciation of the scenery, beautiful on all points of the compass, regardless of the varying qualities of its human inhabitants.

Elizabeth Lamb, with a sideways look at Isabella, observed that Bermuda requires that telephone wires be put underground, and so should this island, but Isabella was occupied in complacent regard of her Victorian features in a pocket mirror and failed to respond.

They passed through demure Somesville, took a right towards Bar Harbor and then followed the road in the direction of Northeast Harbor. Hill parked along the highway in the lee of a little stone church. The party observed, for the most part dispassionately, a wooden sign that announced the top of Sargent Mountain to be a modest 3.1 miles distant. Isabella snorted delicately and announced that the park authorities were as inept as she suspected if they thought that all the torture she was about to undergo could be encompassed in the short stretch of 3.1 miles.

"All out," announced Hill. "To the mountain!"

"I don't see any mountain, not right here," asserted Elizabeth Lamb.

"You will. You'll climb up miles and miles of real estate on one side and when you are up thirteen hundred or so exhausting feet, you'll trudge down miles and miles more on the other side before you get your tea," Isabella informed her pleasureably.

"That's how they talk to all poor little children who are made to climb mountains," replied Elizabeth Lamb haughtily. "They used to poke my father with an alpenstock, too, poor little defenseless boy."

"Probably deserved it, too," decreed Isabella. "I remember well when my brother Peter . . . oh, look, Sarah, our first Mittel Europeans of the year."

"Hush, Issa." Sarah, in the lead, moved aside politely as a stalwart pair of muscular Teutons, clad in thick tweeds topped by tam-o-shanters of ghastly vivid hues, advanced firmly toward them, not moving an inch from the middle of the narrow, rough road. The man marched first, carrying his climbing stick. His wife, burdened with binoculars, camera and berry basket, followed.

"Grüss Gott," they said, distantly but courteously, and Sarah cried cheerily, "A lovely day!" in return.

"I never can determine," Isabella announced in a carrying voice as the party continued on, once more in single file, "why Mount Desert has been invaded in late years by Mittel Europa. One seems to see these types only out hiking, too. Where are they the rest of the time?

"And is it more annoying to my delicate sensibilities to see those impassive countenances barking 'Grüss Gott' at one or to have nasty American youths glaring at or else ignoring us while they drop beer cans along the trails? I must think on it."

"Do so, and save your breath," Hill advised. "We've got to move briskly. It's after one already."

Chapter 14

MOUNTAIN SCENERY

Once started, they stepped along smartly, Jane soon slightly out of breath. The rocky road became a path through a meadow where an abandoned shed and its accompanying building of a somewhat inn-like appearance caused her to wonder aloud if the middle of the island had had bootleg teahouses also? No one answered. The Halsteads and Isabella were on the edge of that deep-lunged euphoria common to those who walk and climb on Mount Desert. They passed a decayed barn on their left and the path again grew rocky. An incongruous wreck of a roadster, driven there perhaps thirty years before, was half-buried in the sweet tall grass beside the way.

There was the slightest tint of an ascent. The path now was slippery with pine needles. Insect song pervaded the sunshine, and, Jane was delighted to see, a swarm of white butterflies hovered over the narrowing trail ahead of them. Past the butterflies, a dirt road crossing their track could be discerned. "We're there?" Elizabeth Lamb cried, in disappointment.

"The mountain is crossed by what some of the Natives call

'Rockefeller roads,' " Hill answered. "They are the National Park's 'carriage roads,' open now, since the demise of carriages, only to walkers and riders — there is at least one stable nearby. And, of course, to skiers and snowmobilers in the winter. Let's say they may be used by anything except automobiles, or 'motors,' as the Rockefeller family terms them.

"In their stronghold, in Seal Harbor, Jane, the entrances to their private roads have the sign 'No motors allowed except those of guests,' and Sarah, in her childhood, read the signs as saying 'No mothers allowed except those of guests' and was puzzled for years."

Sarah said, "Really, Hill!"

Hill went on: "But I believe these are nicknamed 'Rockefeller roads' because, during the Depression, the family paid for the building of many of them. Varner Prouty told me that even later, in hard times, they paid the wages of locals who repaired them. If so, it is a form of very welcome patronage."

Sarah turned in exasperation. "I never heard that, but if it is true, it is extremely nice of them, Hill. I don't know why you always sneer when you are talking about people on this island, rich or poor!"

"Sarah, you know perfectly well that I never —"

Sarah interrupted him. "And it certainly was not I who read the signs wrong; I don't even know if they were there when I was small. It was Cordelia, a few years ago. She refuses to wear her spectacles when driving. She was greatly perturbed and made a scene at a reception in Albany —" Sarah broke off to laugh "— something about discrimination towards the mothers of the poor. It was all just too ridiculous."

They crossed the road, passed a grey wooden sign that read "Giant Slide Trail," and started up an incline. Elizabeth Lamb and Persis rushed off to the left, where a path seemed to lead. Calling them back, Hill said, "Persis, you know you must stick to the trail. Look, there's a strip of red cloth on this tree right above your head."

"I didn't know that was a trail marker, Daddy."

"It isn't a permanent one. It means they're going to put a rock cairn here, or one of those triangular pieces of red metal stuck in the tree that I always fear will someday put the eye out of some unlucky extra-tall walker."

The path was now marked by small piles of rocks. "They always put cairns along unmistakable trails," Isabella complained, "but just get out on a bare slope where you can't see the trail and the cairns are few and far between. I swear the park rangers are lazier each year I come up here. The days when they lugged rocks to make steps up mountains for agile old ladies seem to be gone forever. Nor do they bother to clear away trees that have fallen over the path."

"It's not like that at all." Sarah was offended again. "With all the thousands of tourists milling over the park roads and the campgrounds, the rangers are so busy that the trails have to go somewhat by the board. The new breed of tourists is not all that fond of walking the trails; I suspect most of them don't know that they can buy park maps with the walking trails all marked for them."

"More and more the maps show trails as abandoned, too," put in Hill. "Now, Sarah, that is an observation, not a criticism."

They clambered over a few of the dead trees foretold by Isabella. The narrow trail grew more wet and rough. They were going along a brook bed, as pools of water to their right revealed. Jane tripped over one of the roots across the trail, and muttered a low and ladylike "Damn."

"I suppose it is an act of virtue to climb on Mount Desert?" she asked Hill, who was behind her, bringing up the rear. "And is the accent properly on the first syllable or the second? I've heard both."

"Well, there's the Sahara School and the Sundae School, as a wit said. Actually, he said the Ice Cream School, but I've improved on it. I would say the Sundae School predominates. And as for the act of virtue, don't let Sarah hear you even seeming to criticize any of the island institutions, like walking up mountains.

"You know," he went on in a low tone, "at the time of the Great Fire of 1947, which almost destroyed the eastern half of the island, when the summer kids in their prep schools and colleges heard what was happening, they took French leave, dozens if not hundreds of them, to come up here and help save their island.

"It's amazing the spell the place casts on the children who come up here summer after summer. They regard it as a Blessed Isle, the Elysian Fields — oh, I can't really define it but they have what can only be termed a thing about the place. And their husbands or wives, when they acquire them, soon learn to revere the island or suffer the consequences."

"In Paris," Jane said, "speaking of the fire, one of the newspapers — I think it was the Communist *L'Humanité* though I was barely old enough to read newspapers then — reported that the fire was set by the 'peasants' in revolt against the 'large landlords.' All because it was supposed to have started in a depressed area known as Dolliver's Dump, which they interpreted to mean a collection of peasants' hovels instead of a field for rubbish."

"There's a new theory," Hill replied, "that it didn't start in the dump, but that it is the place usually blamed. Look out, the trail crosses over the brook here."

They continued upward past mossy rocks. Ferns grew from the clefts, and the climb became more steep. Moss cast a green velvet coolness over the trail. One could look up and see, looming above and disappearing into the trees, the landslide of tumbled granite rocks that gave the impression that a baby giant had eons ago slid down the mountain in play.

The trail crossed and re-crossed the brook, amidst, to Jane, a confusion of cairns and rocks, logs and moss. Gus lagged back to help his sister and Elizabeth Lamb. Sometimes steps of flat rock made the going easier. There was a swarm of water bugs in a deep pool, carefully side-stepped by the little girls.

About a half-hour of concentrated climbing up the gorge brought them to a cleft into which they sidled, then dodged under a little rock, scrambled over a mighty one, and then filed right to ease their bodies, sticky with sweat, singly through a crevasse. Elizabeth Lamb slipped and slid to the side of the trail, crushing a giant fern. Isabella turned to arch an eyebrow at her. "Now we won't be able to see you the rest of the way up. Fern seed makes one invisible, you know. An old faery trick."

Persis took her hand comfortingly, as Elizabeth Lamb regarded her once pristine shorts. "I can see you," she whispered. "Aunt Isabella tells stories sometimes."

More clefts, a tunnel, and at last a sign on their left that read, maddeningly, "Sargent Mt. 1.3 mi." They crossed back once more to the left side of the gorge and sank exhausted under a large cedar tree.

"Listen," said Sarah. "A Peabody bird. Hear him say, 'Poor Sam Peabody, Peabody, Peabody'!"

"That's a white-throated sparrow, Ma," offered Gus. "He says, 'Oh, sweet Canada, Canada, Canada.' Mrs. Simons at school told us only Bostonians think he says 'Peabody.' "

Sarah turned a look of outrage upon her first-born as Hill rose to his feet announcing, "No more heresy, Gus. Now let's get up and at 'em. We came up the Slide in half an hour. That's darned good."

They went up a steep path through a little wood. Ten minutes more and they felt a breeze and, turning, saw far to the west the straight blue ribbon that was Somes Sound.

"Only fiord in America, right, Dad?" Gus said with authority. They crossed a brook and climbed on through the now heady mountain air. The path wound through patches of blueberry bushes, the berries still a bluish-white.

"Sometimes they're already ripe on Sargent," Isabella offered. "That woman we passed had a few."

"Oh, no; Sargent Mountain blueberries are the best on the island but they're much later than those at sea-level, always," Sarah replied.

"Nonsense," Isabella answered heatedly. "I remember —"

"Girls," interrupted Hill, "it's too hard to climb and argue at the same time. Whenever anybody talks about blueberries, all *I* remember is that waitress in Bar Harbor last year, when I questioned the menu's 'Home-made Maine Blueberry Pie' quite early in the season when they weren't ripe anywhere. 'Made in Maine, wasn't it? ' she answered, and that shut me right up, as I hope it's doing to you."

Sarah subsided but Isabella turned to say sulkily, "I know what I remember, and, for one thing, I remember it was *Le Figaro* not *L'Humanité.*"

"Girl has ears like a lynx," murmured Hill, to the amusement of Persis and Elizabeth Lamb, who giggled and jumped several times into the air for an ineffectual examination of the Grafin's ears.

They crossed a second road and now a larger vista opened to the west, at which they paused to look while catching their respective breaths. Jane sat, exhausted, on the ground and her daughter and Persis followed suit.

"Look," Hill pointed out, "there's the new high school for the whole island. It cost a fortune already and some genius designed it with a flat roof which I would think decidedly unsuitable for a region that sometimes gets heavy snows. They'll have to repair or replace it in a few years, I'll bet. Too hazy to see Blue Hill, but there are all the islands in Blue Hill Bay. Not quite all; I can't see the Follies where Varner, by the way, Sarah, is raising a horde of rabbits for meat this winter. We might land and get ourselves the makings of a pie. Hey, there's Napoleon's Hat, quite clear."

"Napoleon's Hat?" queried Elizabeth Lamb.

"It's a point of land on Long Island that, with its trees rising up, looks like a side view of his hat. See?"

"J.l.E." observed Isabella, looking at the nearer vistas of mountains and trees between her and far-away Blue Hill Bay. As Elizabeth Lamb opened her mouth, she was hastily forestalled by Isabella; "That means 'just like Europe'; my mother and aunt are fond of saying it of any reminiscent view on the island. Let's go on, Hill. We haven't been climbing for much more than an hour yet and you urge us on whenever we want to stop, so turnabout is fair play."

As Jane struggled to her feet, she suddenly smiled. To Hill's questioning look, she quietly explained, "Just then I had a feeling of pure light-heartedness, for no reason at all. I've felt it only a few times in my life: a flash of meaningless happiness that comes without any cause. It's a sort of feeling that life is just beginning, I think."

"Life always seems to be beginning, but it never is." Hill's tone was, for him, somber. His gaze went ahead, fleetingly, to Sarah and his children. "However, en avant, as your little girl might say; our life for the next couple of hours is limited to getting up and down Sargent."

On again, through wild raspberry and blackberry bushes, the first in flower. There was a vista to the north and in it a sight of the carriage road they had recently crossed, winding around the mountain below them. Down through a wooded ravine, with a brook at the bottom and bunchberries springing moistly along it. A pheasant whirred up and away as they approached.

Soon they were above the trees, the plain grey rock face of Sargent Mountain above them. There were cairns to show the path, fairly near together, but, as Isabella had said, not as near to each other as they often were on an unmistakable trail. A "peabody bird" called. An iron sign, seeming incongruous in the bareness of low bushes and a few small spruce, pointed to nowhere.

"Can we see the top?" called Elizabeth Lamb, looking back at Hill and then at the rocks above them that were now pink, with lichen growing freely. "I hope so," moaned her mother, breathlessly.

Sarah considerately paused to look across at Beech Mountain, now visible with its rangers' tower on top. Sails could now be seen on Somes Sound; a whole new cool and airy world opened up to Jane and the children after what had seemed hours of hot, heart-pounding, unwinking staring at the trail in front of their feet.

The way appeared to lead downhill, to Jane's dismay, then up through a small patch of grass and low trees, more of the grey vegetation, another little ravine, then — could it be possible? — an unmistakable pile of small rocks with a weathered wooden signpost stuck in it. The top of Sargent!

They trod through rather a lot of broken glass to read the "1373 feet" on the sign. The wind was refreshingly cool. With one accord they made for some flat rocks farther along and sank down. Hill lit a cigarette despite Isabella's frown and her announcement that it was bad form to smoke on trails.

They were not alone on the crest of Sargent Mountain. A short distance away several blue-jeaned figures belonging to both sexes stood clustered around a sweet-faced elderly woman seated on a rock. She was clad in a fleecy white shawl over blue trousers and a dashing red shirt and seemed to be holding court with the attentive young people, to whom she was pointing out places of note on a map and telling anecdotes.

Isabella favoured the group with a haughty glare of displeasure, but Sarah waved in recognition of the old lady, who smiled enchantingly and called, "Don't tell my daughter! Having a good climb?"

"Don't tell what, Mummy?" asked Persis.

"That is Mrs. van Pelt, a friend of grandmother's from New York who lives in Bar Harbor in the summer. She is over seventy and climbs or walks every day, but I should think her daughter would worry if she knew her mother climbed Sargent alone, as evidently she just did. She has such charm of manner that she always attracts other walkers, to whom she is pleased to explain the island."

"Really," said Jane admiringly. "I am absolutely half-dead after the climb, and at half her age."

"There was once," said Hill, "an old summer lady in Bar Harbor who lived near a small mountain called The Beehive. She may even have owned it then, although it is Park property now. Anyway, there is a pool on the top called The Bowl, probably because it reminded someone of a punchbowl, and the woman climbed The Beehive every morning to swim naked in the cold water of The Bowl, even when she was quite old. They don't make 'em now as they used to, Jane."

"Does naked mean all-bare, Daddy?" asked Persis, who knew quite well that it did but was determined to ask as many questions as her new friend.

"It does."

Persis lost interest in the all-bare lady and pointed far out to sea where a huge ship under sail could be seen. "Look, Gus!"

"One points only at French pastry," reproved Elizabeth Lamb.

"That's one of those big schooners out of Camden that carries paying guests downeast," informed Gus. "She's coming along the Western Way. And, Miss Lamb, we point at boats and islands, too."

"What a beautiful name — the Western Way," said Jane.

"Yes," Hill answered. "I always wanted a boat called the Western Way until I heard of a summer fellow in Northeast — that fellow who's on teev-ee, as Lem calls him — who had two, *Western Way I* and *Western Way II*, so I renounced my wish as redundant."

"Look at all the cars going up the road over on Cadillac," said Sarah. "What a shame those people are riding and not walking. And, look, Jane, one can see the Porcupine Islands off Bar Harbor. They're called that because they are shaped rather like porcupines and the spruce trees standing up are the quills on their backs."

"Oh, Sarah," yawned Isabella. "You are going to age into another Mrs. van Pelt, boring everyone with island phenomena. I wonder what became of the old lady on The Beehive; I always had the feeling one could step straight into Heaven, or what passes for it, from The Beehive. Perhaps she did." She then rose languidly and began to amble off to the south, following the cairns.

Her sister regarded Isabella's disappearing back indignantly. "Mrs. van Pelt is certainly not boring, and I hope I am not. I just think this is a fascinating place and that people are interested in it."

She looked uncertainly at Jane, who said warmly, "I love hearing about facets of any place where I am. I meant to ask you, Gus, where is 'downeast'?"

"We're 'downeast,' so to speak," Hill answered for Gus. "The prevailing wind along the Maine coast comes from the southwest, so running before the wind in a sailing ship from Boston, for instance, was going down the wind and towards the east. Going up to Maine was therefore going downeast. One says, incidentally, 'sou-west' and 'naw-west' if one is using the Yankee idiom — sometimes, though, a real old-timer says 'no'th-west' or 'no'th-east' — but never 'nor-west' or 'nor-east' as landlubbers trying to sound nautical do."

The Lambs appeared perplexed by all this information but, even though having not the slightest desire to appear correctly nautical, accepted it politely.

"I'm hungry, Dad," said Gus. "Let's go."

The top of Sargent was a flat table-land that they, now rested, traversed swiftly. Hill pointed out the islands far out to sea in the south: the Cranberries — Great and Little, Bear, Sutton's, Baker's, and the on-the-horizon Big and Little Duck. Jane observed timidly that the sea and the islands gave the impression of being in another dimension. "Like that Tom Swift story," said Gus, nodding in agreement.

"Down there is Hadlock Pond, where Northeast Harbor gets its water supply," Hill mentioned. "Lem, whom you'll meet tonight, cherishes a desire, often expressed, to poison it someday since his Cousin Tom's wife, of whom he is not fond, drinks a gallon of water daily for her complexion. We've impressed on him, or tried to, that he might also demolish a number of innocent victims, some of them ex-Marines, and so far he has stayed his hand."

Elizabeth Lamb looked as if she were mulling over Hill's hyperbole, but the party now had reached a confusion of cairns marking several trails, and so she held her tongue. After several false starts they found a cleft and started down through underbrush towards a chorus of what Jane would have sworn were croaking frogs had she not known herself to be almost at the top of a mountain.

She was about to question her ears aloud when the viburnum bushes and trees parted before her and a small pond was, indeed, revealed. In the center of it, to the loud protests of the frogs, a shapely white form floated regally, clutching a pond lily to its bare bosom.

"Well, I'll be go-to-hell," muttered Hill.

"So that's why she wandered off," Sarah said. "Really, I do wish she'd be more discreet."

Two stout lady walkers were marching along one shore, chattering to each other in German and pointedly avoiding notice of Isabella. They nodded coldly to the others.

"Not. j.l.E., I fear," Jane said quietly, "or their portion of."

Her friends and relatives greeted Isabella, who raised a dignified arm in silent reply, and plunged into the woods and so down the moderately steep Deer Brook Trail. Roots and rocks and places of soft muddy earth were in abundance and to Jane, occupied with swatting at black-flies and avoiding a wrenched ankle at the same time, it was both easier and harder than the climb up.

Before the hour or so that it took them to reach the carriage road was up, Isabella appeared behind them looking cool and refreshed. "Really, my dears, the most delightful ranger came along while I was in the pond. I found him charming in every way, and most accomplished."

No one questioned Isabella as to the ranger's accomplishments, but Gus was scornful. "Bet she made that up," he said quietly to his father, who smiled.

"Probably," he answered Gus, helping the women and little girls down onto the road. "Now, look, if we can get to the Pond House in twenty-five minutes, we'll have done the whole trip in three hours and a quarter, and that's as fast as we've ever done it."

They started on the last lap, following the carriage road along the west side of Jordan Pond. The pond, not visible when they started, presently came into view on their left, blue and shining well below them. Several canoes were visible. One had been beached in a little inlet and its passengers ("barenaked," as Persis observed) were gaily splashing in the water.

Sarah was stern: "That's not allowed. Jordan Pond is the water supply of Seal Harbor."

"There'll be pubic hair in the Rockefeller scotch-and-water tonight," said Isabella happily.

"Hush, Issa," said Sarah automatically. "They don't drink, you know. Remember that time we were invited to the Seal Harbor Club by Mrs. — oh, I can't remember her name, that woman from Sutton's — and everyone kept sidling out to their cars for a drink because there was no liquor on the premises, and when we asked why, we were told it was because of the Rockefellers' virtue, or failing, however you interpret it?"

"Oh, Sarah, they must drink. I don't remember that at all."

A desultory discussion of the drinking habits of the rich and/or famous, as far as they were known, occupied Hill and Jane for the remainder of the brisk walk. Sarah and Isabella regarded the gossippers from a morally superior elevation, and breathed deeply of the scent of pine needles warmed by the sun. The children put one foot in front of the other weary foot and thought of strawberry jam on hot popovers.

They crossed a little wooden bridge and ahead of them a pump house placed beside the stream made a sound like distant Indian tom-toms. "That drumming used to frighten Gus; he thought he would be scalped," giggled Persis.

Gus regarded his sister distantly before he bounded into a little wooded path. The rest of the party followed him, to emerge upon the slope of meadowland running from the lawn down to the foot of the pond. People were wandering about aimlessly, pointing out the beauty of the view to each other. Those headed for the lawn and tea did so on a languid tangent, so as not to appear to be putting gustatory pleasures above esthetic ones.

Gus cut a direct swath through the wanderers, swerving nimbly to avoid an old gentleman sitting on a shooting-stick and fanning himself with a white linen hat. He headed straight for a table strategically placed so as to have an uninterrupted view of the pond and the Bubbles — to the older and more plain-spoken, the Bubbies — at its far end. Miss Elbridge occupied it, smoking a Sobranie cigarette and nodding affably to acquaintances.

"Awful glad to be here, Aunt Emily," said Gus, from the heart, sinking onto a bench on his great-aunt's left. He beamed happily upon his approaching family, a seaman safe in a promising port after a hungry and arduous voyage.

Chapter 15

TEA AND ATMOSPHERE

After moving across the lawn in a stately manner, Isabella paused by her aunt's chair to survey the other tea-drinkers with an air reminiscent of Queen Victoria at Balmoral inspecting an unpromising turnout of newly-recruited ghillies. She then wandered off in the direction of the washrooms.

Hill pulled out the benches on either side of the green-painted table for the Lambs and his female relatives, as Gus rose in his best St. Paul's manner at their arrival, and then seated himself facing Miss Elbridge with his back chivalrously to the view of the pond. "Well, Emily," Hill announced, "you thought it couldn't be done but we did it. It's not yet four-thirty. And here comes a waitress, praise be. I see they're wearing lavender this year."

A pretty girl approached and asked in a soft Southern voice what they wished. "Tea and popovers for everyone," decided Miss Elbridge. "I should like my tea with milk, not lemon."

"Could I have ice cream, too, Ma?" asked Gus. "And cookies with the ice cream? And maybe lemonade to start? Persis and Elizabeth Lamb would like lemonade first, too, or maybe iced tea, they're so thirsty. And cinnamon toast with it?"

"Cinnamon toast is a dollar an order," informed the waitress pleasantly but discouragingly. "And that's just one piece of toast."

"Good heavens, why so much?" Sarah asked.

"They don't like to make it, in the kitchen," the girl answered guilelessly.

"Eight orders of hot tea and popovers, please," said Miss Elbridge firmly. "There is another lady coming. Thank you."

Gus sighed but resigned himself. "I like it better when everyone has something different. I like to see them memorizing it. I wonder why they don't let them write it down."

"It dates from back when the place first opened," his great-aunt said. "Most of the customers were well-to-do summer cottage people, who had waitresses at their own tables, in their homes. The proprietor here thought it would make his guests feel more at ease if they took tea in an atmosphere more like their cottages than a restaurant."

At least ten minutes passed in hungry anticipation.

"Charming girls, these waitresses," said Miss Elbridge, making civil conversation. "I'm told they get them only from Southern colleges and house them right here in dormitories for the summer."

Gus turned from envious observation of the basket of large brown popovers being passed around at an adjoining table. "No, they don't, Aunt Emily. Get them only from the South, I mean. A friend of mine at school was telling me about it. He comes from Mount Desert and knows the manager's son.

"They just advertise in college newspapers all over and it's just accidental that most of them are Southern. Last year they had a Japanese girl from California, and some boys from England worked in the kitchen. He told me lots more —" Gus' voice chose that moment to break and he subsided, blushing.

"Then do tell us," his great-aunt said kindly.

"Especially since we have a lot of free time. That waitress must be the slowest damsel ever to cross the Mason-Dixon line," said his father.

"Although," said Isabella, having suddenly reappeared and seated herself, "this interest in food and restaurants is getting to be an obsession with you, my child."

"Well, this place is owned by the National Park but it leases this tea house to a corporation made up of local big-wigs, even some

Rockefeller, I think, and they hire a manager to run the kitchen and gift shop. It's been going since before 1900 and they're only now on their fourth manager; imagine that! The corporation pays the Park a percentage of every dollar taken in, he said."

Gus' fickle voice betrayed him again, but he went on, red-faced and earnest: "I'd sort of like to run something like this, Dad. I'd rather go to a hotel school in Switzerland, anyway, than to Harvard and Harvard Business School." He looked quickly at his father, met raised eyebrows, and turned to look appealingly at his mother.

Sarah was outraged. "Gus, you are most certainly not going to be a cook or run a restaurant. You know you are going to go into your godfather's office on Congress Street. You are a genius with figures, and you know that you have, as you've just shown, a great interest in how businesses operate."

Jane and Emily looked with sympathy at Gus, who appeared to be wishing himself miles away, even climbing Sargent again. He brightened considerably as the import from Dixie put down a tray of teapots and accoutrements and disappeared to emerge again rather quickly with the long-wished-for popovers.

There was a silence broken only by polite requests for the passing of the jam, butter, or sugar. Gus finished his popover and leaned back with a half-replete sigh and an eye watchfully cocked towards the verandah awaiting the emergence of his second.

Isabella was eating slowly and regarding the other tables. "I just saw a motley conglomeration of articles in the gift shop from everywhere in the universe to tempt these people. When we were children, there was just Pine Tree Taffy, and beaded moccasin slippers, and perhaps a birchbark box or wastebasket. Oh, and those little pillows stuffed with pine needles that had on them 'For you I pine, for you I balsam.'

"On our first tea here of the summer, we got a box of taffy and on our last, a pair of slippers, but only if the previous year's were worn-out or outgrown. That was a proper upbringing. Those children in there today are getting everything and anything they clutch at. I thought they were dreadful enough, but would you look at these people out here!"

Jane Lamb glanced about her and saw quite ordinary, presentable persons, for the most part. There was, in addition, one party of loud and sunburned blonde youths, all wearing red Breton sailing pants, whom she classified as quite probably of the despised Northeast-

Harbor-rich-kid breed, and a middle-aged quartet of rather overdressed aspect, the feminine half of which had its heads adorned with large plastic rollers imperfectly concealed under chiffon scarves.

Isabella seized on them: "Really, the tourists from Bar Harbor are worse and worse looking. There was one in the shop without even a scarf over her curlers. I am almost sorry Bar Harbor resurrected itself after the fire to replace the summer families with the motels that cater to that sort of person."

"Come off it, Issa," said Hill. "The fire was a godsend to the old summer families — the inheriting descendants of, I mean. They couldn't afford to maintain those great arks of cottages as their parents and grandparents had. They collected the insurance money and got out, and naturally they were replaced by transients who spend a few days or a week in the motels. Nature abhors a vacuum, you know, and the tourists may not be aristocratic, but, actually, to my observation, most of them are distinctly well-bred."

"Henry says that the locals who became prosperous in the new era — the contractors and the motel and restaurant owners — are the new aristocracy. They lord it over the golf club, for instance, when before the fire they would have been lucky to be able to sneak in and pee on the seventeenth green."

"Hill!" said Sarah sharply, suppressing a smile, and then, curiously, "Why the seventeenth green, especially?"

"Dunno," Hill answered, enunciating through his second popover, the basket of which had suddenly arrived. "Sounded poetic and euphonious, I suppose."

"Cousin Tom's wife just left, accompanied by four fashionable friends," announced Isabella. "There goes Tom to pay for the sumptuous tea they've doubtless consumed. He looks suppressed, as usual. She has him all dressed up in a blazer and an ascot — look at his shorts and knee socks on those bony legs!"

"When I think," replied Miss Elbridge sadly, "that during his first marriage when he summered on our side of the island, poor Amelia was not even allowed to put a sign out on the road so that her friends could find her. 'Not going to provide free teas for all the hags in Northeast Harbor,' Tom would say in his unbearable manner, and Amelia was too sweet to protest."

"Now he's providing free teas with a vengeance," Hill observed. "Also cocktails, luncheons, and dinners. His wife fancies herself the most lavish and courted of Northeast Harbor hostesses. How the mighty have fallen. It almost makes me believe in retribution by the fates.''

"Look, there's Cousin Cordelia," Persis pointed at the nearby verandah but, glancing at Elizabeth Lamb, quickly lowered her chubby, well-buttered hand.

"She's wearing her Scarf," sighed Miss Elbridge. "She allows herself one Liberty scarf at a time, Jane, wearing it until it is frayed beyond usage, although she loves them dearly and has a dozen or so carefully put away. It has been that rose print one for several years."

The thin figure on the verandah, in a nondescript jersey and dark, baggy trousers, a pink scarf tied rakishly around its neck, was surveying the tea drinkers with one hand nautically above its brow, swiveling nervously from side to side. "Oh, dear," it could be heard to say, "not one empty table. Teddie will be so very annoyed. Why didn't I telephone?" It then turned erratically, to the apprehension of a waitress approaching with a laden tray, and darted back into the shadows of the porch, still emitting faint squeaks of dismay.

"Really!" said Sarah. "He sits at ease in the car and lets her forage for a table. Why is she so silly and put-upon?"

"She's perfectly happy slaving for Teddie," Hill declared. "She's happy in everything she does because she was always feckless and, now that she's reached middle age, she does exactly as she pleases and doesn't mind at all looking ridiculous. Absolutely everybody else is afraid of appearing to be ridiculous and it unnerves us to see anyone choosing to do so, and hence we despise her out of our own uneasiness."

The ladies looked thoughtful upon hearing Hill's acute social observation, but appeared to disagree with his analysis. Sarah shook her head faintly. "I could stand her being feckless," she said, "if she just paid less regard to Teddie and a little more to herself. Whenever I get a letter from her, it is economically crammed on to one piece of letter-paper, so that the last few lines are illegible, and they are the ones that seem to require an answer, if one could decipher them."

"And it's so sad the way she skimps on clothes as well as letter-paper," said Emily, her thoughts on the Scarf, "while Teddie is a walking advertisement for Brooks Brothers and the Burlington Arcade."

"Oh, really, Aunt Em," Isabella raised one of her mobile brows and gesticulated about her. "What does it matter? She'd be dowdy no matter how much money she spent. There are no chic people here, or anywhere Cordelia would be likely to go."

She surveyed the crowd more closely, with an expression of regal distaste: "Just look. They're either dreadful in stretch pants and floral shirts that don't quite cover their fat bottoms, or else dowdy Philadelphia-round-pinned."

Jane smiled. There were indeed a number of modest round gold pins on the conservative print dresses and white blouses on the premises.

"Why, oh, why," went on Isabella, warming to her plaint, "do we come here on Saturday, Sarah, when all the locals as well as the round-pinned are treating themselves?"

"God, Isabella," Hill observed. "Come The Revolution, you'll be the first to go. Absolutely no one suits you."

"Come The Revolution," replied his sister-in-law with one of her little gurgling bursts of laughter, "I'll be in the front of the mob, waving a red flag or whatever emblem is politic, and deciding which of you all will be the first to go."

"Well," said Hill, "whoever and whatever goes, I imagine this place will be here forever. I can't imagine Mount Desert without it."

"I must say," Sarah said mildly, "that we were brought up to feel it was immoral to come here for tea without walking or climbing first. We had to earn our treat. I can't imagine what it would feel like simply to put on a dress and a round pin and drive over to guzzle away."

"There's another person in curlers." Persis indicated the culprit with her chin.

"What I can't understand is seeing them over on the backside on a Saturday night — the biggest night of the week for them — in those things," Hill said. "What are they saving it for?"

"Bermuda has laws against curlers in public," informed Elizabeth Lamb, to a groan from Isabella.

"Now there's a hugger, to use the island idiom," Hill remarked, nodding towards a pretty, curvaceous girl attired in a pale pink skirt and a lighter pink shirt of the new transparent type, with its pockets strategically placed. "Mmm, yes, a proper hugger, I would say."

Sarah frowned in perplexity. "Oh, I see — *hugger,* meaning someone to hug, or huggable. I never heard that."

Isabella was disparaging. "I've seen her selling something in some shop on the island; I can't think which. Those shirts are passé in Europe now. So like you to admire the little shop-girl type, Hill, dear."

Jane looked angry. "I've always hated that phrase as being insufferably patronizing," she said bravely but with a quiver in her voice. "It may be because I was once an interpreter at the Galleries Layfayette and learned that shop assistants, of whatever nationality, are often quite well-bred and have surprisingly good taste." She buried her flushed face in her cup of now-cold tea and mumbled into it, "And good manners."

"Suppose we leave," decreed the Grafin. "We seem to be disagreeing on all sides." Isabella stalked ahead of the others, as Hill separated from them to go into the gift shop to pay the bill. As she was forced to step aside to allow three almost comically fat women speaking with pronounced Maine accents to pass, she turned, smiling, with one of her abrupt changes of mood, as Hill appeared. "Now there are three proper huggers for you, dearie."

"Six ax handles wide," Hill agreed.

"What?" asked Elizabeth Lamb.

"A friend of mine heard that at the Bar Harbor town pier one Fourth of July. A seaman was boarding the tender to get back to the navy cruiser that was in port for the holiday, and a petty officer asked him why he was going back so early.

" 'Only two bars in this town,' the sailor replied sadly, in an Arkansas drawl, 'one of 'em so crowded you cain't get in, and if you make it into the other, they beat you up and throw you out. And all the women is six ax handles wide.' "

"Emily, you drive as you'll get the most room that way."

Emily turned to the left as they drove away from the Jordan Pond House and was presently caught behind a car with a New York license plate driven by a white-haired man so short that he was obliged to tilt his head up to see over the steering wheel. After two or three minutes of movement at 15 m.p.h., she politely touched her horn. The man slowed down even more. Another minute and Emily tooted again. The man stuck his thumb into his left ear and waggled his fingers derisively, peering into his rearview mirror and grinning maniacally.

"Damned old idiot!" exploded Hill. "He's just hoping you'll try to pass and get killed on the curve. Ought to be home in New York in a looney-bin."

Miss Elbridge was philosophic. "I do so dislike getting caught behind an elderly man. Now an old lady will dash along at eighty or so or else pull over to let one pass. Never mind, there's a view of the pond now.

"Can you imagine that you walked all that distance along the shore over there, Elizabeth Lamb? And see that rock perched on the South Bubble? Generations of daring young people have climbed up there and tried to push it down the mountain, but it is immoveable although it looks so lightly balanced."

Jane was seated beside Miss Elbridge, with Elizabeth Lamb on her lap. "I seldom see old ladies driving anymore," she offered timidly, and Miss Elbridge smiled, at either Jane's flattery or her poor powers of observation.

There was little attempt at conversation from the back seat, where the five remaining members of the group were fitted into each other like the proverbial (Maine) sardines.

Presently Hill spoke, his voice sounding strange because of the weight of Gus wedged against his solar plexus. "Anyone read any good books lately?"

His relatives did not deign to reply, but Jane nervously responded: "I'm reading Nabokov's *Lolita*. I just read an article in some magazine about him and the man who wrote it was caustic because M. Nabokov, a butterfly fancier, was asked once, by a clubwoman, what butterflies are for. Her question was perfectly reasonable, I think; she just meant what good is collecting them, but the writer chose to regard her as some kind of Philistine who thought butterflies should have a use."

Isabella attempted a disparaging sigh at Jane's effort at conversation, but it emerged as a grunt because of the compression of her ribs between Hill and Sarah, each of whom was holding a child. Jane flushed and bent her head down towards Elizabeth Lamb.

Emily, having finally managed to pass the old New Yorker, was in higher spirits than her cramped passengers. She leaned over Jane to turn on the car radio. "Hey, Emily," Hill spoke loudly above its sound, "I forgot to tell you Mrs. Parker wanted to see you."

Emily made no answer. "Emily?" queried Hill.

"I heard you, Hill," she answered. Her voice was lower and more clipped than usual.

She drove very fast, and it took only a short time to reach the start of the Giant Slide Trail, where the station wagon had been left. Hill unpeeled himself and his wife and Persis from Emily's seat cushions and, taking Jane and her daughter along, left Isabella and Gus to accompany Miss Elbridge back to The Bungalow.

Passing through Somesville, Sarah pointed out a little road going into the woods beside a general store. "Up there is a cemetery, Jane, on a slight rise with a brook just below it. Dora tells us that the cemetery association had a meeting a few years back to decide which graves should be moved out of the way of the brook, which was changing its course.

"The grave of the aunt of one woman present was mentioned, but the niece angrily protested. 'Aunt would not rest if she were moved,' she said. 'Why, she particularly chose that site because she loved the view from it'!"

Jane laughed as expected.

The day was changing. The sun had gone and a cool wind had come up. Chill patches of fog intermittently drifted over the trees in the Somesville woods. Just as they turned off the main road into the narrow one that led to the cove cottages, Miss Elbridge's car came into sight behind them.

"Good," Hill observed. "We'll all be back by six or so. Hey, is that Varner?"

A form ahead of them had dodged into a clump of spruce trees at the approach of the car.

"It is," Elizabeth Lamb vouched. "I saw him and I saw his axe."

"Funny that he's being so stand-offish. Perhaps he's had a dispute with Minnie and doesn't feel gregarious at the moment. Look, I'll drive the car into the garage when we get there so as to leave more room for the guests' cars."

Coming out of the garage, avoiding Miss Elbridge's car, also driven in, they found Junior leaning against the fence, several lobster buoys in a clam hod at his feet.

"When did you get back?" Hill asked.

"About four-thirty. Terrible lot of tourists coming up on the Turnpike, Hill. I was about done in when I hit the island. I took a half-hour's nap down to home before I brought Mrs. Worthington's supplies over.

"Now, don't you two," he turned, smiling, to the little girls, "let on to her, since she told me to come here straightaway. Good thing I did get a little shut-eye, because soon's she saw me, she had me go out to the reef to get these buoys, here, that had washed up. Spots an awful lot of things on those afternoon rows of hers." He pulled the buoys out and began to tie them on the rail fence, standing back to judge his choice of positioning.

"What are they, and what is that thing you had them in?" asked Elizabeth Lamb. "It looks like a big long basket, but I never saw one made like that, out of narrow little boards."

The adults left Junior patiently explaining the significance of the painted buoys, while Persis at the same time described to her friend how, after clams were dug up with a short-handled, curved-prong clam rake, they were put in the slatted hod and swished through shallow water to take most of the mud off.

This was a major task for Persis because of Elizabeth Lamb's complete non-understanding of what a clam was, although after a time she attempted to interpose her knowledge of the cultivation of French oysters. Persis finished at about the same time that Junior gave up on his dissertation on lobster buoy heraldry.

"Junior," excitedly went on Persis, "in my Social Studies book, in the part on Maine, there was a picture of buoys hung along a wharf, and my teacher said they were beach umbrellas. Imagine! A buoy is tiny compared to a beach umbrella and I never saw anybody use an umbrella on a beach in Maine, anyway. And she wouldn't believe me when I tried to tell her about buoys.

"Come on, Elizabeth Lamb, let's go ask Dora for something to eat. I'm starving."

She looked back at Junior, abandoned for food, and said kindly, "We'll bring you something, too, because you must be hungry. Aunt Isabella said that you had hungry eyes, to Mummy. And you know what Mummy said? She said Aunt Isabella's tastes were too fancy to satisfy a plain and honest appetite. I wonder what that meant?"

Chapter 16

DRINKS AND DIALOGUE

Jane emerged from the studio into a world of thick, cold fog. When she had gone in twenty minutes before for a hasty cleaning-up, the day had been still fairly clear and warm, though sunless. Now the guest cottage thirty feet down the path to the main Bungalow was still visible, but only a dim glow of lamplight farther along the path indicated the main building.

She stood shivering for a minute on the granite millwheel that served as the studio's doorstep. Isabella's remarks about her appearance the evening before had caused Jane to array herself in a beautifully draped grey jersey gown. Although the dress possessed a jacket to cover up its low-cut back, being unmistakably dressed by Grés was warming, in the heartless fog of a Maine summer evening, only to Jane's psyche.

She thought yearningly of a hot tub, well laced with bath salts to ease her aching leg muscles. Mrs. Worthington's bathroom in the studio was accessible only through her bedroom and Jane had not dared to knock at the closed door, since behind it Sarah and her mother were having an audibly animated discussion. There was no bathroom, only another lavatory, in the guest cottage, and although the main Bungalow had two bathrooms, one was surely in use by Miss Elbridge, or Gus, or his parents. The other was a makeshift affair that had been carved out of the old nursery and could be entered only through the kitchen: not even the prospect of the Legion d' Honneur for her valor would have tempted Jane to invade Dora's domain. The sounds that had for some time emanated from the kitchen many yards away, even though muffled by fog and a closed door, seemed to her to be ten times as loud, though very like in character, the description of the tigers Little Black Sambo heard wrangling and scrambling around the tree and disputing as to which was the grandest tiger in the jungle.

The prospect of a fire and a warming drink propelled a hesitating Jane towards the main house. She walked slowly, since these rewards would be gained only by facing a large number of people, some of them unknown to her and therefore even more frightening than the known and yet still alarming denizens of The Bungalow.

She turned her head. There was movement along the fringe of trees at the edge of the meadow, to her left. Someone unseen in the fog surely was slipping along there, the soft footsteps almost matching hers.

"Elizabeth Lamb?" she called. There was no answer. She could hear nothing now but the faraway sound of the sea, the tiger noises from the kitchen, and a peculiar sound as of water splashing somewhere near at hand.

Her heart pounding, she ran the few feet to the guest cottage, crept along its west wall and peered around the far corner, towards the woods. Isabella, in full figure, eyes pleasurably shut and head covered with a fearsome polka-dotted plastic cap, was enjoying the blessings of the outdoor shower of the guest cottage. It had been conveniently placed just to the side of the back door so that persons salty from the ocean and clad in bathing suits could rinse themselves off before entering. Isabella, of course, had dispensed with a suit.

"It's hot water," thought Jane enviously, noticing the steam rising into the fog from Isabella's white sloping shoulders. But she quickly drew back, conscious of her Peeping Tom stance. As she did, the unseen walker appeared through the fog, carrying a box in one hand and, at the sight of Jane, holding the first finger of the other to his lips.

She almost called to him, out of relieved recognition, but it was all too plain that he was trying to avoid the bather's notice. In vain. Isabella turned and with a languid effect of majestic ease, made a half-hearted attempt to hold an inadequate towel in front of her.

"Why, Junior," she called fetchingly, "would you come adjust this spray, please? There's really too much force for me." She laughed in her usual bubbling fashion.

Caught, Junior was still resourceful. "Not just now, Isabella," he said politely. "Couldn't see to do it right, in this fog. Can't see one single, solitary thing, actually. Have to get this to the house, anyway."

He joined Jane, who had withdrawn to the path, and they walked together to the glow of light.

"Why were you in the woods?" she asked, still rather frightened.

Junior sensed her fright. "Golly, you don't have to worry about a thing out here on the Cape, Mrs. Lamb," he said reassuringly. "It's not like New York or Washington or other big cities. Everybody here knows who's around and what they're up to. I went down to my store to get something for the kids — picked up a nail in my tire doing it, too — and I was trying to get it to them without that Dora hearing me come down the path.

"I'm about beat, and after I change my tire and get myself a snack to keep body and soul together, I'm headed straight for bed, but if she catches sight of me she'll holler for me to do some fool thing or other, out of pure meanness. They've already nabbed Peyton," he added ambiguously.

"What?" asked Jane, puzzled. Junior did not answer; they had reached the back porch. Slipping across it into the bunkroom, he lit a candle and whispered to her, "Would you go get them?"

Jane turned uncertainly, but the problem of where the children might be was soon resolved. The wrangling and scrambling noise in the kitchen had continued, on a lower scale, but now it reached a crescendo as Dora flung open the door. Gus and the little girls were standing in a row by the sink, emitting pathetic noises of protest and supplication that might have been baby tiger growls. Persis' face was tearful.

"Not one scrap of anything, not one scrap," howled Dora. "If you'd et your dinner, let alone your tea, your stummicks wouldn't need stuffing this early. Now, fill that doorway before I fill it with you."

The children sidled past her and followed Jane's pointing finger to fall upon Junior's offering, uttering cries of thanks. Jane peered over their shoulders as they pulled off the heavy layers of newspapers that covered the bottom half of a cut-down Campbell soup carton that was also lined with the insulating newspaper. There were three miniature beanpots of brown pottery filled with steaming baked beans topped with slices of crisp salt pork. There was a still-warm loaf of newly baked bread, a bar of butter, three doughnuts and three little cartons of milk, straws, plastic spoons and a knife, and even three pale pink paper napkins.

"Put yourselves outside that," said Junior, beaming down at them. "That's Dottie's beans and bread she bakes for us to sell at the store Saturday night."

"Oh, June, you are just the goodest person to us," said the reviving Persis. "Where did you get the darling little beanpots?"

"That fancy cheese from S. S. Pierce comes in 'em. Peyton and I cleaned out a whole case of it one night when we was taking inventory and hungry enough to eat raw bearmeat. You can keep them for your dolls. I bet," he added, swatting Persis lightly on her bottom as he left, "you have pretty hungry eyes yourself, by now. I knew you wouldn't get anything out of that Dora."

"Why did Dora say we'd had our dinner?" Elizabeth Lamb asked, as Jane turned to leave the happy diners to themselves.

"That's what she calls lunch," answered the knowledgeable Gus. "They call lunch 'dinner' because mostly they eat a big meal then. Wish I did."

Dora had slammed the kitchen door after ousting the children, but the beration of some other person had continued. There had been forceful male protests which her voice overrode. Now she opened the door again to glare at Jane and Junior, who had been a half-minute too late to effect their escape.

Junior began to melt away, but Jane stood transfixed by the backstairs drama and observed, in the dimly-lit kitchen, the blonde man she had seen carrying groceries at the Duck Cove Store. He stood there stiffly and unhappily, his red face contrasting with the spotless starched white cotton jacket in which he was attired. His expostulation to his sister, and now to his sister's back, had been part of the tiger chorus.

"Dora, now listen, now. I have purely got to get back to the store. Be reasonable, now. Junior's out on his feet and there's nobody there but Dottie and I promised her I'd only be gone a few minutes. Tell

Mrs. Worthington I just can't do it. If I'd knowed a day ahead of time —'' He made as if to discard his jacket but Dora released Jane from her glare and turned upon him.

"You keep that on, you Peyton, and you listen to me. They's four more people coming than we thought and Mrs. Worthington specially asked for you to stay and mix drinks. There's that Mrs. Woodhue with that lazy husband and that Tom crittur with the whining wife —''

"I know, I know," Peyton interrupted. "But I got to go help Dottie. Never would've come up here with the groceries if I'd knowed I'd be shanghaied —''

"Shanghaied," shrilled Dora, "Well, that's gratitude, that is. After Mrs. Worthington paid for your wife's operation and for Doreen to keep house for you while Dottie was down to Boston in the hospital, you can't help out here a little? Mrs. Worthington never puts on a show, just polite and lady-like and welcoming all the time to everybody, and this one time she wants to do things up brown, you go and say you're too busy.''

She paused to draw breath and continued: "I starched that jacket up myself, with all I got to do around here it wasn't easy. Hasn't been used since Mr. Worthington had that feller up here one summer eating his head off in my kitchen when he was supposed to be helping Mr. Worthington, him with his bad heart and all, or else waiting on table —''

Dora breathed deeply again and forced herself back to present wrongs: *"And* there's things going on I won't stand for any more, bills coming in twice like they used to do years ago to them millionaire summer people in Bar Harbor; oh, I'm wise to you, brother or no brother. Fine goings-on, I say, all over the place, down-cellar and up-attic as Mumma used to say. You heard me, I said —''

Quick footsteps were coming down the path. Peyton, white-faced by now instead of red, flapped his hand warningly at his sister, his starched sleeve crackling loudly.

"Don't you shush me. And you, Junior, out there, if you're so all-fired tired why ain't you down to home in your bed, alone for onct, instead of hanging around here feeding ungrateful kids I never hear a nice word from for all the good food I cook for them. Mis' Blanchard sent that poor looney over to fetch you for something just 'fore you got back and Mis' Parker was looking for you, stopped special on her way to Bar Harbor. There's plenty of honest work for you to do if you feel the urge, stid of wasting time —"

Sarah came quickly on to the porch as Junior faded discreetly into the fog, with a wink and a mouthed, "What did I tell you?" to Jane.

"Oh, good," Sarah said briskly. "Peyton's right here. Dora, Mother wants you to serve ham and salad and some of your biscuits later, as well as the canapés with drinks. She is in such high spirits. She's finished the commission, all but the firing, and she says she feels like celebrating — making a night of it, she said.

"She is really elated, talking about a surprise visitor. I can't think she means Cousin Tom's wife, but perhaps she does, in her present good mood. Peyton, would you go back to your store for a minute and bring up one of those specially-cured hams?"

"No, he don't, Sarah," decreed Dora. "Let him go and you'll never get him back. You'll have to go yourself. Doreen went over to the Blanchards', to get some ice cubes, time she's taking she'll be carrying a pail of water when she gets back."

"Peyton's needed," Dora went on, "to serve drinks starting right now. Your cousin and that big foreign girl's already here and I hear another car up there. And I can't go; I got them chicken liver canopies in the oven fixing to burn up."

She dashed for the door of the wood range, stopping to shove a tray of glasses at Peyton, who unhappily departed on his mission.

Sarah took Jane's arm and guided her to the path leading around to the front of the main Bungalow. With the other hand, she distractedly tucked the pink shirt she had worn to climb Sargent into the waistband of a long blue woolen skirt.

"My, but Mother insisted I talk to her such a long time," she said, in a tone both faintly complaining and pleased. "I didn't have time to dress properly. Now, Jane, my cousin Lem had the title of General, but as he is now retired he thinks it slightly bad form to use it, so please do address him as 'Mr. Alison.' His young friend — secretary, I mean, is a Miss Thurna Thorssen. I mention it because it is sometimes so difficult to remember — why, Isabella, what are you doing? Aren't you cold? Let me take that cushion for you."

Isabella was meandering along through the juniper bushes to their left, making for the path to the shore and clutching a large sketch pad, a box of pastel crayons, and a huge pillow. She was attired in a one-sleeved short white silk jersey dress of toga-like appearance, more suitable for the Attican climate than the Maine. She wore white sandals and a Grecian band around her hair, which hung down in black curls to her bare shoulders. There were, Jane noticed with some amusement, still some spots of angry red colour on her cheeks.

"I'm going down to spend fifteen minutes doing a quick sketch of the rocks in the fog," she answered tartly. "What does it look as though I'm doing? And do leave my cushion alone, Seizer. Really!" She disappeared down the path to the shore.

Jane and Sarah entered The Bungalow living room to the tune of a lively political discussion in which Miss Elbridge and Hill seemed to be playing largo to General, or rather Mr., Alison's forté.

"And so I said to him," finished Cousin Lem, "— couple of years ago this was, of course — 'Well,' I said, 'the Adams family was the last family of gentlefolk to guide our fortunes, I'm sorry to say, but bad as things are, I still won't have any lace-curtain upstarts telling me what my country asks of me. Go back to the White House and tell that to your boss,' I said, and he answered not a word. Heh-heh."

"Gentlefolk? What about the Roosevelts, both branches?" asked Hill mildly, but the General bent a fierce look upon him and answered, "Only one branch counts; other branch *cost.*" Hill smiled affably and reached for a martini from the tray the drafted Peyton pushed against him.

"May I get you a drink, my dear?" asked the General of a stalwart young lady who sat in a rocking chair looking up at him adoringly. She had extremely large and protuberant deep blue eyes, enormous feet and hands and all other physical features to match. Her hair was blonde and short and she was wearing a grey woolen robe with white runic characters woven along the long loose sleeve and bottom hem edges.

She spoke not a word but went straight to the work of beamingly accepting a martini from Lem and tossing it off at a draught.

"Lem, how good to see you," Sarah said warmly. "Jane, my cousin Lemuel Otis Alison. Lem, this is Jane Lamb, who is mother's secretary. She lives in Paris, usually, but her work takes her over here, sometimes."

Lemuel Otis Alison took Jane's hand with feeling and smiled genially. She observed a tall spare man of about sixty, his face lined and tanned, his pale blue eyes clear and intelligent and his sparse brown hair combed so as to make the most of it. A powerful aroma of Frances Fox Hair Tonic arose from him, mingled with the scent of bay rum. He wore a rumpled blue-and-white seersucker suit and a plaid madras bow tie. His movements were both smoothly sweeping and awkwardly loose. "He reminds me of Walter Matthau playing Governor William Bradford," thought Jane, who was a cinema buff and, surprisingly, considering her European upbringing, conversant with American history.

"And may I present My Secretary, Miss Thurna Thorssen," announced the General. My Secretary, Miss Thurna Thorssen offered a powerful hand to Jane, never removing her eyes from Lem's face and, with the other hand, extending her empty glass towards him in a forceful and demanding manner.

Emily had been sitting quietly in a chair by the fireplace drinking a martini rather quickly (for her), and she also extended her glass towards General Alison, who gestured to Peyton.

"Pitcher's empty, and there ain't no more ice neither, Lem," said that functionary. "I'll just go see if I can't find where Doreen got to." He left discreetly by the door to the front porch. Hill opened the kitchen door to explore for more liquor and through it came a howl from Dora as she ambushed her brother at the start of his run for his truck and freedom.

"What in the world can be going on out there?" asked Emily of Hill when he emerged with a heavy pine ice bucket, followed by Peyton, once more in servitude.

"Doreen evidently took almost an hour to get to the Blanchards' for ice — got lost in the fog and just got back, brought along by them. Dora burned the canapes and is blaming her, somehow. Here come the Captain and Kitty, and I swear she's been drinking, Emily," answered Hill, simultaneously pouring Miss Elbridge a drink, pushing Peyton back into the kitchen, and turning to greet the Captain and Kitty Blanchard at the front door.

The Captain came in smiling jovially, his brick-red face set off healthily by the white tennis sweater above the white flannels he was wearing. Mrs. Blanchard trailed printed chiffon beside him and, except that she leaned rather heavily on his sturdy arm, did not seem to add likelihood to Hill's observation of her. They greeted the company, heartily on the part of the one, charmingly on the part of the other. The Captain behaved himself when presented to My Secretary, Miss Thurna Thorssen, contenting himself with offering a subdued "Humm-umm" after repeating her name.

No sooner had the Blanchards been provided with drinks by

Peyton and charcoaled chicken livers wrapped in dark-hued bacon by Dora, whose expression brooked no refusals of her wares, than the doorway framed a pleasant-looking couple, in their thirties or early forties. They were similarly garbed in white shirts, navy-blue blazer jackets, and grey-flannel trousers. Identical red and blue printed foulard scarves were tucked into their open shirt collars.

Glad cries of "Henry" and "Betsy" greeted them, and they were warmly kissed by Mrs. Worthington who emerged from the kitchen, where an Armistice of sorts had settled, due, no doubt, to her appearance there.

Mrs. Worthington's appearance belied, more than usual, Hill thought, her seventy-plus years. Her black hair was knotted low at the back of her neck and diamond earrings blazed beside a face discreetly and attractively made up and radiantly happy. She wore her favourite white linen, of ankle-length above red kidskin slippers, and an enormous navy, red and gold Hermes scarf was carelessly tied about her shoulders.

"Cordelia called us, Cousin Elizabeth," said Henry's wife in a pleasing, girlish voice, "and asked us to tell you that Teddie feels most unwell and that they can't make it over tonight. She was terribly upset, and quite incoherent, but I gathered that he had somehow not got his tea at the proper time and that had disturbed his 'dietary clock' as she called it, whatever that is."

"His 'dietary clock,' dammit," said Lem irascibly, "never interfered with his accepting any offer of free food or drink before this. Must be getting old, or maybe feeling his lack of exercise and discipline. We old Marines are still able to make it to chow, not to mention bed and all that sort of thing. Heh-heh." He mused and added, as an afterthought, "Don't know about the Navy, though."

Miss Thorssen looked even more adoring. Miss Elbridge reached for another martini and shook her head slightly at the General.

"What have we here, the Gold-dust Twins?" asked Isabella's clear voice, from behind Henry and Betsy. "Thank you, Peyton. Lem, darling, a kiss for your cousin. Ah, you've slightly lost the touch — must be practicing on amateurs of late. Oh, thank you, Dora; Chicken Livers Othello tonight, I see."

Having managed to antagonize at least four-and-one-half of her listeners, ("one-half" because Dora was not quite sure of who or what Othello was and would therefore be obliged to consult her daughter's University of Maine textbooks, which it was powerfully apparent she was making a mental note to do) Isabella then leaned gracefully upon the fieldstone mantelpiece to talk prettily to her aunt.

"You'll all stay to supper, I hope?" invited Mrs. Worthington, "But let's relax with Peyton's expert cocktails for a while, first. Sarah, have you arranged about the ham?"

Sarah moved to consult with her mother. Hill glanced out of the window.

"The fog is even thicker tonight than last," he said. "Almost time for high tide, and Gus tells me a record one is expected."

"Oh, lord, my things!" exclaimed Isabella, making for the porch door. "I left them where the tide will surely cover them, thinking I had time to finish my sketch after seeing all you lovely people for just a minute."

"You didn't bring Horatio," said Miss Elbridge to Kitty Blanchard, with a not too distinct tinge of relief in her tone.

"No, he was very much occupied with his project. He had a construction project assigned to him by his school for his summer in Maine, and do you know what he chose to build?" Kitty signalled for another drink to Peyton, who was regarding her dubiously.

"I cannot imagine," Miss Elbridge replied, with sincerity.

"He is building a replica of Buckingham Palace entirely out of shand-sand-dollars, and to the exact scale of one inch to one foot. What do you think of that, Emily?"

"It must be very difficult — and large."

"Yes, but he is very much attracted to shand-dollars —"

"I thought it was coat-hangersh," Hill murmured, turning safely away from the Blanchards to get Sarah a drink.

"— however, I really think I shall go back to get him. Freddy, may I have the car keys? But I'll have another martini first, I think. I've had only two, Freddy."

"Dear, I'll go. I really think I should."

"No," Mrs. Blanchard insisted, swallowing her drink whole and reaching for Emily's. "I'll go. Freddy, the keys, please."

"No, dear, let's leave him," said the Captain, alarmed at the disintegration of his wife's speech from a pretty Southern drawl to an attractive Southern slur.

"Er," he said, turning to Hill, "boy's a bit of a monarchist, you know. Strong feeling for royalty. He'd be most upset if we interrupted him tonight, Kitty. He's on a most important part of the palace. He'd regard it as lèse majesté, or some such. Why, he is determined, you know, Hill, that no one but a young man of royal blood shall marry his sister. Gets quite violent if we disagree with him about it."

The Captain took a strong pull at his glass and hastily added, "All in jest, of course."

The assemblage received this ingenious explanation in good faith, feeling that most likely there was some truth in it, though Lem gazed at the Captain and muttered, "Bushwah," albeit admiringly.

His remark was disregarded by those members of the company who, aware that Horatio never jested, turned to look pityingly at Pherousa. Pherousa blushed and sipped her ginger ale. She had slipped in just behind her parents, simply dressed in a pale sea-green cotton frock, and had found a corner where she had remained unnoticed.

"Kitty, I've got to run down to the Duck Cove Store," said the practical and resourceful Sarah in a matter-of-fact tone. "I'll drive you as far as the path to your place and pick you and Horatio up on my way back in twenty minutes or so."

Mrs. Blanchard, swaying a little, agreed to this arrangement and they left, she clinging to Sarah's arm and tearfully assuring her that really, truly, Sarah, honey, Horatio's thoughts were all beautiful, as was his soul, and his artistic efforts with glue and sand dollars.

"Tight's a teddy bear," said Peyton to Hill, in none too low a voice.

"I heard a good story today," said the General in forceful tones, giving Peyton a military shove that rattled the glasses on his tray. "Old fellow who hangs around the wharf in Sow-wow — that's what some of The Natives call Southwest Harbor —" he explained kindly to Jane, who, as usual, had begun to look terrified at hearing an expression new to her, "was watching a tourist yesterday afternoon doing a painting of the harbor at high tide. One of those little shopgirl types she was, you know, who come up here on their vacations hoping to see a lot of aristocrats at play. Heh-heh."

Jane's expression, which had changed from terror to courteous attention, became a look of mild outrage that was, in turn, replaced by a watery smile as Hill winked at her.

The General went on: "She came back this morning to finish the picture and was all in a fluster because the tide was low and her painting wouldn't jibe with what she'd done on it before. Asked the old codger where the water was. 'It's them hotels over in Bar Harbor,' he said. 'They use up all our water twice a day, suck it right up. It'll all be back this afternoon when they let the water out of their fool bathtubs and swimming pools and such. They're a powerful trial to us poor folk over here.'

"And she ate it right up! Said she would sit right down and write a letter of complaint to the Bar Harbor Chamber of Commerce. Heh-heh."

"They love to do that," Henry said. "If they don't agree with one of those stupid ratings put on movies, they say they're going to complain to the Chamber of Commerce. I give them the address and the name of the secretary."

"One of 'em came into the store last week," rejoined Peyton. "Demanded native blueberries. We said they wasn't in yet. Then wanted native raspberries, then strawberries, then was going to settle for native plums or apricots or Gawd knows what. Finally Junior told 'er the only native fruit we had was bananas. 'Oh, where from?' she asks. 'Town Hill,' says June, 'center of the island where it's warmest.' And she bought ten pounds."

Peyton then looked bashfully around at his laughing audience and made as if to sample one of his own wares, out of a feeling of bonhomie. At once the door to the kitchen was opened by Persis and Elizabeth Lamb who came quickly in bearing the message that he was wanted by Dora. "And immejitly," added Persis helpfully. "She's been listening to you through a crack and grinding her teeth awful loud." She smiled engagingly around at the adults, clutching, as was Elizabeth Lamb, her little beanpot, now scrubbed and shining. They wandered over to the tray that Peyton had hastily abandoned.

"Jane, would you get me my red cardigan, please?" asked Mrs. Worthington. "I believe it is on the chair by my bed. Old bones need more warmth than even Hill's excellent fire is providing," she added, with an enchanting smile that would have done credit to one forty years her junior.

"The fog is thicker than ever," Hill said, as he opened the door for Jane. "Strange how sound travels so clearly over the water, even in thick fog. I can hear old George Paine's boat radio quite clearly, all the way from Mrs. Parker's mooring."

"He's deaf's a pirate, you know that," pronounced Dora, who had taken over Peyton's post for the moment and was dashingly mixing drinks and tossing ice more or less accurately into them.

"Couldn't hear it so plain if it wasn't turned up to a hundred dessybills or some such. A person could get murdered right on that dock and nobody could hear the screams over the ruckus of them ball games he's so fond of. Dore-e-e-n, come out here and clear up this ice I spilled all over creation."

"Jump on it," advised the General. "That's what they do in the Navy, hey, Freddy?"

Quite unnoticed, Persis and Elizabeth Lamb had obtained a pitcher of martinis from Peyton's deserted tray before Dora had begun her bartending and had secured ice cubes as some skittered over to their corner. These they gravely placed in their beanpots and then lavishly filled them from the pitcher just in time before Dora, mumbling as to where in tarnation Peyton had hidden it, retrieved it.

Captain Blanchard had responded in robust nautical tones to the General's aspersion, which appeared to refer to some incident meaningful only to the two of them. Conversation became lively and little twosomes formed to carry it on, split up and formed into other twosomes. Peyton reappeared and went about his duties in a marked silence, saying "Sir" and "Ma'am," his eye on the kitchen door, more often than was necessary. Gus wandered in from the kitchen with a bulging cheek. A roar from Dora followed him, indicating that the oven had betrayed her again.

The two little girls sat relaxed in their corner, screened by the high basket of firewood, and sipped luxuriously at their beanpots. The warm lamp-lit room filled with cigarette smoke and blurred pleasantly before their eyes. "The late-late show," murmured Elizabeth Lamb. Persis nodded agreement, although her television viewing had always ended at six p.m. Snatches of hazy dialogue drifted to them, first near and loud and then swimming far away:

"Yes, Emily, we went to New York for our bi-enniel treat. Henry and I especially wanted to see Julie Harris in '40 Carats.' Believe it or not, plays and movies do copy life, as well as the reverse. There's a woman in Bar Harbor —"

"Still got that beard, your boy Horatio? No? Wait — wait —could do one of my rhymes about that. Let's see —"

"Food prices in Northeast Harbor are just ridiculous, Elizabeth. Bar Harbor too. Still, the Natives have to live and have only ten weeks to make their money, as I even heard one of 'em say, so I don't complain when I shop. I do it to save Kitty the trouble and —"

"Well, Henry, you may be an agnostic but good Biblical grounding is helpful in life. Fellow who did that history of the Navy wrote that some brass 'comforted with flagons' him and some other officers after a battle in the Pacific. Told him quotation he was referring to went 'Stay me with flagons, Comfort me with apples' and he faced up and changed it. Knowledge of the Bible very necessary to an historian; helps me with my history of The Corps. I had good teachers and I'm a mere Unitarian. He's an Episcopalian — one of God's frozen people, as the feller said. Heh-heh.''

Isabella returned, pink-cheeked and breathless, and cast an observant and sardonic eye upon her niece and Elizabeth Lamb who were even more flushed than she and smiling happy, glazed smiles as they sipped. She held her peace towards them, however, and contented herself with muttering something like "Cow" over the oblivious head of Miss Thorssen, who was still masterfully drinking and looking with silent adoration upon her employer.

The little girls, unaware of being detected by anyone in their vice, sipped and listened away:

"Well, okay, then, Henry; you're not just a monkey-wrench sailor, though that's what Dad calls anyone who runs a motorboat. I like motorboats myself, because you can stow away a bigger lunch on 'em. How come Boston Whalers have a special status, as I guess one'd call it? I admit they're good, but with a strong northwest sea —"

"Ha, that reminds me of a rhyme I did about you, you young seadog. Listen to this:

> 'Isn't it a lovely day?'
> Young Gus asked, heading up the bay.
> But, gosh, there was a northwest chop —
> And parts of 'Gustus still wash up.

Heh-heh.''

"But, Elizabeth, why do so many consider men in their forties still young and dashing and women of the same age passé? It was even worse, I admit, when you and I were growing up. I was reading a magazine, once, that referred to President Kennedy as 'our young president' and in the same issue a woman of exactly his age was called an 'aging actress.'''

Miss Elbridge then turned away from her sister, took a sip of her sixth martini, and burst into quiet tears.

"Emmy, dear, why don't I get you a nice glass of water. Clear your head and all that sort of thing. Heh-heh."

"Well, darling brother-in-law, aren't you ever going to tell your wife about your little fling in Cannes? Talk about the Primrose Path to the Everlasting Bonfire, as I think Mencken put it! You'd better confess, before I decide to do my sisterly duty. Did you know that in Mt. Auburn Cemetery there's a Primrose Path? They can bury you beside it, sweetie, and hopefully before your damned ego gets as big as your —"

"Yes, ikons are always done on gesso panels; Betsy, dear, gesso is pronounced with a soft 'g.' The Siennese school? It stayed static until well into — oh, Jane, thank you. What a long time you've been finding my sweater for me, poor thing. I'm sorry. Now, Betsy, the Siennese school —"

"The manners of some of 'em are abominable. Wish they'd get drafted into your Corps; that'd straighten them out. They just can't see why they shouldn't throw their thick lummoxy legs over the back of the seat in front of them. When they argue, I tell 'em: 'Those seats have lasted almost thirty-five years and I intend them to last until you're let into another authentic Art Deco theatre, which might be never. Feet down or you're out' —"

"Well, but middle age, as Elizabeth and I were told by Uncle Saville when we were girls, is 'fifteen years older than one is.' Really, Lem, you should begin to understand that you are too far into it to keep on this —"

Sarah entered, rather out of breath with her hair damp from fog and hurry and possibly from the effects of the beration which followed her into the room from the kitchen. The burden of its complaint seemed to deal with the length of time she had been absent and the large figure on the price tag on her purchase. Her eye touched upon her daughter and Elizabeth Lamb, now lying flat on their backs and giggling. Before moving towards them, however, she dutifully went to her mother to report on the success of her errand.

The gigglers, though supine, still heard the dialogues, now through a glass darkly:

"God, Jane, I absolutely fear Emily is getting looped. Or getting 'tight's a boot,' as my friend Varner would say. Keep an eye on her while I warn Sarah —"

Miss Elbridge turned with careful dignity. She addressed Jane: "Although my New England guilt conscience has been an impediment to me in that it forbids me to read for pleasure before nightfall, it is also a help because it tells me when to retreat gracefully. And now I think I shall lie down for a bit before dinner."

Miss Elbridge moved in a stately manner that would have reminded any movie-goer of a Caesar proceeding to his coronation. She reached the door, carefully and with a chilly smile putting aside Hill's helping hand, although she bumped into Betsy, spilling her drink, as she made her exit, and majestically apologized.

"Oh, that's all right, Emily — Yes, I did love 'Goodbye Columbus' but I couldn't understand what the title meant. What? Isabella, why do you say such things about Wellesley? Well, indeed —"

"Got it! How about this:

>   Horatio has lost his beard.
>   It happened just as we had feared.
>   When Varner's sight commenced to fail
>   He shot it for a moose's tail.

You Navy people may sail the seas but it takes The Corps to be literate. Heh-heh."

"I was only just down to the store, Mother. When I got back, I waited a few minutes for Kitty, but she didn't come. I mainly took so long because I felt I should help Dottie out a mite. Crowd was fierce there, and all demanding groceries like they was going out of style — stop laughing like that, Hill! I know, I know; I'm very susceptible to speech patterns —"

"I do the same thing at the theatre, Sarah. Let a Southerner, for instance, ask me a question and in my next few sentences I go pure corn-pone. They think I'm mocking them —"

"Ah — ah — are standard typewriters used in Iceland? Ah — I learned to type on a Swiss machine which had the 'y's' and 'z's' transposed from the American models and my — my first employment was with an American author who brought me along back to New York to help with a novel she'd started in Europe. That's — that's how I, ah, began to work on both sides of the Atlantic. Well, her heroine's name was — was Zelda and —"

Jane, along with everyone else, stopped talking at a shriek from Sarah, who was smelling the breath of her small daughter.

"Oh, Persis, darling, what have you done? You've never been so naughty as in the past two days. I cannot believe what a bad influence that child — that child — well, never mind. Now, the two of you come with me to the bathroom at once and when you, Persis, feel better I want you to go out by yourself to look for the great horned owl you think you may have seen last week. It's only eight o'clock but he may be out. And by yourself, I said. I don't want any more —"

Persis opened one eye. In a high carrying voice she pronounced: "Eight o'clock and all is well and those who ain't can go to hell!"

Sarah shrieked again. Mrs. Worthington looked over and, seeing her granddaughter's condition, gently put Sarah into a chair and herself got the children to their feet. With a firm hand at the nape of each little neck, she escorted them to the kitchen, calling to Doreen. She came back, smiling reassuringly at the white and speechless Jane, and secured a drink from the goggling and scandalized Peyton, which she pressed upon Sarah. She then addressed her silent guest.

"I am so very glad my cousin brought you over tonight. Are you enjoying Maine? There must be some similarities to Iceland. Have you had time to see any of the really beautiful places on our island?"

Miss Thorssen got respectfully to her feet and, nodding and smiling massively and politely, sketched a kind of Norse curtsey. She then put her empty glass into her hostess' hand and spoke the first of the three words she was to speak all evening.

"Please?" said Miss Thorssen.

Mrs. Worthington, a little nonplussed, gestured to Peyton and then turned away, to listen with some amusement to the splashings of cold water and the faint moans issuing from the bathroom off the kitchen.

Kitty Blanchard tumbled in, her chiffon fluttering damply and her eye wild. She breathlessly began to explain to her husband that Horatio was nowhere to be found: "I looked everywhere, Freddy. I really did, even on the roof. Oh, Freddy!"

The Captain eased his wife on to the divan next to Lem, who was holding a kind of state audience with Jane and Betsy and Pherousa, with Miss Thorssen, still drinking and still adoring, now leaning on his knees from her seat on the floor.

Despite the considerable weight of his secretary, Lem lept to his feet and clutched Peyton as the latter again attempted to edge himself toward the porch door and freedom. He spoke as a Marine N.C.O. might speak to the most hopeless raw recruit in boot camp.

"Enough of that, you," Lem bellowed. "Right now, a cup of black coffee, and tell Dora to put a shot of clam juice in it. And fast. Jump!"

He turned back to Kitty. "My own private remedy," he said. "Fixes me up every time. Not" — he rolled an eye towards Captain Blanchard — "that The Corps ever needs much fixing up. Got harder heads than the rest of the services. But this gives a push to the liver and the adrenals and all that sort of thing. Heh-heh."

Kitty reached up to clasp his hand. She spoke tearfully. "Do you know what Mrs. Parker has done? It has made me so frightened, dear Lem, and that's why I drank so much. That terrible woman has actually persuaded a Child Guidance Association in Bangor or Ellsworth or somewhere to send down a case-worker to investigate Horatio and our handling of him.

"She claims he is dangerous and is trying to have him taken away from us. She had the effrontery to write me to tell me an investigator is coming. My poor boy! She should be put away somewhere, Lem, in a dark, dark hole. She is a horror. If poor Mr. Parker were only still —"

"Now, now," Lem interrupted. "She can't do that, Kitty, call in someone to check on you no matter how much she contributes to the do-gooders. Doubt it's legal. They'd refuse.

"Now, look, my dear, with your permission I'm going to run over to your cottage for a minute to call my place. I've an old friend coming up for a visit who should be getting to Northeast Harbor any hour now, and I want to tell my housekeeper a few more things before she leaves for the night. Expected to be home by this time, you see, but you are all so congenial and Elizabeth wants us to stay for supper.

"Be right back. I'll take a cast around for your boy. Thurna, sweet, look after Mrs. Blanchard for me."

Miss Thorssen, upon Lem's departure, seated herself beside Kitty, nodding with gigantic reassurance. She reached down into her sizeable bosom and produced a small pewter vial from which she poured a minute amount of a dark liquid into Kitty's coffee cup.

"It fix," she said in a deep voice, and applied herself once more to her glass, gripping Kitty's chiffon with one ham-like hand so that her charge should not escape her.

The Captain had been appropriated by Hill, who was engaging him in an erudite discussion involving the alleged peccadillos of Mr. Fortas. Hill, from a base of Mr. Fortas, evolved into an abstruse consideration of the changing morals, public and private, of the age. The Captain began to shift uneasily from one sneaker to the other.

"Yes, yes, yes, my boy," he boomed. "Whole country is going to the dogs. I'll just leave you for a short time, I think. Want to run up after Lem and try to find Horatio. Kitty's uneasy."

He escaped.

People began to change partners, as must be done at cocktail time. Henry moved over to Jane, who had said little, of course, and was still engaged with her first drink.

"Do you like Mount Desert Island, Mrs. Lamb?" he asked politely. "I suppose you haven't been here long enough to answer that. Betsy and I loved it when we were what the Natives call summer complaints, but now that we are forced to live here year round, it is awfully confining. The Natives themselves get what they term 'cabin fever' round about February, but we're beginning to get it even in the summers."

Jane answered shyly. "Yes," she murmured, "I should think there would be a great many problems of acclimation. Still, you chose to live here, didn't you? I would think you really don't have to. As the Spanish proverb goes: 'Take what you want and pay for it, says God.'"

Her voice was much more loud and firm as she quoted. Mrs. Worthington, hearing, glanced over and smiled. Henry took Jane's glass from her and gallantly went in search of a refill.

Gus had for some time been reading Morison's "Admiral of the Ocean Sea" by the light of a lamp on a table a little removed from the main action of the late-late show. Occasionally he had surreptitiously transferred something from his trouser pocket to his mouth, but his searching hand had encountered only crumbs on its last few missions.

Now he pathetically addressed Mrs. Worthington. "Grandma, could we please have dinner? I've never been hungrier. Please?"

Mrs. Worthington touched his blonde head consolingly. "Would you see to it, Sarah?"

Sarah had been quietly drinking and brooding. With a sigh she tentatively approached the kitchen door and, summoning all her considerable resources of breeding and character, passed through it in a manner reminiscent to Jane, who watched with sympathy, of the hero of "The Lady or the Tiger?"

Dora was heard to greet her. "Lands sake, Sarah, can't you tend to them damned dogs? Whining and howling in at me through the screen, they've been, for the last hour or so. I give them all the canopies that wasn't et and now they're at it worse'n ever. Well, if you don't want 'em given perfectly good food, why don't you take some care of them? What do you mean 'burned' —"

The door slammed shut and the living room conversations went on, a little more subdued since hunger was settling upon more of the company than the ever-starved Gus.

Betsy's good manners moved her to address Pherousa, who was still silently sipping her ginger ale. "I hear you are entering Radcliffe this fall."

"Yes," Pherousa whispered. "Iwasveryluckytobeaccepted."

"But why not Wellesley? The girls there are so much prettier and better dressed. The Radcliffe student body is simply not admired by the Harvard men, you'll find, I'm afraid."

There was another whispered reply from Pherousa.

"Well, yes," Betsy admitted, "it is true that a large percentage of them do marry 'Cliffies', but I've never understood that."

Another whisper from Pherousa.

"Your father insists you major in history at Harvard because he wants you to be a naval historian?" Betsy's sweet high voice went even higher. "Oh, you poor child!"

Betsy went over to stand beside her husband and inform him of Captain Blanchard's iniquitious behaviour to his only daughter. Hill sat down beside Jane.

"Since you know Cannes, I think it might amuse you to hear the truth of what that blasted sister-in-law of mine keeps implying. You know the Hotel Metropole, and how the rooms are all named instead of numbered? Well, after the Korean War I was in the navy, and had got a weekend leave. Checked into the Metropole with plans to do nothing but sleep; didn't know a soul in the place, male or female, and didn't want to. Of course, Isabella was on the premises, under another name, probably.

"Anyway, this charming jeune fille had the room next to mine. It was called 'Mistral' while mine was titled 'Mirabelle.' Well, I was bone-tired and had drunk a liter of vin rouge at dinner and when I went up to go to bed — oh, Lord, excuse me for a moment, Jane. Peyton's behind the bookshelf, finishing all the drinks on the tray."

Hill left to escort Peyton into the kitchen, as the Captain came in the porch door, puffing and snorting like a dolphin, of the officer class, of course.

"Boy's in his bed, Kitty, sleeping soundly. Completely tuckered out. Didn't disturb him."

"In his bed, Freddy? Oh, good."

"Well, in his room, that is. Couldn't see hide nor hair of Lem. Must have come the long way back, by mistake."

Dora entered, bearing a succulent-looking Smithfield ham, finely sliced. Doreen followed with a huge mahogany salad bowl of the favoured leaf lettuce, scattered with small chunks of Roquefort cheese, and an enormous basket of little biscuits, only a few of which showed her mother's charring touch.

A subdued Elizabeth Lamb, hair damp from Doreen's masterful handling of the cold water faucet, carried napkins and an assortment of small trays. Gus handled a tray of goblets of water.

The three Dalmatians entered on Gus' heels, whining and crawling on their bellies. They leaped upon Sarah, who was annoyed.

"Will you please take them out and feed them, Peyton?" she asked. "Dora will show you where their food and bowls are."

"Tried already, Sarah," answered Peyton, hiccupping. "They wouldn't eat. Just want to sit and yelp. Here, if you'll open these bottles of wine, I'll try again." He ushered the dogs out to the porch, where they sat and moaned, staring in at their mistress.

"Come, everyone, it is self-service," declared Mrs. Worthington, setting an example by choosing a tray and beginning to assemble her dinner upon it. "Sarah, why are you holding those bottles of burgundy? I told Peyton to get some champagne out of the ice-chest, if anyone wants it. Nothing else is anything but wasted with ham.

"And would you please get Hill to open it; we won't wait for Lem. Oh, good, here is Emily."

"I fell asleep," Miss Elbridge confessed. "I must say it seems strange to me to nap at this hour. A nap after lunch I have always considered perfectly proper, but before dinner, a bit self-indulgent."

With appetites whetted by the chill air, the sight and smell of Dora's offerings, Peyton's skill at bartending and their own efforts at conversation, the company pitched in heartily.

Dora, in a fit of masochism, attempted to question Sarah as to whether or not a raisin sauce would have been desired with the ham. Sarah rolled her eyes to heaven and muttered one word: "Redundant."

Miss Elbridge inquired of her sister as to why she persisted in using a mahogany salad bowl, when a porcelain one of the type preferred by knowing salad fanciers had been presented to her as Miss Elbridge's guest present. Mrs. Worthington rolled her eyes to the kitchen door and muttered one word: "Broken."

General Alison entered, blowing briskly on his hands. "Unbelievable that this is June," he observed. "Made my call, Freddy. Thought I heard you stomping about the place. So many porches and parts and exits and entrances — sounds familiar, that; wonder why? — I couldn't be sure who it was. Certainly heard someone.

"There was a peculiar clicking noise," he went on. "Would have sworn wire coathangers were being clashed about. Couldn't have been, of course, but it reminded me of a friend of mine who has a dry-cleaning plant. Awfully nice fellow —"

Hill, visions of Horatio's clicking coathangers dancing in his head, amidst fumes of all the gin and vermouth he had consumed, burst into discreet but beserk laughter until pulled up by Sarah's frown. He busied himself with helping Dora hand around platters of hot buttered pilot crackers spread with guava jelly. "Our favourite Bungalow dessert," he assured Jane Lamb, who had accepted a piece with some hesitation and a frightened look.

Coffee was poured and handed about by Dora and Doreen. Snatches of conversation went on. Elizabeth Lamb, held somewhat in disgrace by all except Mrs. Worthington, who smiled at her frequently, stole unnoticed over to her mother.

She took Jane's hand and spoke quietly. "We are doing very well, Mummy," she said. "We will handle everything we must do with style, just as you said. I'm proud of you."

Jane looked nervously around. No one was listening. "And I am of you, Elizabeth Lamb, except perhaps of your behaviour an hour ago. It was a bit too reminiscent of your father, and it disturbed me for that reason and because, as you must realize, it was most unbecoming. But we will see everything through."

She hugged her daughter. Elizabeth Lamb patted her mother's cheek and slipped out of the room.

She waited a moment outside the kitchen door. Persis had not returned to the bunkroom, their agreed-upon meeting place, so Elizabeth Lamb wandered along the path towards the meadow. The fog had lifted so that she was able to see as far as the fence beyond which several cars were parked.

No sound came from the woods indicating the advent of her friend, and so she sat down upon the doorstep of the guest cottage to contemplate the evening. It had warmed considerably as the fog had dispersed. Nightfall was imminent, but the fog's lifting permitted her to see a red glow in the sky over Blue Hill Bay.

"Red sky at night, sailor's delight," murmured Elizabeth Lamb, who remembered more than one of the sayings of her long-gone father. She leaned back upon the shingled wall and half-dozed. She woke to hear water running, and got up to peer around the corner of the cottage as her mother had done a few hours earlier.

Junior was standing by the outdoor shower, rinsing off a clam hod and rake. He jumped as Elizabeth Lamb appeared, and turned, frowning. His expression changed to pleased surprise as he shut off the water and greeted her gaily.

"Thought it was the Grafin sneaking up on me again," he explained. "Man can't turn his back around here without her jumping out at him, sometimes buck-naked."

"What are you doing?" asked Elizabeth Lamb, smothering a yawn.

"Went down to dig myself some clams," Junior answered. "All those places on the road today offering fried clams — which are nothing but clam necks out of cans, or so a feller told me — sort of gave me a craving for some real ones. Thought I'd gather a few and get Peyton's wife to fry 'em up for me fast before I fell into a long summer's nap."

"Get any?"

"Nope, too tired to dig 'em properly. Changing my tire about finished me. Practically collapsed on the mud. Gratefully. Figured I'd drown or smother then and there and it'd show everybody a thing or two about how valuable I was, onct I was gone.

"However," he went on soberly although his eyes, in the fading light, were twinkling, "my baser nature took over and I struggled up here, denying myself the pleasure of looking down from Heaven to hear Dora wailing at my funeral. So I'm going home to revive myself with a can of soup, if I have the strength left to open it, and I advise you to head for your bunk. Your elders and betters look like they'll carouse all night, by the sound of 'em. Where's Persis?"

"Her mother sent her into the woods to look for an owl."

"Into the woods, at this time of night?" Junior was startled. "What's Sarah thinking of, anyway? Now I suppose I ought to go look for her; must be almost nine o'clock, or is it nearer ten? Can't be, it's too light. Which way did she go?"

"She's all right. Look, there she is."

A small sweatered form came trudging out of the trees. It fell upon Elizabeth Lamb, they embraced, and headed toward the main

Bungalow. Persis turned to wave goodnight to Junior, who regarded her gravely, shook his head at her mother's heedlessness, and, clutching his equipment, strode up the path to his truck. None of the three noticed the figure on the porch of the main house, which had been watching them for some time. At the little girls' approach, it slipped quietly into the kitchen.

The children advanced to the window looking in over the divan and peered sleepily through it at the assemblage. They had no thought of going to bed; Persis had had too many years of the shame of having her bedtime set at two hours before Gus' to miss this unusual chance of viewing adult entertainment. As for Elizabeth Lamb, adult entertainment was meat, if not, as she had found out during the evening, drink, to her.

They leaned heavily into the window, and on each other, and prepared to be diverted. Through the slightly opened casement at the side, bits of dialogue drifted to their tired ears:

"Elizabeth, next to the food at the Somerset Club, which we Bostonians know is the best in the world, comes yours. Indisputably. Heh-heh."

"— but — but you are discounting the effects of utter despair. There is a dead calm that comes with it that makes — that makes creation possible. I know; I have endured that despair and discovered that — that calm. What have I created? Well, ah, for one thing, a livelihood, a rather unique livelihood. For — for another, a child. A rather unique child. Sarah, I know you think she —"

"No, my surname is spelled with one 'l'. Long story about that; came about because two brothers in Scotland named 'Allison' had a falling-out, centuries ago. Suppose with a name like 'Lamb,' you have no problems as I do in shops. Shopgirls really are the limit — they say, 'Yes, sir, one 'l' but how many 's's'?' They are just too —"

"Excuse me, Lem, but I had to leave Jane very rudely before. Well, Jane, to get on with What Happened in Cannes, after I opened the door of 'Mistral' by mistake, and, of course it was pitch-dark inside —"

"Speaking of moorings, Gus, this rich summer fellow in Bar Harbor, see, is a volunteer member of the town fire department, as I am, and he's very generous with all the other members, regular or volunteer. Betsy and I went up to his place to borrow one of his endless moorings for our Whaler, but couldn't find him or his caretaker. I asked one of the men working on the place about it, and was sent to the greenhouse.

"Nobody and no moorings were there, so we went back and tried again with the fellow who'd directed us. 'Well,' he said, 'I don't know all the plants Harold has but I'm sure he's got some English Morning.' 'No,' I hollered, 'I want an endless mooring; who said anything about a plant?' 'Why, then,' he answered, 'why in tarnation didn't you ask for a moo-ren in the first place?'"

"Het or hove? What do you mean, 'what do you mean'? I said shall I het up your cup, Miss Isabella, mam, or do you want I should hove out what's in it and start fresh? Listen, now —"

"Do you think the National Park can use the right of remnant domain to appropriate the off-shore islands? Henry says he hopes it does before the Natives cover them stem to stern with beer cans. Oh, yes, I suppose he did say 'eminent'; Sarah, you Radcliffe people are so clever excepting in —"

"Of course I agree with Lem. Betsy's related to the Adams family and it had integrity and a tradition of using political power for the public good. These millionaire upstarts who buy their way in are what will ruin us, along with — hey, Fred, wake up!"

The eyes of all the company turned towards Henry and Captain Blanchard. Feet planted on the floor as firmly as on a pitching quarterdeck, head thrown back over his chair pillow, and mouth wide open, the Captain had made a clever retreat into sound slumber.

His wife rushed to him and ungently patted his cheek with a practiced touch that showed she must have had to take such punitive action at many a military get-together. The Captain leaped up, rubbing his hands together briskly, and announced loudly, "Heard every word you said and agree utterly. Utterly, my boy!"

Peyton put his head in through the kitchen doorway and inquired of Dora, in what he may have thought was a discreet tone, "Godsakes, ain't it time they was going?"

Taking the hint, exclaiming at the lateness of the hour, and expressing thanks for the evening's entertainment, the lady guests began to assemble their belongings, male and personal. Miss Thorssen, still silent, showed her appreciation with many white-toothed smiles and powerful handshakes. The efforts toward departure were spurred on by Dora, who stood watching with folded arms and chilly eyes.

Gus was active at the table, disposing neatly of any lingering biscuits and polishing off the remains of the salad. He strategically moved to kiss his grandmother as Dora turned upon him.

"Please see to the dogs, Gus," Sarah requested. "I cannot think why they have been behaving so badly this evening. And after you help clean up, I want you to go straight to bed with no more to eat."

Hill escorted the guests to their cars. Miss Thorssen lingered behind to swallow the contents of a glass left on a table by the door. Mrs. Worthington bade her family goodnight.

"Remember that church is at nine tomorrow," she added. "We'll breakfast at seven-thirty, Dora, please. Peyton, my purse is at the studio, so would you come there with me, and then would you wait a few minutes to run Dora and Doreen home?"

Sarah, Miss Elbridge, Jane, Doreen, and Gus hastened to get the dishes, glasses, and ashtrays out to the kitchen, where Dora received the assortment in a towering temper.

"Worst collection of cultch I ever saw," she raged, scraping remnants of food from the plates into a bowl to abet the dogs' next dinner. "That living-room looks like a Prouty dooryard. Can't see why a body has to show off and have people in to eat and drink themselves senseless. Inconsiderate for the hired help, I call it."

Elizabeth Lamb and Persis watched the cleaning-up operation from the back porch, noses pressed to the screen door.

"You wouldn't have a job if people didn't eat and drink and have parties sometimes," observed Elizabeth Lamb, yawning tremendously.

The kitchen helpers stood motionless, waiting for the storm to break. For a full half-minute there was no sound except the noises from the uneasy dogs in the woodshed near the back door. Then Dora laughed loudly.

"That's a fact, Miss Girl," she said heartily. "You've got gumption as well as good sense. Remind me of somebody, you do. Probably somebody whose picture's in the post office," she added to herself and the dish-filled sink.

The even-song was uttered by Hill, prayerfully to himself, as he ambled back down to the kitchen to get a glass of milk, after genially waving each car away. "Thank God," he intoned, "for small mercies, or should I say, large ones; Cousin Tom and Wife never showed up."

Chapter 17

CONVERSATIONS BY CANDLELIGHT, 2

Gus appeared in the doorway of the bunkroom as the little girls were trundling into their warm nightclothes and giving their faces perfunctory swipes with washcloths dipped into an enameled basin containing water that had been hot when Doreen had poured it from an old-fashioned English brass can an hour before.

"Wow, does *this* place ever look like a Prouty dooryard," he said disparagingly. "I'm glad Dora didn't look in here. Don't you ever hang anything up? Say, did I happen not to eat my doughnut Junior brought?"

Elizabeth Lamb dredged about under a pile of sweaters. "You ate yours but you can have mine. Here."

Gus accepted it gratefully. "Fuzz adds to the texture, if not the flavour," he said thoughtfully, enunciating around doughnut and mohair. "Elizabeth Lamb, where are you going to go to school?"

"Where we can afford to send me, I guess."

"What about where I go, St. Paul's? You'd do okay there. And I bet we could get you a scholarship. You're pretty smart."

"Gus," Persis said, "they don't take girls."

"They will, I bet, next year or the next. All private schools'll have to. Lots of parents are sending their boys to public schools or day schools near home because tuition at boarding schools has gone up so much. Besides, they have to save lots more money for college tuition now. So the schools'll have to let girls in, to keep going. I hear the masters talking."

"But she's only eight, Gus. They won't let girls into the Lower School."

"Oh, well, in a couple of years, then. She could go to that crappy school you go to till then. Ma could get her in."

"I don't think she would," Elizabeth Lamb said sadly. "She thinks I'm a bad influence."

"We'll make her come round. I like you. You're something like Persis, in a way, and she's okay."

Persis beamed proudly. Gus wandered back to his room, prompted by a vague recollection of an ancient chocolate bar in one of his jacket pockets.

As soon as he had gone, Persis' expression turned with almost comic celerity from a pleased look to one of great worry.

"Elizabeth Lamb," she said timidly.

"What's the matter, Persis? Tell me."

"You know what Aunt Issa said about the fern seed? Well, I didn't quite believe it, but when I went over to Mrs. Parker's woods I found a big fern and I shook some seed all over me."

"Why?"

"Well, we're not supposed to go there. She doesn't like children and Mummy doesn't like her. But I've always wanted to go over there, and I thought maybe the fern seed would make her not see me."

"Well, did it?"

"I don't know. I sneaked right up behind a workshop kind of place near the cottage. She was there, around in front of it, and having a terrible argument with somebody, like a fight. I was scared."

"Who was it?"

"I couldn't see, and whoever it was talked real low and the man out on her boat was playing his radio real loud. She was yelling, sort of, things like 'to remember all this time' and 'not so proper, are you' and then she stopped, all of a sudden. Then she screamed, really screamed, 'Oh, no, God, don't. Oh, God, don't, God.' Those were the words she said, though maybe not just that way. I was awful scared."

"Oh, Persis, you just heard the radio and got all mixed up."

"But there was a thudding, sort of, and then she stopped yelling and sort of moaned. I ran away."

"It was just a radio play, or maybe one of those religious programs. What time was this, anyway?"

"Oh, Elizabeth Lamb, I just don't remember. You see, I did it twice."

"Did what twice?"

"Went over there twice. I did the fern seed thing both times. First I went over there right after you and I and Gus finished the supper June brought us. It was while you and Gus were playing cards. Then I came back and you and I went in and drank that stuff and then I went over again."

"Well, but Persis, which time was it you heard all that, or think you did?"

Persis began to cry. "I just don't remember. That awful stuff made me feel funny, confused, as Aunt Isabella is always saying. It's just like I was dreaming, except I remember some parts and some I don't. One time I didn't hear anything and the other time was what I told you.

"I don't remember which time was which. I was scared to go over both times. Something made me, like a witch put a spell on me the way they do in fairy tales," said poor Persis.

"Well, I don't see how you can remember you went over there but not which time it was you got scared."

"Well, I just don't. I told you I was scared both times anyway, and when I get scared I just can't think right."

"Maybe you didn't really hear anything either time. That was awfully strong liquor. I thought it might be like wine but it made me feel sick and dizzy till Doreen made me throw up. You couldn't, so I guess you felt worse than I did."

"Do you think I should tell Mummy?"

"Well, not now. Tomorrow, if you want to, though I bet you'll see that lady in church tomorrow, perfectly all right. But now your mother wants to go to sleep in peace and quiet, I should think. Peace and Quiet, Merry Christmas, Happy New Year."

"What?"

"I read that on a fence in Nassau last winter, when my mother was there doing some work for a man who writes songs. Somebody had painted it in pink paint. My mother laughed. Now go to sleep. I'll tuck you in."

Persis obediently climbed into her bunk and shut her eyes. Elizabeth Lamb pulled up the coverings and patted Persis' head reassuringly before she blew out the candle and climbed into her own bunk.

"Goodnight, Persis. Sleep tight."

"Thank you. Peace and Quiet, Merry Christmas, Happy New Year," replied Persis.

"Hill," said Sarah.

Hill turned from an attempt to survey the profile of his stomach in an inadequate pine-framed mirror hung above a low oak chest of drawers.

"I wish to Heaven I wouldn't eat so much up here," he replied. "What is it?"

"You're perfectly flat. Hill, why couldn't Lem write a novel and make some money? His conversation is so very witty, don't you think so? And those girls could type it up when not typing the Marine history. He doesn't have anything else for them to do to fill their time."

Hill regarded her with disbelief. Sarah was brushing her hair in bed. She had on a rose-sprigged flannel nightgown and looked very pretty, earnest, and innocent. He suppressed the answer he had been about to make.

"Well, I suppose some people might consider him witty. He couldn't write a novel, though. He's a Bostonian."

"What does that mean?"

"Well, they can't write dialogue. They're so used to laying down the law and not brooking any discussion that they couldn't possibly invent a two-sided conversation."

"Really, Hill."

"It's true. Has any Bostonian except Marquand ever been able to write dialogue? And he was originally from Newburyport, I think."

"Oh, Hill, you are so sarcastic."

"No, truly, it isn't seemly for a Bostonian to write anything but history. Not a proper Bostonian, anyway, and whom else would you and I be discussing? From Parkman to Morison, there's been an unbroken tradition of historical writing, not novel writing. Can't buck tradition in Boston.

"And it's a good thing, too, that there is that tradition, because not one mother's son of 'em — nor mother's daughter — can invent dialogue, not dialogue that anybody'd want to read. I stand by my statement."

"Hill, you're not being fair."

"But I do know what would go over tremendously, and maybe I'll write it. Lem wouldn't dare. You know how people love to read about sex and how they love to read about Boston. Anything with 'Boston' in the title has a good chance of becoming a best-seller, so a man at my club who's in the publishing business told me. And we all know what happens to anything when the word 'sex' is prominently displayed. In fact, I once saw a sign S—E—X outside an auto body shop, and under it, it said 'Now that we have your attention' and then it listed all their services.

"Well, I'll write an epic documentary entitled 'Erotica Bostonnia.' I'll even have a great time doing research for it. You can help, too, if you want."

"Hill, you are absolutely the limit. Or the living end, as Isabella says. I'm really very angry."

Sarah blew out the lamp. Hill laughed and moved to her in the dark. There was subdued conversation and activity not quite proper to reveal . . . and then, Peace and Quiet, Merry Christmas, Happy New Year.

Mrs. Worthington was also brushing her hair. Emily tapped on her door and went in.

"A good party, Elizabeth," she said, "although I have a dreadful headache to show for the pleasant time I had."

"I hope everyone enjoyed it. Emily, forgive me, but you are not feeling unduly possessive of Lemuel, are you, after all these years?"

"No," answered her sister, somewhat sadly, "but why are men such fools?"

"I don't think they are essentially more foolish than women," Mrs. Worthington replied. "They just have more leeway to exhibit their foolishness. At the present time, anyway. I look forward to this new movement for women's liberation. Perhaps soon we shall have the freedom to be just as silly as men are."

Emily laughed her pleasant laugh. "Elizabeth, isn't the *Hilda* getting rather decrepit?"

"I suppose so. I don't think even Bobby's boatyard can caulk and repair her successfully after this season. Junior will be hard-pressed to keep her afloat even this summer.

"I do so hate to give her up. She was, as you remember, a wedding present to Otis and me from old Hilda Swenson, who was Mrs. Worthington's maid and waitress all through Otis' youth. The fifty dollars Hilda put out for that skiff made a great hole in her life's savings, I fear."

"Well, if you must replace her, could we name the new skiff *Thurna*? Then I shouldn't feel so much compunction if Persis ran her on the rocks, as is her habit."

Mrs. Worthington smiled. "Cheer up, Emily. There will be a diversion soon, and you'll enjoy it. Good night."

Jane was sitting at the writing table in her room. A letter lay there that had gone unnoticed when she had hastily changed after the Sargent climb. She opened it with trepidation, looked surprised and happy while reading, and then sat staring at the candles thoughtfully. At a sound from the window she started, and pushed the letter under the blotter.

Isabella was outside. Her face, even reflecting the glow of candlelight from the room, was pale and uneasy. "Are you going to bed," she asked politely enough, "or would you like to come for a walk?"

"Well, I think I shall go to bed. It is not very late, but I am tired. Aren't you?"

"I am, rather. I was going to walk but perhaps I won't. I really feel most upset, and can't imagine why. I'm sensitive to atmosphere to an unusual degree, but I see no reason for this uneasy feeling tonight. Strangely enough, this is the way I feel when I paint best, but I am not up to doing the cove by lamplight. Lamp-black would be more like it, you know?"

Jane laughed.

"I just remembered that Hill told me your father was a painter. No one else would have known lamp-black was a pigment."

"Yes, he was, a portrait painter, chiefly."

"I've often wondered how portrait painters feel about their subjects."

"They like them; they always do. After they're into the portrait, that is. My father said it's impossible not to like someone you're taking so much trouble with."

"If my husband had ever sat for him, he would have been the exception to that rule. Well, good night."

"Good night, Isabella."

At the Blanchards', Kitty sat in the kitchen drinking whiskey and water and sobbing quietly. Pherousa sat at the table beside her mother and gently patted her hand. The Captain stood at a window, hands clenched behind his back, staring out into the darkness. Upstairs, under his bed, Horatio slept. No one spoke.

At the Gambels', a party was in damp progress, in the conversation pit. The guests wore bulky tweeds or hand-knitted dresses and sweaters in murky tones. All the women were minus waistlines and all the men were minus scalp hair, either in front or on top.

The participants dipped with limp potato chips into depressing-looking bowls of creamy substances and drank warm Scotch. The conversation was languid, erudite, possibly subversive, and carried on in German and Russian.

At Mrs. Parker's, old George Paine woke up in his bunk on the *Hesperus* around midnight, perhaps at the loud sounds of guests departing from the Gambels' establishment across the cove. He turned off his radio, wondering sleepily at the absence of lights in the Parker cottage, but decided his employer had gone off to Bar Harbor again.

He settled back into sleep. With the disappearance of the sound from the radio, there was deep, deep quiet all about the Parker property. And, possibly, peace.

Chapter 18

BY GUESS AND BY GOD

Evidently there had been heavy rain during the night. There were pools of water on the clamshell path as Jane went down to the main Bungalow for breakfast. The juniper and blueberry bushes beside the path were sodden and left wet marks on the skirt of her pink linen suit. Someone, doubtless Dora, had freshened and pressed it since her arrival, no small task as the only pressing equipment at The Bungalow was old flat-irons heated on the top of the wood stove.

She glanced in at the children in the bunkroom, thinking how remiss a parent she must appear to the Halsteads, who would not realize that Elizabeth Lamb had more or less taken care of herself with great resourcefulness on two continents for several years now.

The resourceful one and Persis were assisting each other into the printed lawn dresses they had worn Friday night.

"Why don't you wear one of your own frocks, Elizabeth Lamb?" Jane asked.

"They are too chic, Mummy, and Persis doesn't mind if I wear hers. Why don't I have a smocked Liberty print?"

"We must get you one," Jane answered absently, her thoughts on the letter she had opened the night before. "We may be going back to Europe soon, and it's possible I won't have to work any more."

"I don't want to! I want to stay here and learn to row!" Elizabeth Lamb clenched her fists and shook her silver-gilt head violently. She desisted at once and pressed her hands to her temples.

"Why do Persis and I have headaches, Mummy?"

"It's called retribution. Promise me that you will never again drink anything unless it is offered to you. It is very bad form to do what you did and Mrs. Halstead is still very angry, I fear."

The children promised fervently. Jane ushered them to the dining table in the main Bungalow, where breakfast was waiting. They passed Doreen, who was slowly conveying a tray up to Mrs. Worthington in the studio, and humming abstractedly.

The rest of the family was at the table, sipping orange juice and listening to Sarah and Dora, neither of whose tempers had been improved by a night's rest.

"Doreen's bringing in the deer liver in just a minute, Sarah," called Dora from the kitchen. "Bacon to go with it's not quite crisp, yet. That liver might be kind of high, you know, since none of you troubled to put it in the ice chest Friday night. Good thing a game warden didn't put his head in the kitchen door."

Sarah sighed.

"See that loaf of bread right beside you?" went on Dora. "Slice it for me, can't you, and get them kids to toast it over the fire in there; I got enough to do out here. Then you could butter it and put it on a plate and I'll put it in the oven for a minute. Help out a little, won't you? Took some doing for Doreen and me to get here this early. Wasn't nobody around to give us a lift into the Cape."

"I can't spread anything with butter because I don't see any butter," rejoined Sarah tartly. "I realize we used up most of the butter last night and that the remainder went to fry up the liver, but why couldn't you have brought in a pound or two from the store? You stopped to get a loaf of Dottie's bread."

"Because there was margarine down here, sitting in the ice chest where that liver should've been sitting, that's why. It's right there on the table. What's wrong with margarine? Us poor folk eat it all the time."

"Well, I don't have a coloured television set, as some poor folk who have to eat margarine do, and I like butter," answered Sarah, more or less reasonably.

"I do like a little bit of butter to my bread," muttered Jane and Hill in unison, and burst into laughter.

Doreen appeared with the rest of the breakfast and relieved Elizabeth Lamb and Persis of their toasting forks. Quiet enjoyment of Varner's offering prevailed during the meal. Sarah ate the golden-brown toast proffered by Doreen unbuttered, or, rather, unmargarined, and this abstinence was noted by Dora, who loudly uttered "Humph" each time she peered from the kitchen.

"There was a red sky last night but it's all downcast and grey this morning," Elizabeth Lamb volunteered.

"The fog will burn off by eleven, always does when it's foggy this early," Gus replied. "It's going to be a bright day after that."

Elizabeth Lamb and Persis went out to sit on the porch. They had eaten a moderate amount of breakfast and felt less queasy.

"I'm awfully thirsty," Persis whispered. "Let's go around to the kitchen and ask Doreen for ginger-beer. Ginger's good for the stomach, and Doreen has a kind heart, I heard Aunt Emily say."

Gus wandered down to the rocks along the shore where he sat, uneasy in his tie and tweed jacket, and pondered, looking out at his beloved Bullseye in which he had not sailed for almost thirty-six hours.

Their elders lingered at the table over their coffee cups, smoking and waiting for the time to leave for church. Mrs. Worthington came in, her dark red linen dress complemented by a flat black velvet bow pinned across the knot of shining black hair at the nape of her neck, and by the small prayer-book she carried.

"I'll have some more coffee with you," she said. "Dora and Doreen are coming with us. We'll have to take your car, too, Emily. I do wish that wretched garage would finish that repair on mine."

"Going to wear my new Monkey Ward outfit," announced Dora from the kitchen, over her usual crescendo of dish-washing. "Doreen's above all that dressin'-up, she says. Her money goes into the bank so's she can go to Paris for a year after her second year at the university up to Orono. That'll be next year, you know. Mostly she wears things she makes up herself out of blue denim. Looks like a brakeman most of the time, is what I say."

"To Paris?" asked Jane, entranced. "Why do you want to go to Paris, Doreen?"

Doreen was pouring coffee for Mrs. Worthington. "Everybody

must want to go to Paris, Mrs. Lamb," she answered, her round white face animated for the first time in the view of anyone in The Bungalow. "I want to see how to dress better and I want to take some cooking lessons. I want to be a good cook and not have to live in Maine and —" She broke off, her face recovered its usual stolid impassivity and she carried the coffeepot back to her mother in the kitchen, whence came a loud sniff, either of pride or disdain. With Dora, it was hard to say.

"Mis' Parker might help," said Dora, coming to the doorway and looking harshly at Isabella, who had raised her eyes to Heaven. "Doreen told her her plans, onct, and she said she'd leave Doreen five thousand dollars in her will. Her husband loved Paris, seems like. 'Course, Doreen'll be to Paris and back and even finished the university before Mis' Parker dies, doubtless, but it'll come in handy, nevertheless."

"But this is fascinating," murmured Mrs. Worthington, ignoring the mention of Doreen's benefactor and moving to the kitchen, where Doreen was giving mugs of ginger-beer to the little girls. "I had no idea. She must be encouraged and helped."

Her conference with Doreen took some little time. Dora had finished the dishes herself and was tightly encased in a pale blue dress with eyelet embroidery trim, very simple, and, thought Jane, though obviously inexpensive, very attractive. She jammed a small straw hat of a matching blue down over her frizzy curls as she stamped about the living room looking at her watch and sighing heavily, to the annoyance of Isabella, who was half asleep over her coffee.

Doreen finally emerged from the kitchen. While still conferring with Mrs. Worthington, she had gone into the bathroom off the kitchen to change into a plain, well-fitting, blue denim princess dress, its simple lines emphasized by darker blue stitching. She had knotted a large red bandanna over her blonde hair and looked smart and cosmopolitan and completely different from her usual nondescript self. Both Jane and Isabella regarded her with surprise and appreciation. Dora, however, muttered "Boston and Maine," to Jane's puzzlement.

They finally embarked upon their godly quest. Both Hill and Emily drove fast, but the opening hymn was in progress when they arrived. Sharing a hymn-book with Persis, who was heartily rendering "Onward, Christian Soldiers," Elizabeth Lamb looked about her.

The little church was attractively plain, with cream-coloured walls and dark wood trim, but there was a good print of an Italian madonna on one wall, which she viewed with recognition.

The back rows were the domain of the Natives, who were dressed in their Sunday best and wore expressions of Sunday reverence. The front rows were occupied by the summer people, whose Sunday best was more expensive and whose expressions were both reverent and obtrusively charming. The priest, a rotund little man with a bald pate, was attended by an acolyte whose chief concern seemed to be with not falling over his large feet, which, encased in brown deck shoes, protruded beneath his red cassock to an unbelievable distance.

The service proceeded pleasantly and piously. The handing-around of the collection plate was supervised by Junior, who had evidently had a good night's sleep at last. He looked handsome and tanned, his light hair beautifully brushed and his navy-blue blazer and grey flannels extremely well-tailored, Jane noticed. His eye was solemn but he managed a discreet wink at Persis, who giggled, to her grandmother's annoyed perplexity. Mrs. Worthington had had the foresight to slip fifty-cent pieces into the little girls' hands in the car, and these they proudly handed over to Junior's care.

The sermon dealt with money, and the effects of an inordinate desire for it. The rector was earnest and logical and his thoughts followed one another smoothly. He had taken the trouble to verify and insert a number of witty quotations having to do with his subject.

With the benediction, timed for exactly 9:57, the service ended and the children leapt to their feet. Mrs. Worthington remained seated for a few minutes, listening to the very good organist, and then followed her group to the vestry, where the rector was making pleasant farewells to his congregation.

"Look," said Miss Elbridge, "there is Cordelia in her Scarf."

Cordelia, in rumpled green silk shantung, her head covered by her rose-print Scarf, was taking an inordinate amount of time over her farewell. The priest was courteous but fidgety. Finally, Teddie took her arm forcefully and herded her down the steps to their car.

"Most energy he's expended in ages," murmured Isabella. "His dietary clock must be signalling for lunch. Doesn't Cordelia look dreadful?" she added, looking complacently down at her own faultless white Couregges ensemble.

Greetings were being exchanged in the parking lot. Junior had been captured by an elderly man in sailing khakis, black necktie, and a duck-billed khaki cap, to whom he was apologizing.

"I just overslept, George," he said. "I was dead tired and barely got up in time to make it here. Now, don't get all bent out of shape; it wasn't deliberate. It's the first Sunday I've let you down and it'll be the last."

"WELL," shouted the old man, who appeared to be George Paine, Mrs. Parker's yacht hand, "I WAITED AND WAITED ON THE DOCK FOR YOU TO SHOW UP. FINALLY ROWED OVER TO THE BLANCHARDS' AND HITCHED A RIDE WITH THE CAPTAIN. NONE OF THE REST WAS COMING, SO HE WAS GLAD OF MY COMPANY."

"I got to get home to see that Red Sox game on the t.v., George," said a Native, overhearing, a not difficult accomplishment. "Got a stop or two to make first, but I'll give you a ride back in to the Cape."

"NO SENSE RUSHING; THEY WON'T WIN," old George responded. "MY BOY'S PITCHING AGAINST 'EM. GLAD OF THE LIFT, THOUGH, BECAUSE THE CAPTAIN'S GOT TO GO TO THE DRUG STORE IN SOUTHWEST FOR SOMETHING AND I GOT TO GET BACK TO THE BOAT."

"I'll take you back in, George," Junior assured him. "Being gone yesterday, I'm behind with the Cape cottages. I'll have to go back to the house to change, but I'll be bound you could stand to drink a beer while you're waiting for me."

"Do you see that lady?" asked Elizabeth Lamb of Persis, who was looking about her with a troubled frown.

Persis shook her head. The Bungalow company exchanged their last Sunday civilities with their friends and acquaintances and got into the cars. Persis nestled against Sarah in the back seat of the Halsteads' car. "Mummy, there's something I want to tell you," she said.

"Just a minute, dear," answered her mother, who was involved in a discussion with Jane provoked by the sermon. "It is indefensible, Jane," she went on, "to maintain that money can make one what one is not."

"That is not what I said," Jane retorted. "I never said money can make you what you are not; I said it makes you what you are. Perhaps I should put it another way: the lack of money makes you what you are."

The argument continued. Persis sighed and rubbed her forehead. In the front seat, over the head of Elizabeth Lamb, Mrs. Worthington and Hill were discussing the virtues of the rector.

Persis felt trapped and confused by the talk. The car was hot from the sun, which had appeared before Gus' predicted time. Nausea began to rise in her throat.

"Mummy," she said pitifully, in a pause in both conversations. "Mummy, please listen to me."

The car fell silent. "What is the matter, Persis?" asked her grandmother. She put down the window on her side so that a breeze blew in.

Persis began to cry. "I don't want to tell you," she answered through sobs. "I'm afraid. I feel sick."

Elizabeth Lamb drew a deep breath. Turning to Mrs. Worthington, she said, "I'll tell you. Persis went over to Mrs. Parker's woods last night. She heard an argument. She thinks somebody hurt Mrs. Parker. I think someone should go over there and see that she's all right so Persis can stop worrying."

"There couldn't be anything wrong with Mrs. Parker," Hill was beginning, but his mother-in-law interrupted.

"Stop at the turn to her place, Hill," she said. "I'll drive us home and you just run up to her cottage and make sure. I have been noticing all morning how unwell Persis looks. It is best to settle her mind."

Mrs. Worthington drove her party back to The Bungalow. Church clothes had been doffed in preparation for a pleasant day on and in the water when Hill appeared at the kitchen door. He leaned against the door-jamb and watched Dora and Doreen, once more in the pink uniforms favoured by the former, beginning preparations for lunch.

"You may as well stop, Dora," he said. "We won't be eating till late today."

Mrs. Worthington, who was in the kitchen obtaining matches for the firing of her kiln, looked closely at him. "Why not?" she asked.

Hill was calm and expressionless. "Because," he answered, "Mrs. Parker is dead. Half inside the workshop door, with an ugly bruise on her forehead — more bruises than one, I would say. My guess is that they couldn't have been caused by a fall. I called the police. They're going to her place first, of course, and then they'll be coming over here, and to the Blanchards' and Gambels', too, I suppose.

"We'd better prepare the children. And, for God's sake, will somebody give me a drink?"

Chapter 19

ENTER THE INVESTIGATOR

The adult occupants of The Bungalow sat on the porch sipping sherry, their usual Sunday-after-church tipple. The beautiful scene below and before them, the sun glinting on the blue water and the white sails of an occasional yacht gliding past the mouth of the cove, served to cheer them somewhat.

The children were in the kitchen with Dora and Doreen, consuming warm gingerbread and milk. Dora's heart had been softened by the woeful Persis and she had volunteered to make her aunt's famous gingerbread, from a closely-guarded family recipe. Gus, who had applied his eye to the knothole in the wall of his great-aunt's bedroom that looked into the kitchen, had ascertained that one of the secret ingredients was vinegar, but several other strange substances, whose identity he could not discern, had also been tossed into the bowl. The secret recipe remained secret, but no less appreciated, by Gus and the little girls.

"How long do we wait, Hill?" Sarah asked. "What is happening? What did you do when you were over there?"

"I called the Southwest Harbor police. They're the nearest. They won't be over; this area isn't under their jurisdiction. They called, or maybe radioed, the Sheriff's Department in Ellsworth. The Sheriff's Department will notify a deputy sheriff down here. He'll come in, with an aide, to seal off the area."

"The whole Cape?" asked Miss Elbridge. "Or just Lettie Parker's place?"

"I really don't know. I imagine they'll seal off from below where the road branches out to the three roads going to her place, to the Blanchards' and to here."

"Then what?" asked Isabella.

"Well, I'm not an expert on Maine police procedure in homicide cases, but —"

"Homicide?" Mrs. Worthington interrupted. "Why do you say homicide?"

"Because," Hill answered patiently, "that's what it is, Elizabeth. She was no doubt killed, either intentionally or unintentionally. In either case, it is homicide."

"Well, you can't be sure, Hill," Sarah said, "and so you really mustn't speculate. I should think a lawyer would know that. Maybe something fell on her."

"Maybe an eagle dropped a rock on her, or a seagull a series of clams," agreed Hill. "I stand corrected, my learned opponent. Anyway, the deputy will notify the coroner — or maybe he's now called the medical examiner — in Bar Harbor to come over. The County Attorney must be present, I believe."

"Where does he come from?" asked Isabella.

"I think Bar Harbor; anyway —"

"Everybody seems to be from Bar Harbor," observed Isabella, with a tinge of sarcasm. "I hope the murderer was."

"Isabella," began Sarah, "you shouldn't say 'murderer' —"

"We know, we know, Sarah," Hill said forcefully. "Well, then, as I was trying to say, the Sheriff's Department will take pictures of the body and the scene and a special homicide investigator will come over and state troopers will be sent from Bucksport —"

"Oh, for heaven's sake," said Isabella. "Not that I'm not susceptible to state troopers — I do so love those uniforms, especially the hats — but can't you get to the gist of it: how long before they can remove the body, question us, and get it over with?"

"How can you, Isabella?" cried Sarah. "Talking about susceptibility at a time like this!"

"For God's sake," rejoined her sister. "Don't pretend you're mourning that miserable old wretch."

"Isabella, be quiet," said Mrs. Worthington. "Hill, go on."

"Well, I can't go on very far, not with any assurance, anyway. I believe that, under the new law, the body must stay here until an assistant attorney general arrives from Augusta. It's Sunday, and that might take several hours, at the very least. The body will be sent in a hearse to Bangor for an autopsy by a state pathologist.

"However, long before that, the first officer who arrived on the scene, the deputy sheriff, could be freed by the arrival of some of the others so that he could come over here to take our statements. Since, although I discovered the body, we know practically nothing, that won't take long."

"Well, but," Isabella said uneasily, "they might dredge up all sorts of things. In books, these investigators take forever." The rest of Hill's audience looked apprehensively at him.

He laughed, with a return to his usual sardonic manner. "Surely," he answered, "none of you are thinking that we're going to be grilled by a tough Los Angeles private eye the police find standing, by chance, on the Southwest Harbor town dock? Or that a little Belgian who uses his grey cells is visiting in Somesville and will descend on us and quiz away? Or that a distinguished member of the British nobility and his wife Harriet will come into Bar Harbor on a yacht today and volunteer to come over and Solve the Case?"

He laughed again and suddenly gesticulated out at the cove. Both Miss Elbridge and Jane, who were listening intently, jumped slightly before their heads turned to follow his pointing finger. "Or," he went on, "that the henchman of a fat man with a taste for high cuisine is suddenly going to row around the point there, come ashore and demand some of our mussels, which his boss has heard are the tastiest on the whole coast, and stay and catch the culprit for us? Really, ladies, you read too much fiction!"

"You're right, of course," Sarah said, though with a glance at the point around which an Archie might appear. "We won't be held up very long, since none of us knows anything about it. Gus and I want to sail over to Bartlett's in *Coacher*."

"Forgive me," Jane said quietly, "but what about Persis?"

The company fell silent.

"Yes, of course, Jane." Mrs. Worthington said finally. "Well, this may be difficult."

"Hill," Emily asked, after a while, "you didn't leave the — Lettie, that is — alone, did you? I thought one wasn't supposed to do that. Did the police, I mean the deputy sheriff, get there so quickly? You weren't over there very long."

"Oh," Hill answered, "I forgot to explain that. Junior and George Paine drove in just as I was telephoning. I asked permission to leave and the police said it was okay as long as I told the two of them to remain, both together, by the body, and touch nothing.

"I suppose I might have stayed, too, probably should have, but I wanted to prepare you. It was a young, new policeman by his voice. I hope he doesn't get chewed out for telling me I could go."

There was the sound of a car door being shut by the garage. Hill leaped up and peered from the edge of the porch.

"Here he is," he said. "June came over with him. It's Buzzie Higgins. Those damned dogs are snapping at him. Oh, Lord."

"Buzzie Higgins?" asked Miss Elbridge. "Oh, dear. I heard Junior being very unpleasant to him about our missing weathervane when he came down last week."

"Well," said Hill, "he is suspected of being light-fingered. They say, and this may be merely one of the typical Island rumours, that he has some relative who is a fence, in Bangor. More things disappear from the cottages and camps in this area than can be laid at the Proutys' doorstep. They say —"

"Hill," said Sarah sharply, "you mustn't. That is slander."

"Oh, God, Sarah, you're right, of course, but must you —"

"Hush, Hill."

Mrs. Worthington rose and spoke rapidly and firmly: "Both of you hush. Not only have I known Buzzie Higgins since he was a child, not only am I a fairly good judge of character, but Varner Prouty has assured me that Buzzie is absolutely honest.

"Oh, yes," she continued, to surprised looks, "I often meet Varner, in my walks, and he tells me many things. When a Prouty has a good word to say for a law officer, one may be sure that the officer is completely straight. Be quiet; here he is."

Buzzie Higgins, who appeared on the porch with Junior behind him grasping the dogs, was a tall, thin, sandy-haired young man, most unimpressive to the viewer. His pale eyes behind wire-rimmed spectacles blinked nervously. He wore khaki work clothes to which he had added a red and black plaid hunting shirt, worn as a jacket for warmth, although the sun was now high and the day almost hot. On the wool shirt was pinned his official badge.

He greeted Mrs. Worthington respectfully and nodded pleasantly to the rest of the company.

"Junior and I were talking about that weathervane, coming down here from Mrs. Parker's," he said mildly. "I'm still working on it, Mrs. Worthington. As I told him before, and more'n once," he added with a touch of asperity and a sharp glance at Junior.

Junior received the glance with some composure. "Dora's got no pressure in the kitchen sink, Hill," he said. "I'd better go start the pump. The latch on the pump-house needs fixing, too. Buzzie has to question me again, he says, but he can do it here after he talks to you all. He figures I won't make a run for it, I guess, till he piles up some evidence against me. Buzzie's good at evidence." He then returned Buzzie's sharp glance.

"Well, you go fix the latch before somebody steals the pump, Junior," rejoined Buzzie. "I'll see you and Dora and Doreen later."

"Now, then, Mrs. Worthington," he said, turning deferentially to her, "I guess it's just you folks here I need to talk to. No sense bothering the kids."

Sarah drew a deep breath of relief. Her mother began to assume a demeanor that could only be described as one of Well-Bred Bostonian Lady Preparing to Do Her Duty. Hill forestalled her.

"Actually, Buzzie," he said, "my little girl, Persis, was over in Mrs. Parker's woods last night and heard something. We'd better have her tell you first and then you can ask the rest of us what you have to ask. Where would you like to sit? And would you like some sherry?"

Buzzie agreed to this proposal, refusing the sherry, and seated himself on the porch steps, producing a small black notebook and a pencil. Persis was summoned and came out followed by Elizabeth Lamb and Gus, the latter still clutching a healthy-sized piece of gingerbread.

"Now, tell me what you saw last night, please, Persis," said Buzzie.

"I didn't really see anything," responded Persis, "but I'll tell you what I heard."

She very calmly related her story, omitting mention of her debauch with the martini pitcher. Elizabeth Lamb nodded approval.

Buzzie turned to her. "And where were you when all this was going on?"

"Well, we really don't know when it happened. Persis told you she got all mixed up. We were both very tired from climbing a mountain, as she said. The first time she went over was after we ate some supper. Maybe that was around quarter of seven; I don't know. I looked at my watch when we started to eat and it was six-thirty. Maybe it was seven when she went. I was playing cards with Gus and then helping him check his boat while she was out. She doesn't like to play cards so that's why she took a walk.

"She was gone a long time because we didn't go into the party until she came back, and then it was getting near eight o'clock, I think. I *think* because I'm sure we weren't there long before we left and it was eight o'clock then. I remember because of something Persis said to her mother."

Sarah blushed.

Isabella looked severely at Elizabeth Lamb. "You were there quite a long time before eight. Time flies when you're having fun."

Buzzie frowned at Isabella. He finished noting down what Elizabeth Lamb had said, read it over and frowned even harder at his notebook.

"What time was the second time she went over there, then?" he asked of Elizabeth Lamb, whom he seemed to hold in some regard.

"I don't know. After eight o'clock, is all I know. We were both sick from something, something we ate at the party," said Elizabeth Lamb unblushingly.

"After we felt better," she went on, "Persis went into the woods for a walk again and I went back to the party to carry things in for Dora when it was time for dinner. Then I went out and talked to Junior awhile and then Persis came back and pretty soon we went to bed. That's when she told me what she'd heard."

Hill stirred. "Buzzie, you aren't supposed to take hearsay. You're supposed to ask Persis directly."

"Well, I know, Hill," said Buzzie, somewhat abashed. "I'm not really sure as I'm supposed to question little kids at all. It never came up before."

"Buzzie, look here," Mrs. Worthington said helpfully. "Since Persis agrees with what the other child says, why don't you put it down as if she'd said it herself?"

"Mother," sighed Sarah, "you are not supposed to tell the deputy what to do."

"Actually," Isabella said, "we don't have to say anything at all to him, do we, Hill? I mean, we aren't charged with anything, or are we?"

"No, ma'am," Buzzie answered for Hill. "You don't have to answer anything. If you don't, though, I'm supposed to put that down. I think I am, anyway," he said uncertainly.

"I know I can put down my own observations," he added with more assurance, "and that would be one of them. Now, I'm also supposed to ask you if all of you intend to stay in this here vicinity for a while?"

"Of course," Mrs. Worthington answered firmly. Jane looked uncertain.

"I may not," she said timidly. "I received a letter yesterday from my husband. I may have to join him." She looked appealingly at Mrs. Worthington, who regarded her with astonishment. Her other listeners looked almost as surprised.

"Well, I can't order you to stay. One thing you have to do, ma'am," Buzzie said turning to Isabella, "is agree to be fingerprinted. The Sheriff has to do that. He's in Blue Hill working on an accident over there and may not get here till tomorrow morning, or maybe tonight."

"Good," Isabella said surprisingly. "I always wanted to be fingerprinted." She put her small white hand on Buzzie's plaid sleeve. "I have lovely fingers for it, don't you think so, officer?" Buzzie blushed and moved slightly away.

"Why fingerprints?" Hill asked. "Was the weapon left lying around? There *was* a weapon, wouldn't you say, Buzzie?"

"I'd say as how there'd have to be, Hill," agreed Buzzie. "Don't see how she could of got in that shape without somebody bashed her. Was a lot of internal bleeding into the brain, the doctor thinks.

"'Course," he went on, "we don't know that the bashing killed her. Lying there in that heavy rain — half in it, should say, she might've died of exposure. Won't know for sure till after the autopsy in Bangor."

"What does the medical examiner think was used to hit her?" asked Hill.

"Well, there weren't nothing laying around. There's a lot of things in their rightful places in that workshop, though, that might've done it. They'll go over them all for prints. Junior says he doesn't think there's any of them missing, and George Paine, who spent a lot of time there fussing over things he repaired for the yacht, says the same. It was some kind of heavy, blunt thing, the doctor says, that she was hit with. Iron or wood, most likely."

"Not the famous 'blunt instrument'!" exclaimed Jane, in a low voice, to Hill. "I've encountered it in a hundred mystery novels. I never thought I'd actually be hearing about it, in the flesh."

"Wasn't in the flesh, ma'am," said Buzzie, overhearing and not quite understanding. "No traces of anything on the lady's skin, no foreign substances, as they put it. Just the bruising, with some blood from scrapes, like. Just abrasions, the doctor said, but the forehead was caved right in."

"Are you supposed to be telling us all this?" asked Sarah, who seemed to be setting herself up as a model of rectitude. "Aren't we suspects?"

"Well, Mrs. Halstead, I wouldn't say suspects, but everybody who was anywhere around the Parker place last night, that we know of, has to be questioned. Anybody might've done it. Most likely one of them hippies that hike along the Cape Road did it.

"We just have to eliminate, so to speak. I'll ask you who was over here last night between six in the evening and one in the morning; hope you'll be so kind as to tell me, with no offence taken."

"A number of people were," Hill answered. "We were having a sort of party, a social gathering, as I imagine the Boston papers will describe it, if it ever gets to them. But why do you limit the time of the crime — or, yes, Sarah, the happening — to between six and one?"

"Well, old George Paine saw the car drive up a little before six. He was out in the yacht tender, fishing from a hand line, and happened to be where he had a good view of the car coming into the parking space. So many trees around, it's lucky he had drifted to where he was, right in a spot where he could see through 'em. She'd been over to her place in Bar Harbor and left there, we found out from her daughter, about five-fifteen, so that jibes."

"If I were her daughter," murmured Isabella, "I'd have done her in long since, when I was eight or so. A black thread across the top of the stairs is highly effective."

Her mother looked severely at Isabella. "But it may not have been Mrs. Parker in the car," she observed to Buzzie. "Perhaps she was already dead and the murderer was driving."

"Mother," said Sarah, "you mustn't say murderer."

"Shut up, Sarah," Hill said. "Mrs. Worthington may be right, though, Buzzie. Perhaps Mrs. Parker wasn't driving."

"Well, George saw her on the porch of the house a few minutes later."

"Why didn't you say that, then, in the first place?" cried Isabella.

"I just hate all this," poor Buzzie answered. "I get all confused. Wisht I'd stayed a full-time fisherman, like my father. What I'm trying to get at, Hill, is that Mrs. Parker was seen alive at six and when her body was found, it was soaking wet. The part of it that was outside the workshop door was, that is."

"So?" asked Hill.

"So, there was no rain after one o'clock in the morning. I know that for a fact, myself. It started raining around eleven-thirty, a downpour it was, and stopped completely by one. Didn't rain one drop after that, not one. I've got several verifications of that from several fellers who were on duty last night.

"So, if she was killed — died, that is," amended Buzzie, looking at Sarah, "after one o'clock, her body wouldn't have been found soaked through."

"Dew couldn't have done it?" Mrs. Worthington asked.

"No, mam, not to that extent. So I have to find out what everybody in the neighborhood was doing between those hours and what they might've noticed. Could I ask this young man?" He turned to Gus, whose mastication of gingerbread was proceeding at a rate of unusual slowness, due to the fascination of watching on-the-spot detection at work.

"I guess I'm through with the little girls," went on Buzzie. "I have a sort of idea what they did. Sort of," he repeated gloomily.

"I was around here all evening," responded Gus. "Didn't see or hear anything you'd be interested in, I guess. I played cards with young Elizabeth, here, and then we went down to the shore to look at my boat. The tide was at its highest and I was worried she might drag her new mooring. The fog had lifted enough so that we could see she was okay without having to row out. Didn't see or hear anything unusual.

"Then," Gus went on, "I was in my room for a while listening to my radio. Then I went into the living room and talked to the guests and read a book. Then I had dinner — had had just a snack with the kids before. That's all I did, except go to bed. Didn't go off the place."

"Well, that's clear and simple," said Buzzie, much relieved at such a coherent story and making rapid shorthand notes. "You kids can go do whatever you're planning. Make sand-castles, or something. Look, Hill, would you list everybody's name here, on this piece of paper? Full names, that is, so's I know who I've been talking to and who I still have to look up."

The children left the porch, Gus repeating "sand-castles" to himself with some scorn. Buzzie continued writing for some time. Elizabeth Lamb and Persis collected some of Persis' fashion dolls from the bunkroom and sat themselves down in the juniper bushes, out of sight but not out of hearing.

"Here's the list, Buzzie, with all the guests' addresses," Hill said. "Well, now, what can we tell you? The party started around six-thirty, when the first guests came. We all, we who are here, got back from Seal Harbor around six. I'm sure none of us left the place between six and six-thirty."

"Who was the guests?" asked Buzzie, licking his pencil.

"My cousin, General Alison and his secretary, a Miss Thurna Thorssen," replied Mrs. Worthington. "They came over from Northeast Harbor, but they arrived first. Then there were the Blanchards and their daughter; their son did not come. My cousin Henry Wasgatt and his wife Betsy. Two other couples had intended to come but did not appear."

"What time did the party break up?"

"Around ten-thirty," said Hill. "Maybe a little later. Since I didn't know there was going to be a murder — be quiet, please, Sarah — I wasn't noticing time, especially."

"Daddy," wailed Persis from the bushes, "I can't get my dolly's head to stay on."

"Go find June," Hill answered. "I'm busy, Persis." Persis and Elizabeth Lamb departed for the pump-house.

"Well, now," said Buzzie, "where was I? So you were all here together, in the living room, I guess it would have been, from six-thirty till it all broke up? Of course," he added delicately, "some people might have left the room for a minute or two, I guess, but no longer than that?"

"No," said Isabella.

"Yes," said her mother.

Buzzie looked from one to the other. "Hill?" he asked, worriedly.

"Well, let's see," pondered Hill. "Isabella came in some time after the party started. She also left for a while later on to pick up the painting things she'd left down by the shore."

"Thank you so much, Hill, darling," Isabella said sweetly. "Come to think of it, he's quite right, officer."

"What were the times?" asked Buzzie. "Do you know how long you were gone, about?"

"I haven't the slightest idea," Isabella replied coldly.

"Do you usually leave a party your mother's giving?" asked Buzzie.

"What does that mean?" Isabella was shrill, as a Victorian fishwife might have shrilled. "Sometimes I do. I'm what is known as a free spirit, officer." She produced her little bubbling laugh.

"Well, but, mam, why was you late getting to it?"

"I was painting a picture and before that I was washing and dressing. Some of us do dress for an occasion, you know," replied Isabella, her eyes fixed on Buzzie's plaid shirt.

Buzzie coloured slightly but persisted. "Didn't notice nothing when you were out? Where'd you go, exactly?"

"Down to the rocks above the water to get my things. I had left them there a little before, meaning to go back and complete my sketch."

"Finish the picture?"

"No, as a matter of fact, I didn't."

"Could I see what you've done on it?"

"I can't seem to find it," Isabella answered vaguely. "Probably one of the children made off with it. Things seem to tend to disappear around here lately — within the last day or so."

Evidently Persis and Elizabeth Lamb had returned to the juniper bushes. They rustled indignantly. Mrs. Worthington tightened her lips and regarded her daughter sternly. Isabella gurgled prettily and smiled out at the cove.

"And you didn't see anything out of the way going on, nor hear anything?"

Isabella sighed. "No-I-did-not," she answered, enunciating clearly. "All-I-saw-was-a-lot-of-fog."

"And you don't know how long you were out?"

"No-I-don't."

Since no one could, or would, enlighten Buzzie on that point, he pressed on.

"Mrs. Halstead?"

"I went down to the Duck Cove Store for a ham," Sarah replied. "My mother had more or less suddenly decided to ask the guests, who had been invited for drinks, to stay and have dinner. It was a spur-of-the-moment thing. I don't know how long I was gone. I helped Dottie out for quite a while; she was very busy and all by herself."

"We asked Mrs. Dorr if she'd noticed any strangers coming into her store," Buzzie said. "She hadn't, but she did mention your helping her. Said it was only for about ten minutes, though."

"She is mistaken," Sarah said sharply. "There were a great many customers milling about and she must be confused about the times. It was for a half-hour at the very least. Maybe longer."

"Could you name any of the people you waited on?"

"I don't think so — oh, yes, there was Mrs. Chatterley, who has the cottage out on Oak Point. She was very unpleasant because she had ordered a pot of beans to be reserved for her, and we couldn't find it. We must have sold it. I don't remember anyone else; there was a good deal of confusion and I was slow and Dottie was racing about, harassed, and people were impatient. It was a horrible half-hour." She added firmly: "Actually, it was probably longer than a half-hour."

"You can't remember even a couple more people who came into the store, if 'twas that long a time?" asked Buzzie, with a tinge of disbelief in his tone.

Sarah drew herself up. "Since it seems to be so important to you to verify what I have told you, I'll try to think." She suddenly dropped her head and chewed nervously on her thumb. Hill and her mother looked surprised at Sarah's lapse from her usual firm demeanor.

There was a silence. The others looked at Sarah and Sarah gnawed her cuticle and looked up at the porch ceiling. Isabella smiled happily and Hill got up to reach for the package of cigarettes on the table beside her, managing a smart kick to her ankle as he passed her.

"Ow," cried Isabella. "Damn you, Hill. You get more clumsy by the day. You probably killed the old lady by courteously opening a door for her in your mawkish fashion and knocking something down on top of her head."

Jane giggled nervously.

"Hush, Issa," Sarah said. "I do remember, Mr. Higgins, that old Mrs. Calley came in, the one with the idiot boy, or man, as I suppose he is now. He tried to bite open a can of sardines."

Jane giggled again. Mrs. Worthington poured more sherry for her: "Jane, drink that and compose yourself."

"I'd say the Calley feller would be hard to overlook," observed Buzzie seriously. "I woulda thought you'd remember him right off. We'll ask his mother about what time they was in to the store."

"If you must," Sarah answered coolly.

"Anybody else, Mrs. Halstead?"

"I just can't think. Oh, yes, there was that German man, the one who has the cottage down behind the church. He bought the last loaf of Dottie's bread and insisted on a certain kind of cheese, for an omelet. Really, I am glad I don't have to make my living running a store. People are so demanding."

"German man?"

"From Connecticut, I think. The one who goes about gathering mushrooms. One is always coming across him in every likely field or wood. He's been down here."

"Last night?" asked Buzzie quickly.

"Of course not last night. He was in the store last night, I'm trying to tell you. He was the last person I waited on, come to think of it."

"I can't seem to place who you mean," puzzled Buzzie.

"You certainly ought to," Hill said solemnly. "You had to rush him over to the hospital at least three times last summer to have his stomach pumped."

"Oh, yeah, him," answered Buzzie, with a sigh. "Well, that's more clear, then. We'll just place the time you left the store by asking him when he was in, about."

Sarah maintained an indignant silence. Hill laughed. "He'll probably be okay for questioning since he evidently had bread and a cheese omelette for supper last night, instead of toadstools. I wonder why an old bachelor like him doesn't give up all these fancy little things and just open a can of beans?"

"Beans, beans, good for the heart; the more you eat, the more you —"

"Hush, Issa," interrupted Sarah sharply. "I really seem to say that more than any other phrase all summer," she muttered to herself. "Well, officer, that's all I remember."

"Did you see anybody at all around when you drove out or back in here to the Cape?"

"No, I did not, and I am tired of this inquisition. I merely went out to buy a ham and stayed to help a woman who was worked to death, and I resent having to defend myself," Sarah answered, her voice rising. Mrs. Worthington poured her some sherry.

"Well," Buzzie said calmly, "I've written down what you said. You, Hill?"

"I was here, in the living room or kitchen, before witnesses, the whole time. So was my mother-in-law. Neither of us left for even a minute. Good training shows, you know," said Hill, poker-faced.

Buzzie blushed but wrote stolidly. "And you didn't notice anything strange, or hear anything?"

"Only George Paine's boat radio. We heard that all right."

"It wasn't turned off for a while?"

"Now, what does that mean?" asked Isabella. "Do you really think he'd turn it off if he were going to row ashore to whack Mrs. Parker over the head? This is getting ridiculous."

"No," Hill answered, "it wasn't turned off. It was still on when I went to bed. But I must agree with my sister-in-law; what could it mean if it had been turned off?"

"Well, might be a clue," Buzzie answered absently. Isabella snorted with regal delicacy.

"As for me, officer, I was indoors the whole time and neither saw or heard anything unusual," said Mrs. Worthington clearly. "That is my statement."

Buzzie was writing. "Yes, mam. Guess that's plain. This young lady, now. Mrs. Lamb, is it?"

"I never left the party at all," Jane stated.

"Oh, yes, indeed you did," corrected Isabella. "You came back with my mother's sweater, I noticed, and I remember she remarked how long you'd taken to bring it."

"Oh, yes," said Jane, miserably. She sighed. "I had to go up to the studio for the sweater."

"Had trouble finding it, did you?"

"Y-Yes, I did."

Mrs. Worthington looked at Jane quickly, opened her mouth, closed it, and held her peace.

"Where did you finally find it?" Buzzie asked.

"To tell the truth, I found it right away. What I did was, what I did —"

"Yes, ma'am?" Buzzie prompted, as Jane subsided, blushing.

"Well, I was cold and very stiff, so I ran a tub of hot water in

Mrs. Worthington's bathroom in the studio and just sat in it for a few minutes."

Mrs. Worthington laughed gaily. Isabella frowned.

"Took a bath?" asked Buzzie incredulously. "With company here, and all?"

"Yes, I did!"

The juniper bushes rustled again. A clear little voice, showing signs of the power it was already rehearsing to command drawing rooms, press conferences, and the halls of Congress in twenty years, emanated from them. "Officer," it said, "please remember that my mother does not lie. My father and his family do, but my mother does not."

Buzzie pursed up his mouth and wrote in his notebook. "Now, Mrs. Lamb, I know you haven't been here long. Junior told me that you and your little girl arrived just day 'fore yesterday, so you aren't familiar with the place, but did you notice anything that seemed suspicious, that made you uneasy, like, last night? Sometimes a stranger takes more heed of his surroundings, see what I mean?"

"No," Jane answered. "I couldn't say that I did. Earlier in the evening, before I came down to the party, I thought there was someone in the woods, but it was only the caretaker."

"Junior?" asked Buzzie sharply. "When was this?"

"Why, exactly at 6:20. I had just looked at my watch to see how long I'd taken to dress. He was only coming back from the store with a box of supper for the children; he knew everybody would be busy with party preparations and that the children would be hungry. He was walking along the edge of the woods —" Jane glanced nervously towards the screened door to the living room where a pink uniform might have been lurking — "because, ah, because he wanted to surprise them."

Buzzie looked thoughtful and a shade triumphant.

"No, Buzzie, it won't wash," said Hill. "He didn't leave for the store until after we all got back here, around six. That's not long enough."

"No, I guess not." Buzzie showed his disappointment. "Dottie said he got there about ten after six, picked up some stuff quick and set straight out again. She says he often makes up little treats for these kids. Oh, well."

"If she can be that exact about Junior, I don't see why she can't remember how long I was there," said Sarah bitingly.

"Not so feudal after all, are they?" murmured Hill.

"Well, but, Mrs. Halstead," said Buzzie tactfully, "she wasn't so busy then. Said if she'd knowd how many people was going to pour in later, she'd have asked Junior to stay. As it was, she told him she could handle the store herself, if Peyton didn't get back. Anyway," Buzzie added, avoiding Sarah's eye, "she is exact as to the time you were there, like I told you, mam. Says it was about ten minutes. But no need to get upset; we realize that in the rush she could've lost track of time."

"I hope you do!" Sarah chewed her thumb again.

Buzzie wrote. "Anybody else leave the party?" he asked.

"My cousin General Alison did," Mrs. Worthington answered. "He went over to the Blanchards' cottage to call his place in Northeast Harbor. Something about a guest who was expected to arrive before he could get home."

"Take long?"

"Fairly long. We started to eat dinner without him."

"Phone here not working?"

"We don't have a telephone," Hill answered. "Mrs. Worthington prefers not to have one up here."

Buzzie looked incredulous but wrote away. "Well," he said, "I'll have to speak to General Alison direct, later on. Maybe he saw something helpful whiles he was out. Now, that all?"

"Well," Hill said, "both Captain Blanchard and his wife left, at different times, to go up to their cottage to look for their son, who was supposed to have come with them but who had disappeared. I gather he hides around the place at times."

"Oh, yes," Buzzie said gloomily. "Horatio. I'm supposed to go over there next. Don't relish the prospect, I don't mind telling you. That young feller called up the Sheriff onct and said he'd recognized me as a kidnapper wanted in Louisiana. Swore up and down he had a secret communication from some source he couldn't divulge to the effect that I was a desperate criminal."

"Now, how long was the Captain and his wife gone, would you say?"

"Oh, lord," Hill said. "We really weren't noticing. People were drinking and eating and talking and nobody was expecting to have to account for himself or anyone else. And it does seem to me now that not everybody was here at the same time. What I mean is, somebody was always absent, come to think of it."

"Yes," agreed Buzzie, "from all I can make out, there was a lot of coming and going. Place was more like a Greyhound Bus Station than a cocktail party, far's I can see. However, you and Mrs. Worthington and the Wasgatts, who run the movie over to Bar Harbor, don't they, and General Alison's secretary and this lady here" — he nodded at Emily, "Miss Elbridge, stayed put. That right?"

"Yes," Emily agreed. "That's right."

"My sister left to lie down for a little while, I believe," said Mrs. Worthington.

"Oh, yes, I forgot that," Emily said. "So I did."

Buzzie sighed. "How long was you gone, Miss Elbridge?"

"I really couldn't say. I didn't feel very well and I simply went to my room and slept for a while. I don't think it was for very long."

"It was something my aunt ate, officer," put in Isabella with a smile. "Probably the canapés. Whatever it was, it must have had the same effect on the two children."

The juniper bushes rustled again.

"Did you see or hear anything you might think was strange, like, Miss Elbridge?" asked Buzzie.

"No, not a thing."

Buzzie sighed again. "Now, nobody really saw anything out of order or remembers when anybody left, nor for how long? Is that right?"

"That's quite correct." Mrs. Worthington was firm. "No one was gone long enough for us to think it unusual. Isn't that so, Hill?"

"Yes, Elizabeth."

"Well, mam, you'd be surprised how little time it takes to bash a lady's skull in," rejoined Buzzie. "But I'll have to leave it as 'tis for the time being. Now I'll go talk to Dora and her daughter, and Junior. I thank you for your patience. We'll keep you posted.

"Oh, one more thing, Mrs. Worthington. I guess I ought to ask you if there was anybody that had any grudge, like, against the deceased, that you know of?"

"We all admired her," Mrs. Worthington answered, and Isabella, Emily and Sarah joined in chorus to murmur, "Indeed we did." Hill and Jane smiled.

"Then that's that," pronounced Buzzie, and left for the region of cookery.

Dora greeted him mildly. "Seen any weathervanes lying around anywheres lately?" she inquired.

Buzzie reddened. "All I come for is to ask you your whereabouts yesterday evening," he said with dignity.

"I was right here, hanging over this cussed stove, the hull time, till Peyton took Doreen and me home, a little 'fore eleven," she answered.

"Peyton stay in the cottage all evening?"

Dora smiled grimly. "He did."

"Doreen, too?"

"That's right, Doreen, too."

"Doreen went over to the Blanchards' to get ice, Dora," called Elizabeth Lamb helpfully. She and Persis were now sitting on the back porch in front of their bunkroom door, dressing and undressing Persis' dolls. "You were taking on about how long she'd been gone. I heard Peyton say that."

Dora, in her turn, reddened. "So I was. Don't think she really took so long, though. I was just fussing because this blamed stove was acting up. Always does when there's a downdraft."

"Where's Doreen now? I'm supposed to talk to her direct."

"She just left to go down to the spring to get some water for lunch. Miss Elbridge looked like she had a headache, this morning, and I know how she likes that spring water when she don't feel so good.

"We might," she added bitterly, glaring at Buzzie and then at the kitchen clock, "get around to serving lunch around five-thirty or so, or whenever you decide we don't know nothing criminal and get your behind out of here."

Junior came into the kitchen with an armful of split wood for the stove.

"You, Junior?" asked Buzzie.

"Me, what? You asked me over to the Parker place all my actions and observations about last night, and you asked me again coming down here. You wouldn't be hoping to trip me up, now, would you, Buzzie?"

"Well, I got to ask you official and write it down. What was you doing yesterday from six p.m. on?"

Junior sighed. "Before or after I murdered Mrs. Parker?"

"Now, that's enough of that, June. I have to ask."

"Like I said, I was right here in the afternoon doing some things for Mrs. Worthington after I'd got back from a run to Boston for her. Went down to the store around six or so to pick up some stuff for the kids' supper. Wasn't gone more than fifteen-twenty minutes. You can ask Mrs. Lamb when I got back; she saw me. I picked up a nail in my truck tire on my way back so I changed the tire — the Captain saw me at it when he came over to the party. Then I was fixing to get myself something to eat —"

"Junior" wailed Persis from the porch. "My dolly's head came off again."

"Persis," said Junior patiently, "you'll have to find your father. I'm busy right now. Where was I — I hope you're writing this down, Buzzie, because I ain't aiming to go over it a fourth time — well, then I talked to Elizabeth Lamb a while till Persis came along, then I went home and fell into bed. No witnesses to that, I'm sorry to say. I don't know what time it was, didn't think to look at the clock and my watch'd quit on me last week. Hill'll verify that."

"Mrs. Young, next door to your place, saw you pull in a little afore nine and didn't hear you go out again. Guess she watches everything in the neighborhood pretty close. Now, did you see anything funny going on last night?"

"Always knew that busy-body'd be good for something, some day. And, no, I didn't see anything funny going on, except there was a lot of happy drinking and talk going on down here, but that's usual, at a party."

"How long'd it take you to change your tire?"

"God, Buzzie, I didn't have a watch. All I know is, the Captain saw me doing it when he came, and I was still at it when he come back the second time, had run up to his place for a while. You'd better ask him."

"What'd you think of Mrs. Parker?"

"What I think of any good-paying employer. Enough so that I wouldn't have hiked four miles back in here after I got home and four miles back, shape I was in by the time I drove my truck into my dooryard, to kill her. Now she's dead, her daughter'll close the place up, doubtless, and I've lost some income. And speaking of losing, I wish you'd come up with that lost weathervane Mrs. Worthington set so much store on, and quit trying to figure out a reason why I should exert myself to dispose of a woman who was a source of money to me."

Dora laughed appreciatively. "Nor do I have a reason, 'cept I really couldn't stand those arrogant ways of hers, when it came right down to it. And she was nothing to me, so suppose you stop looking for a reason and look for that weathervane."

Buzzie tightened his lips. "When it comes right down to it, as you say, in a case like this," he informed her, "we always ask 'who benefits?'"

"What's that mean?" Dora asked.

"Well, who hated her so much it interfered with his sleep, or who did she have something on, or who was left money in her will, for instance," Buzzie answered.

"Her will?" Persis asked, coming in with her doll in two pieces. "Dora, I heard you this morning saying something about Doreen and Mrs. Parker's will. Junior, Daddy says he's going out of his mind and would you please fix my doll again?"

"Oh," said Buzzie, "Mrs. Parker's will? What about it, Dora?"

Dora was red and indignant. "Why, nothing," she said. "Persis, you skin right out of here with that doll. I'm trying to cook your lunch. Scat, now, and you, too, June. If you please," she added more politely.

Persis, Junior, and the doll left for the porch, Junior smiling slightly at Dora's obvious discomfiture. Buzzie regarded Dora carefully. His eyes by no means blinked as nervously as they had when he first arrived at The Bungalow. He looked sharp and alert and nobody's fool.

He snapped his notebook shut and made for the door. "Well, enjoy your lunch," he said politely. "We'll do a little checking with Miss Parker and the lawyer and so forth. We haven't got the autopsy report yet, either. We'll probably find it was all some kind of fool accident and nobody was up to anything. I better get back to Mrs. Parker's now. I'll be back later to take Doreen's statement. She might've noticed something on her way to or from the Blanchards' cottage."

Dora blanched. "No need to talk to Doreen. She didn't notice nothing and you shouldn't worry young girls with all your fool goings-on about murderers and reasons and wills."

"Well, we'll see," said Buzzie. He paused on the back porch to survey Junior and Dora, turning to include in his gaze Isabella and Sarah, who had come around the corner of The Bungalow.

"Let's hope," he added, "that we'll soon have some idea of which way the wind blows. Even without a weathervane. Good afternoon."

Chapter 20

TIME AND TIDE

Lunch had not been a success. Dora had essayed a cheese soufflé that had been burned as well as flat. She had made another, smaller one for herself and Doreen and Junior —with whom she was maintaining a kind of nervous truce, evidently under the "all in the same boat" theory — and that had been a duplicate of the soufflé served to the family a little earlier.

Junior had then endangered the truce by asking for baking soda. Dora had angrily replied that he couldn't be already suffering indigestion from such a small amount of perfectly good food, "just a mite brown," especially as he was still engaged in eating it.

"Wasn't thinking of indigestion — yet," Junior answered. "I read somewhere that baking soda takes away the burned taste."

"That's for using in burned pots, Junior," Doreen corrected him. "It doesn't work on food." She looked reflective, thinking, no doubt, of the soufflés to be eaten in Paris.

"Well, it's good, anyway," said Junior, manfully swallowing the cinders. He then asked for milk instead of coffee, "to put the fires out," and Dora became completely enraged. He was told to leave the premises without dessert and went with calm resignation, having viewed the dessert, which was a black-and-brown apple tart.

He could now be seen on the float, working strips of oakum between the leaking floorboards of the *Hilda* and chewing on licorice slipped to him by Miss Elbridge, for whom a British doctor had years ago prescribed it for unhappy stomachs. She always provided herself with a goodly amount of it for her weeks at The Bungalow.

The family lingered over lunch, which had been eaten at the table on the porch.

"That deputy sheriff appears to be an intelligent young man," Emily observed.

"He can't be very intelligent," Isabella replied, "or he'd be down checking on Varner's movements. I should think that the imminent fear of being ousted from one's home would be a reasonable motive for murder. He was very upset when I was with him the other night. And we saw Varner skulking around with a hatchet, yesterday, on the way in from tea. He ducked when he saw the car, but Gus noticed him in the bushes off the road when we drove past. The side of a hatchet head is a blunt instrument."

"How would Buzzie know about the house?" Sarah asked.

"He does, though," Hill replied. "Evidently Varner was well into his cups at the beer parlor in Southwest Harbor yesterday afternoon and railing about Mrs. Parker. This got to Buzzie's ears — you can't breathe on this island without someone's counting your rate of respiration and reporting on it — and he went to Varner's place with June, before they came down here this morning."

"What happened?"

"Minnie said Varner wasn't there, June told me. He's sure Varner was, though, hiding. All the kids were behind Minnie in the doorway, clutching on to her skirt and looking back and forth from Buzzie to the chicken house, scared to death."

"Poor Varner," said Miss Elbridge. "If he did it, you'll have to help him, Hill."

"Of course, and I think I could get him off, though hitting an old lady with a hatchet is a pretty serious proposition. We — and he'd have to have a local lawyer — could prove he was drunk to the point of not being responsible, which would be true enough, assuming he did do it."

"What would he get?" Isabella asked.

"Hard to say. Maybe ten or twenty years for manslaughter, with pardon possible before that, I suppose. I'm not an expert on Maine law, as I told you."

"Poor Varner," said Miss Elbridge again.

"All of you have got Varner in jail and requesting pardon for killing a woman we don't even know was murdered," Sarah objected.

"For God's sake, Sarah," answered Hill. "Did you ever know a woman more likely to be murdered? She made enemies all her life.

"Just look at the few of us here, on this porch. You think she poisoned your dogs. Some really fanatical dog-lovers, — and you are a dog-lover, not to the extent of doing murder, of course, — would kill because of that. Isabella, well, Isabella disliked her —"

"Never mind me, just now, Hill," Isabella said, looking at her mother.

"Emily," went on Hill, "nursed a resentment of many years' standing, unless I am much mistaken."

Miss Elbridge looked bleakly across the cove at the *Hesperus*. "I did," she admitted, "but it is most unlikely I'd kill her over it, after all this time."

"Elizabeth and I," pursued Hill, "had no motives, at least none that anyone's noticed, and no opportunity. We never left the party, let alone the place."

"Dora and Doreen had a motive," Isabella pointed out. "Money. Five thousand dollars for Doreen."

"Right. Dora's out, having been occupied all evening burning up the comestibles, but Doreen took four times as long as she should have getting the ice from the Blanchards."

"The Blanchards!" cried Sarah. "What about them? Horatio was their motive and they both left here for long periods."

Her audience thought this over and agreed, refraining from pointing out to Sarah that if there had been no murder, the Blanchards were guiltless.

"Horatio, himself," suggested Mrs. Worthington. "The boy is undoubtedly mad and might kill anyone, or so I am beginning to fear. And Emily tells me Lettie Parker was responsible for having his diving helmet taken away from him. If he did kill her, it would almost be a mercy; I mean by that that he would be confined where he could do no more harm, and yet he would not be hurt, and it would be, in the end, a great relief to poor Kitty and Fred."

Hill was not so certain that poor Kitty and Fred would be relieved at Horatio's possible confinement, but let it pass.

"Junior?" Sarah asked, getting into the swing of the thing. "Perhaps Mrs. Parker was going to leave him something, as well as Doreen. I think he's rather fond of money."

"Who isn't?" rejoined Hill. "But there'll be no legacy for him. Mrs. Parker was extremely put out when she found her husband had left Junior several thousand in his will, since he had worked for them only a year or less when Wilson died. She told June he needn't expect a cent from her.

"Junior was rather witty about it; told me he guessed there was no sense poisoning her Saturday grocery order on the weekends she was here, though he'd often been tempted, for the reason that it seldom consisted of more than one lamb chop, three eggs, and two tomatoes and had to be delivered."

"What about Lem?" Isabella asked. "His career was blighted by her niggardliness. He was gone from The Bungalow for much longer than a telephone call should have taken."

"Not Lem," Miss Elbridge objected. "It's just not possible."

"No," Hill agreed. "He wouldn't kill her; he'd do a Bungalow Rhyme about her. Funny thing, come to think of it, that he never has. I don't know," he added thoughtfully, "that that's a healthy sign."

"Oh, for heaven's sake," Sarah said. "We're taking this much too much to heart."

"A woman is dead, Sarah," her mother reminded her. "A neighbor of long standing. It should be taken to heart."

"What about Jane, Hill?" asked Isabella.

"Don't know," Hill replied, regarding Jane gravely. "Maybe Mrs. Parker injured her, at some time, or her father or husband. Or maybe she is really Wilson Parker's natural daughter, and his wife wouldn't give her any rights. Could be. People often aren't who they say they are."

Jane looked, predictably, terrified. "I never heard of her until I got here," she said quietly.

"That's just what you would say," pointed out Isabella. "What about that alcoholic iceberg of Lem's, Hill? She could have known or been related to old Nosy — old Mrs. Parker."

"She never got ten feet away from Lem or the liquor supply," replied Hill. "Look, this is getting out of hand and we're scaring the children."

"Persis," said Sarah, "I want you to go to the bunkroom and

write a little essay on the hermit thrushes you've been watching. Grandmother is looking forward to reading about them."

Persis obediently rose to her feet. "I will later, Mummy. I think now I'll get the binoculars and maybe lie in the meadow. Junior says he thinks there's a larks' nest there. I don't feel very good and I just want to lie down."

She lingered a moment, twisting a lock of hair around her finger. "Mummy?" she said wistfully.

"What is it, dear?"

"Mummy, is God close by?"

"Well, of course," Mrs. Worthington answered for Sarah. "He watches over us."

"Well, but can you talk to Him?"

"When we pray," said Sarah.

"Well, that lady —" Persis lowered her voice and spoke into her mother's ear, "— that lady talked to Him. She said, like, 'Oh, no, no, God, please don't.' I think He hurt her and I'm afraid He will hurt me."

Sarah put her arm around Persis and gently led her off the porch. She walked along the path talking earnestly to the child.

Elizabeth Lamb remained quietly near her mother, playing with the dolls and holding low, intimate conversations with them. Sarah returned and sat down, watching her.

Gus appeared. "Ma, I'm going down to the store on my bike," he announced. "Captain Blanchard gave me a dollar last night. I thought I'd go get some ice cream. Lunch wasn't very good," he added regretfully.

"I don't know, Gus," Sarah said, frowning worriedly. "Hill, do you think he should?"

"There are troopers all over the place, Sarah," Hill answered. "Just stick to the road, Gus, and don't go crawling through the underbrush playing boy detective. It's entirely possible that Mrs. Parker was killed by some vagrant on a drug trip, or something like that, so just stay in the open."

"Poor Lettie," said Mrs. Worthington. "Do you think that is at all possible, Hill?"

"Anything's possible," Hill answered, "as lawyers and clergymen and doctors find every day. I really think, though, that she was killed because of what she was, not as a result of a happenstance of fate.

"The more you know about murder, the more you realize that

persons who get murdered are not very meritorious people. Good people are haplessly killed, of course, and nowadays more often than ever before, but, in a normal situation, those versed in murder will tell you, having been killed is not a fact that leads them to regard the person killed as one who was of high moral values, filled with loving kindness and good will. Someone who gets himself murdered is usually a pretty despicable character, vindictive and self-satisfied."

"I don't understand that at all," replied Isabella, "and if I did, I don't think I'd believe it. It sounds like something you cribbed from a book on crime and got wrong."

"It does seem, Hill," said Sarah, "to be a very harsh judgment. I don't think it's true, either, necessarily. And we still don't really know that Mrs. Parker was murdered."

"Dora," shouted Hill, "more coffee, please. Sarah, I implore you not to use that line again. We'll soon know, I hope. Is that Buster Griffin out there pulling his traps on a Sunday?"

Dora appeared with the coffeepot.

"No, he's not, Hill," she said. "Don't you start any more rumours; they's enough floating around this island already. Sunday lobstering's illegal in the summer and you know it and Buster knows it."

"What's he doing, I heard him at church inviting a bunch of his in-laws to a lobster bake out on Bar Island. He keeps a supply of them — lobsters, not in-laws, that is — in a car tied to a buoy in our cove, for when he gets a taste for them. Safer here than most places, with those Proutys rampaging around."

She poured coffee and glanced over to the Parker dock, where several figures were embarking in rowboats.

"They're going out to question George, looks like," she went on. "That'll be a treat. We'll hear the hollering clear over to here. Hope they've got more sense than that Buzzie Higgins. He has a nerve, talking to me the way he did. What he'd ought to do is go around looking for clues down-cellar and up-attic, as my poor old mother used to say. I said —"

"Dora," interrupted Miss Elbridge loudly, "would you make me a piece of plain toast, quite dark? It's very good for the stomach and mine feels a little upset."

Dora immediately took umbrage. "Don't know as why you should feel any such way, Miss Elbridge. My food's plain but wholesome. Finest cook on the backside, I'm known as, now that my poor aunt's in her grave. She cooked summer after summer for the Comforts, who owned Elk Island and had upwards of twenty guests to a weekend —"

"— who, after dying of indigestion, are all of them buried down-cellar and up-attic," finished Hill. "I really think I am going to go bananas. Dora, please make the toast for Miss Elbridge."

"Well!" exclaimed Dora. "I never expected any such talk from you, Hill. I'm only a cook, I know, and you're a smart Boston lawyer, but smart Boston lawyers don't know everything. I was going to tell you something you don't know, but now I see as how I'm not supposed to speak around here."

"Dora, please don't say any more just now," Mrs. Worthington requested gently. "I really don't think any of us feel up to a wrangle. Just make the toast."

Dora immediately left the porch, shutting the screen door sedately behind her, disappointing the company, which had, to a man, stiffened in expectation of the slam it had anticipated. As soon as the door closed, however, she burst into loud, effective sobs which accompanied her all the way to the kitchen.

Isabella rose, muttering under her breath, and went to stand beside one of the upright square posts on the edge of the porch, which supported its shingled roof. She absently reached up and struck the camel's bell hanging under the eaves.

"Issa, don't," said Sarah. "You know we ring that only when guests come by sea."

"Oh, for God's sake, Sarah. It was hardly a criminal act." She yawned. "I'm going down to lie on the rocks around the point. Without my bathing suit. You don't object, Ma*ma?*"

"No one's expected," Mrs. Worthington answered, "and I'm sure Junior's innured. Take a towel, though, Isabella, in case someone drops in or Buzzie comes back."

The rest of the occupants of the porch sat drinking their coffee and thinking their own thoughts.

"Had you ever considered a little flower garden here, Elizabeth?" inquired Miss Elbridge of her sister. "Just so we could have something for the table? I get bored with bunchberry and Indian paintbrush and daisies."

"I think Junior has enough to do putting in the vegetable garden," Mrs. Worthington replied. "If the children would plant a flower garden and take care of it, perhaps we might have a small one.

"I do think, though," she continued, "that a cultivated garden is redundant at a Maine summer place. The native ferns and grasses and wildflowers are so lovely, and such a refreshing change for us. I think the earth itself has more sweetness and fragrance in Maine than anywhere else in the world."

"Cousin Tom used to say that," Emily agreed. "That was when he was married to Amelia and used to relieve himself just outside the door of the cottage, claiming the earth was so sweet it destroyed any scent."

"Ha, I'll bet he doesn't say that nowadays!" Hill said explosively, with a loss of his accustomed calm. He had been quietly sitting and simmering since Dora had called him a "smart Boston lawyer."

"Tom's place in Northeast is so expensively overplanted with everything from catnip to orchids that one piss would cost him fifty dollars in damage. At least. If his wife ever permits him even to unzip his pants outdoors, which she wouldn't. Poor old Tom. I wonder that she even gives him enough leeway to come over here for church some Sundays. Probably that's when her lover calls."

"Hill, really," said Sarah reprovingly, glancing at Elizabeth Lamb. "Look, Elizabeth Lamb, there's a plane coming in over the cove."

"It's a sea-plane," said Elizabeth Lamb. "Why is he flying so low?"

"It's a Sea and Shore Fisheries official looking for lobstermen pulling their traps on Sunday," Hill informed her. "He's a kind of game warden. If a lobsterman's breaking the Sunday law, the warden can swoop down and land beside him and write him out a summons."

"Well, Buster's clear, according to Dora," Sarah remarked, "and I haven't seen any other lobster boats out today. What is Buster Griffin's real name, Hill? I always wondered."

"It's Orient," Hill answered.

"Orient?" inquired Jane. "I can't believe it."

"Oh, there are a number of wonderfully unusual first names among the Natives. Just naming men, there's Harvard, Royal, Gardiner, Oral, Bion, Sabin, Aldine, Millard, Fairfield, Alvah — oh, I could go on for minutes. And these are only names whose owners I know personally. There must be dozens more."

"Buster Griffin's father's name isn't Orient," mused Mrs. Worthington. "I know him. His name is George and he has a son younger than Buster who is named Everett but always called Junior. I can't think why."

"Yes, why should that be?" Jane wondered.

"Can't imagine," Hill answered, "but, also, Junior Noyes — that's our Junior, Jane — had a father named Robert and yet June was christened Gardiner and nick-named Junior. Perhaps it is just that a boy child is referred to as Junior even though he isn't one, strictly speaking."

"I'm glad of it, in our Junior's case," Mrs. Worthington said. "I would have to pronounce 'Gardiner' each time I wanted to address him. 'Junior,' or, as you often say, Hill, 'June', is quick and succinct."

"One of the things I found most annoying about poor Lettie Parker," announced Miss Elbridge, "is — I mean was — her habit of conserving her energy by addressing her friends or employees only by the first syllable of their names. She always refused to use nicknames, but would use nothing but the first part of Christian names.

"Perhaps it made things easier in her rope factory, but she did it everywhere. She might refer to me as 'Emily' but she always addressed me as 'Em.' Isabella was "Izz"; Sarah, 'Sare.' Junior's father, who used to work for her, was 'Rahb,' in that dreadful South Boston accent of hers. Peyton was 'Peyt' —"

Hill began to grit his teeth, wondering if it would be Dora's histrionics or Miss Elbridge's repetition of points already made that would finally drive him off the deep end. Mrs. Worthington came to his rescue. "Yes, Emily, yes," she interrupted. "It was all very annoying; still, I am sure we all wish she were still alive to continue the annoyance. I must say," she added, "that Lettie never called me anything but Elizabeth."

"I suppose," her sister answered, "even she balked at calling anyone 'Eee' and 'Liz' would have been a nickname, which she abhorred. Oh, dear, may she rest in peace, with all her dislikes and unpleasantness and idiosyncracies."

"Your idiosyncracy, dear Hill," observed Isabella, who had wandered back, draped in a towel of inadequate size, "is to ignore your rather low first name of Frank and to use your middle name, which is certainly more posh. At least, they didn't name you Frank Earnest Halstead. Frank and earnest, so dreadfully tacky and certainly inappropriate for one so devious as you." She smiled prettily and wafted herself away to her sunning.

"Speaking of nicknames, Jane," said Hill, successfully rising above his sister-in-law's interposition, "the island is just as resourceful in them as in unusual first names."

"Just the island," Jane questioned, "or all of Maine?"

"Probably the whole State of Maine, but I'm familiar with only the island. I know fellows who are called Shad, Chubba, Toss, Mukka —"

"Hill, stop it!" ordered Sarah. "You are driveling on and on and I feel much too tense to endure another monologue about names."

"Well, I'm trying to divert our thoughts from the activity across the cove. What should I talk about, now that I may not go through my repertoire of island names and nicknames? Names of boats? Can't think of any at the moment."

"Names of boats?" asked Elizabeth Lamb.

"How about names we always wanted to call boats? I always wanted a fast sloop called *Helangone*. How about you, Sarah?"

Sarah yawned and deigned no reply.

Dora appeared on the porch, carrying a large tray. Her eyes were red but her face showed the effects of a recent washing with cold water and her voice was determinedly cheerful.

"Here's your toast, Miss Elbridge," she announced. "Made you a pot of tea to go with it. Made a fresh pot of coffee, too. Hill, I threw together one of them frying-pan coffeecakes you're so fond of. Here you are.

"Doreen and me's going to take a walk pretty soon," she went on, composedly. "It'll calm our nerves, sort of. We'll be back in good time to fix supper, even though we're supposed to have the evening off. I figure we'd best stay here through supper, too. No telling if some of them police might come over and then you'd need a buffer, so to speak, to hold 'em at bay whilst you eat."

She withdrew, leaving surprise and gratification rampant on The Bungalow porch.

"Good heavens," said Miss Elbridge. "Is she turning over a new leaf or has she suddenly got religion? It all amounts to the same thing, I suppose. Well, let us be thankful."

"Maybe," Mrs. Worthington said, "she did the murder and is afraid of leaving the scene of the crime. A habit of murderers, in fiction, at least. Isn't that so, Jane?"

Jane agreed, laughing. Sarah seemed on the verge of reproving her mother's and Jane's levity. Hill quickly distributed plates of the frying-pan coffeecake.

"Another of Dora's aunt's secret recipes or 'receipts,' as she called them. That old lady was a genius. This bakes in a skillet in minutes and is pure ambrosia. With a piece of it in one hand and a cup of fresh coffee in the other, I'm happy as a clam at high tide.'

Elizabeth Lamb was also delighting in Dora's offering. "It's awfully good," she said. "It tastes French. What was that you said about being happy, Mr. Halstead?"

"Oh, that I feel happy as a clam at high tide, now that my sweet tooth is appeased."

Elizabeth Lamb giggled. "What does that mean?"

"Sweet tooth?"

"No, I know what that means. I mean about clams."

"Well, it's a picturesque seacoast figure of speech. A clam at high tide is happy because the water over the clam flats is as deep as it'll ever get and a digger can't operate. Not for six hours or so, when it's low again. The expression wouldn't apply at the moment — to clams, not to me — because it's just an hour, about, after dead low tide and the mud can be walked on and the clams dug up. So right now *they're* worrying, but *I'm* happy. Have another piece of cake."

Elizabeth Lamb gladly accepted and, the cake in one hand and a doll in the other, made her way down to the shore. She picked up a pastel crayon, wet and soggy, from a niche in the rocks and stored it carefully away in her special pocket for treasures. As she passed under the big beech tree high on the bluff above her, she waved at Persis, who had abandoned her meadow site and was perched, with her binoculars and bird book, on one of the beech's lower branches.

Gus' Bullseye lay placidly at her mooring about a dozen feet out from the line of rocks rimming the shore. The tide was still so low and the water in the cove so transparent that the mushroom anchor holding her could clearly be seen on the bottom, about four feet below her hull.

Junior was rowing the *Hilda* away from the float, standing up in his favoured rowing stance and peering at the floorboards as he rowed to see if the oakum with which he had mended her seams was holding.

He hailed Elizabeth Lamb. "There's a little place where I can land right over there," he said. "See where I'm pointing? Scramble over and I'll beach her and pick you up. Might's well have company. Think I'll be rowing a good hour before she swells properly."

Elizabeth Lamb did as directed and caught the *Hilda*'s prow as Junior headed her in. "My sneakers are getting all muddy," she complained.

"Take 'em off. Only way to walk on a clam flat is in bare feet or hip boots."

"Is this a clam flat?"

"Sure. It's little, but it's the best place for clams on the cove, except right off the reef, maybe. See that little hole — there's a squirt of water coming up. Mr. Clam is sitting right beneath it. We might dig a few. Got my hod and rake right here in the boat."

"Is this where you were looking for clams last night?"

"Why — yes."

"You couldn't have been, Junior. It was high tide just before I saw you, well, an hour or so before. All this was deep in water. Gus and I were down here looking at *Coacher*. Last night the water was way up to those rocks above my head, where Isabella was. She left a paint stick there."

"Why did you lie, Junior?"

Junior laughed easily. "Now, then, I didn't exactly lie."

"You did, too. You couldn't have been clamming. I didn't know about tides and clam-flats last night or I would have realized it. Why were you washing off the clam hod in the shower?"

Junior's eyes were no longer merry and crinkled, as she had so often seen them. They were an opaque slate-blue. He moved a step toward her. His hand reached back into the skiff and then stopped. The hand holding the heavy hod dropped to his side.

"Come on, Elizabeth Lamb," he said calmly. "Let's take a row out to the reef and dig for clams there. At low tide there's millions of 'em. Even at high tide you can get some. That's where I was last night, come to think of it."

"That's not so, Junior, and you know it. You weren't digging clams at all and I'm going to tell Mr. Halstead and that sheriff man you lied to me."

Junior's face hardened into decision. He glanced quickly up at the rocks above them. No one was in sight. They could not, he knew, be seen from The Bungalow porch. Only the branches of the beech tree showed a little movement, as from a stirring of wind. He raised the hod and swung it.

In the second before it touched her, Elizabeth Lamb realized what had been the cause of the bruises on Mrs. Parker's forehead. She ducked quickly to one side, but she was not fast enough. She avoided the full force of the blow but she felt the heavy wood crack into the side of her skull. The blue, shining world turned dizzy and black and she fell to the ground, half in the water.

Junior picked her up and deposited her in the bottom of the skiff, tossing the hod and rake on top of her. He pushed off the *Hilda,* leaped in and began to row for the mouth of the cove.

Persis, in the beech tree, cried out. Sarah had been standing on the steps of the porch, something nagging at the back of her mind: Emily's tale of how Mrs. Parker abbreviated proper names, how she would have undoubtedly shortened Junior's correct name of 'Gardiner' to 'Gahd,' as she would have pronounced it, and how Persis had recounted the dead woman's cry as being something like 'No, no, God, don't'. She saw Junior, seemingly alone, rowing out in the *Hilda* as Persis screamed, "Mummy, Mummy, Junior hit Elizabeth Lamb with the clam hod and threw her down into the boat."

While the others on the porch were merely showing astonishment at Persis' cry, Sarah had covered half the distance to the float. A few seconds later and she was in Mrs. Worthington's punt, had cast off the line that secured the punt to the float and was with shaking fingers positioning the oar-locks and preparing to row in pursuit.

"Thank the Lord," she thought of her craft, "that no one had pulled her on to the float and that the oars were left in her. But, even so, I'm going to be too late. He's had too much start; he'll row around behind the reef and throw that child into the water and hold her head under and we can never prove a thing. But why is he doing this? Why? God, he must have gone mad."

Sarah glanced desperately over her shoulder as she rowed. The *Hilda* was almost at the reef. She could discern no one but Junior in the skiff. For a moment she wondered if Persis had accurately observed what had happened. She wavered in her stroke, briefly, then thought of Mrs. Parker and rowed desperately, heavy with the knowledge that if Junior's intentions were as she had surmised, she would not be in time.

And then it happened. She had been aware, in a far corner of her consciousness, of a sound that almost drowned the pulsing of the blood in her ears and the throbbing of her heart. The sound increased to a roar, and she looked up to see the Gambels' Boston Whaler careening across the cove, wildly out of control. Two of the Gambel children were in it, jerking at the throttle and shouting, half in fright and half in excitement.

It seemed certain to Sarah that they were heading straight at her. She dropped the oars and waved her arms, screaming, "Watch out, watch out, turn to port!" The older child, eyes widening in terror, heard. He jerked his head to look toward her, letting go the wheel. The other boy seized it and frantically tugged it towards the right, not the left. The boat turned sharply, now on a collision course with the skiff rowed by Junior.

The Whaler hit the *Hilda* squarely amidships. There was a splintering of ancient wood and a cry from Junior. Almost before the sound of the impact came to the stunned watchers on The Bungalow porch, Sarah had kicked off her shoes, pulled off her skirt, and dived.

Thirty strong strokes carried her to the small figure floating face down amidst the fragments of the skiff. The two little boys in the motorboat, who were now wailing loudly, had managed to turn off the ignition, and the Whaler wallowed some yards away. Sarah grasped Elizabeth Lamb and pulled her through the water for the short distance that lay between them and the rocks of Dead Man's Reef.

There was no sight, nor sound, nor sign of Junior Noyes.

Chapter 21

SOLILOQUY, WITH ANSWER, BY CANDLELIGHT

It was almost nine o'clock at night. Sarah, playing Russian Bank with Isabella in a candle-lit corner of the studio, thought wearily that it seemed to be, at the very least, about three in the morning. Her eyes blurred and she rubbed them, dropping her cards. Isabella exclaimed impatiently, glanced over at her mother, and held her tongue.

Sarah played mechanically, her mind going over and over the events of the memorable day not yet over. It ran through her mind like the screenplay of a silent movie. She remembered all the actions but could not be sure of the words spoken by anyone after she had rowed out in the punt and rescued Elizabeth Lamb.

When she had gained the reef, she had lain panting for a few minutes, the child beside her, still held protectively in her arms. Elizabeth Lamb was unconscious but, after she had coughed and spat up some water, her breathing had become regular and almost normal. Sarah had struggled to her feet to look for what help might be on the way.

The two Gambel children were engaged in trying to gain mastery of their boat. They succeeded in starting the engine and, without another look at Sarah or at the wreckage of the *Hilda* floating all about them, had roared away over the water to parental analysis and protection.

Hill was visible on The Bungalow float. Sarah had realized that he was preparing to swim to *Coacher,* the only craft now available to him. She also realized that, with the wind so light, his progress to the reef might be disastrously slow. She lay an anxious hand on Elizabeth Lamb's forehead. It was cold, and the child's limbs were trembling.

There was no sign of anyone at the Parker dock or on the *Hesperus,* but there was activity at the Blanchards' float. Horatio and his father were in the rowboat that had an outboard motor on its stern. Captain Blanchard neatly cast off as Horatio pulled the starting cord of the engine, which instantly caught. They reached the reef in but a few minutes. Horatio lept nimbly out, competently picked up Elizabeth Lamb and carried her carefully to the boat, in which his father was standing, clutching on to one of the jutting rocks of the reef. Then Horatio helped Sarah aboard. His eyes were no more sane than usual, and he was whispering to himself in an unnerving manner, but his actions were sure and gentle.

"Perhaps," Sarah had thought, dazedly, "the mad should be let loose in moments of catastrophe. Perhaps that's what lunatics were designed for. It seems to make sense."

The movie *The King of Hearts* flashed into her mind, seeming to corroborate her theory and then her tired mind lost the tenor of her thoughts, which had seemed to her — in the same fashion in which like enlightenment comes sometimes to conversationalists at cocktail parties after their fourth drink — to have in them the essence of all the wisdom in the universe, if only the thinker could express them before he forgot them.

The boat had arrived at The Bungalow float.

The next few hours were a jumbled mass of confusion in Sarah's mind. Somehow, as Elizabeth Lamb was being carried by Hill up the slope from the water, Lem had appeared. With him had been the enigmatic Miss Thorssen, massive and pale in light green jersey and slacks, and Lem's house guest, a mild-looking middle-aged man, all of them out for a Sunday drive.

Behind them strode a young state trooper, angrily berating Lem for a number of things including driving past a police car when ordered to stop. Lem was paying not the faintest attention to him. With a quick martial grasp of the situation, he had ordered Elizabeth Lamb wrapped in blankets and had then instructed the trooper to radio for help. This had come within minutes, in the form of the medical examiner who, as the officer had intelligently realized, was still at the Parker cottage.

This functionary, in Sunday golfing outfit, calm and competent despite his game's interruption by homicide-already-engineered and now apparent-homicide-just-prevented, had examined Elizabeth Lamb and given the opinion that, despite the head blow, there was no concussion. He insisted that the child be taken to Bar Harbor for an X-ray of the skull, but was outnumbered by Jane and Mrs. Worthington, who pointed out that Elizabeth Lamb was now attaining intermittent periods of sleepy consciousness during which she was fearful, and, since they trusted his judgment as to the lack of concussion, maintained that she should stay at The Bungalow where she would be in familiar surroundings.

Since the child was now out of shock, and had only a slight rise in temperature, the doctor permitted himself to be won over, but only after making sure that it was understood that if there were the slightest change in condition, an ambulance should be obtained at once. He promised to return very early the following morning, as a surety, and left, murmuring to himself that if the country were run by old ladies from Boston, it would be hell to live in but not quite such a mess as it was at present.

Lem and his followers had also taken themselves off, Lem loudly congratulating himself, as representative of The Corps, for having been the instrument who, by having defied mere civil authority, had been the means of having a doctor almost instantly produced at a dwelling so misguided as to have no telephone connection with what passed for civilization. Mrs. Worthington, still shaken, had heard him out in apologetic silence.

The house guest had listened to his host and been quiet, apparently stunned by the events a Sunday drive on Mount Desert Island could produce for his diversion. Miss Thorssen, impassive as ever, had, while Lem's speech was going on, efficiently consumed the greater part of a bottle of rum left on the kitchen table by Dora, who had got it out to flavour a chocolate pudding. Captain Blanchard, meek under Lem's robust observations to the effect that the Navy might bring in the casualties but it took The Corps to save their lives, had left in his boat with Horatio, the latter still whispering.

More police — Buzzie and a superior officer — had come, observed, and taken statements from Sarah and Persis. Elizabeth Lamb was able to whisper a few words to them. The Gambels' motorboat had been requisitioned, despite loud mention of "police brutality," and the cove and the adjoining waters and shores of the bay fruitlessly searched for any sign of Junior Noyes. Scuba divers had been summoned from the Coast Guard base in Southwest Harbor, and they, too, had searched.

Persis had told of Junior's hitting Elizabeth Lamb with the clam hod, and the intelligent Buzzie, sensing it had been the murder weapon, had directed the searchers to look for it, or any fragments that might have survived the crash of the boats.

Hill had had a conversation with Buzzie. Words of it drifted to Sarah, and she had questioned Hill. She was too tired to assimilate his answer, which had implied that anyone who thought about it would have seen Junior's motive, and he had possibly said something about the same gain. Or maybe it was pain. Sarah had been lying on her bed as Hill spoke, and had fallen asleep.

A quick supper of ham sandwiches and chocolate pudding, the latter slightly burned, had been eaten. Dora and Doreen had been taken home by Hill, Dora loudly observing that now a body could sleep at night, with murderers where they should be.

They had been reluctant to abandon their posts, and had consented to go home to bed only because, as they were assured by Mrs. Worthington, their services would be needed even earlier than usual in the morning, since the doctor was expected, and wouldn't it be nice if he could be given the treat of a real backside breakfast, cooked by the best cook on the backside, instead of the inferior meals that must be his portion over there in Bar Harbor?

Sometime later, Varner, alerted by the Native grapevine, had appeared with a collection of fresh herbs sent by Minnie. Isabella, using only a very few of her pretty Victorian mannerisms, had stewed them under his direction and Jane, surprisingly to Sarah, had consented that her child be persuaded to sip the brew. She had almost instantly become less feverish and now slept more quietly. At each time of awakening, a procedure the doctor had insisted on, she was still fearful but more clear in mind and relaxed in muscle.

"And now," thought Sarah, her reflections up to the present, "we can go to bed, some of us, at least, and I mean to be one of those who do."

Hill and Emily and the two Halstead children were in the main Bungalow, doing the supper dishes and setting the table for breakfast. Isabella and Sarah, Mrs. Worthington and Jane kept vigil in the studio. Elizabeth Lamb had been placed in the extra bed in her mother's bedroom. The door to this was open, and occasionally one of the watchers would move over to it to view the little figure lying in one of the Hansel and Gretel beds, candles burning brightly beside it.

Mrs. Worthington and Jane sat on the small red sofa in front of the Franklin fireplace in the center of the room. Jane's head was thrown back, resting on the top of the low sofa, and her eyes were closed. Mrs. Worthington sat calmly reading a volume of poetry by the light of the oil lamp on the table beside her. From time to time she gazed thoughtfully into the flames of the fire and patted Jane's hand, which lay lax on the cushion between them. Two of the three Dalmatians were stretched out near her; the third slept beside Sarah's chair.

The dogs lifted their heads at the sound of footsteps on the path outside. Isabella and Sarah also listened, then resumed their game as the footsteps passed, going down to the main building. Mrs. Worthington did not look up from her book, and Jane remained asleep.

There was the sound of loud voices from the main house as the visitor opened the kitchen door. Snatches of song could be heard. Sarah frowned in bewilderment. A door slammed, the sounds from the kitchen ceased, and quick footsteps came back up the path.

The studio door was thrown open. A tall, heavy-set, black-bearded man, brown of face, with hair so short it was merely a dark stubble, stood glaring at them. His eyes, behind tortoise-rimmed spectacles, were indignant as well as bleary and red. He wore, despite the warm June night, a British naval officer's duffel coat and he was burdened down with numberless canvas satchels slung carelessly about his large person. A Burberry was tossed over one shoulder.

The dog beside Sarah rose, growling. The man kicked it accurately and casually and it subsided.

The apparition spoke. "Jesus Chronicle Christ!" it exclaimed. "Have I come into some kind of looney-bin? There are cop cars all over the Cape road and some idiot in one of 'em had the effrontery to stop my taxi and ask me who I was. I soon settled him; reminded him of how we used to steal candy from Seth's store together. And in the kitchen here —" He broke off and seemed to choke, looking angrily about him.

He fixed his stare on Mrs. Worthington, who regarded him with a smile from under raised eyebrows. Fumbling in one of his many pouches, he produced a small wash-leather bag, which he tossed toward her. It landed on the sofa between her and Jane, who opened her eyes and gave a low cry of fright at the sight of the dark figure in the doorway.

"You can share that, Ma," said the intruder, "between you. Hello, sweet. We finally made a killing in that mine, as I wrote you, Ma. After three God-damned years. There's not one stone in there less than two carats. I carried 'em through customs in my raincoat pocket as we used to smuggle those liquor miniatures in from Bermuda when I was a kid."

He switched his look of fury to Sarah and Isabella, who were staring at him, open-mouthed. "Got another bag for you two," he announced, "somewhere. Not as good as those and you won't be satisfied, no doubt, but nothing to sneer at, either."

He turned back to Mrs. Worthington. "Are you aware," he asked, more calmly but still loudly, "of what is going on down in that kitchen? Emily and Hill are drunk as skunks and singing the worst French song I ever heard. They've got two little kids drunk, too, probably yours," he again glared at Sarah. "Some mother you must be.

"They're all of them slugging whiskey and warm milk, Ma," he went on, "and trying to tell me they just saw the ghost schooner sail out of the cove. They're so far gone they can barely enunciate. I think the d.t.'s have set in: how the hell could the caretaker have been lost at sea? And why, in the name of sweet Jesus, should they think somebody got murdered? I haven't slept for thirty-six hours and a bitch of a homecoming this —"

He fell silent as the old school-room clock on the wall struck nine. Elizabeth Lamb, fetching in a pink nightgown, eyes overly bright but face composed, stood in the little hall outside Jane's bedroom looking at him.

She spoke severely: "I'm a little child who must have rest," she asserted. "I heard them say so. I uncovered a murderer and was nearly killed. I need peace and quiet. Don't swear any more, please."

She made as if to go back to bed, halted, and looked over her shoulder at the figure in the studio doorway. She smiled sweetly at it and spoke again: "I'll see you tomorrow. I must say you're looking well. Good-night, Daddy," said Elizabeth Lamb Worthington.

THE DOCUMENTS
AFTER THE CURTAIN

Miss Emily Elbridge to Mrs. Henry Wasgatt:

Dearest Betsy,

We were all so very sorry to hear of your mother's serious illness. What a shame that you and Henry had to rush off to Oregon just at the beginning of your busy summer season! I do hope that young Sam and your employees can cope efficiently with the running of the theatre. I am sure that your and Henry's presence will give your mother's convalescence the impetus necessary to make complete recovery come in a much shorter time.

Yes, as you wrote, the newspaper accounts of our excitement here on the Cape must, indeed, have been confusing to you. We, right here on the scene, were hardly less confused for a number of hours. It barely seems possible that it is only a week since the dreadful events took place. Your letter arrived this morning and Elizabeth has asked me to answer it and give you the information you requested, as she and Hill are very busy trying to organize things so that she can get on with her summer's commissions and the writings she has promised to complete before the end of August.

Well, as you know, Mrs. Parker, our neighbor here on the cove, was brutally killed last Saturday night, actually during the time you and dear Henry and Lem and the rest of us were enjoying ourselves here at The Bungalow. It was our, and her, caretaker who did it. Perhaps you remember him — a tall, attractive young man whom the newspapers referred to by his correct name of Gardiner Noyes. We always called him Junior, or June.

I am afraid greed was at the bottom of it all. Mrs. Parker had a magnificent collection of wines and spirits in her husband's cellar beneath her cottage, and Junior had been selling off the contents, he and his partner Peyton Dorr. The latter is our Dora's brother, and they ran the local store. Evidently they had some arrangement with a man in Bangor who was connected with wealthy oenophiles in New York and Boston. All this has been corroborated by Peyton, who was questioned by the police because of his connection with Junior. The cellar was found to be almost depleted. I rather believe that they were also responsible for disappearances from cottages here, but I do not know if that has been admitted or proved.

Mrs. Parker had evidently discovered the condition of her wine cellar the night before her murder, the very night that, I am afraid, we here at The Bungalow were consuming one of the stolen bottles of champagne. Her lawyer received a letter from her written that night. I fear that Hill was the one who pointed out to Junior, who was over here with us for a while that evening, that Mrs. Parker was down in the cellar, where no one but Junior, who had found Mr. Parker's key, ever went. Hill saw the light, you see, from the cellar window. We observed Junior to be shaken and upset, but we put it down to concern over her safety. She was over seventy.

Junior had to leave at once, to go to Boston for Elizabeth; actually, Hill conducted him as far as Ellsworth to rent a car and, because of heavy fog, it took them hours to get there. Therefore, it was quite impossible for him to return and confront Mrs. Parker that night. He took the chance which, really, circumstances forced him to take: that she would make no move without talking to him. He may even have felt that he could charm her out of taking any action.

Junior stayed very close to our place next evening, although he was obviously very tired from his drive to Boston. When he did steal over to Mrs. Parker's, it must have been made plain to him that she would announce his thievery, and this would have ruined him. Persis heard an argument over there, but did not see who was speaking to Mrs. Parker. Sometime during the evening, little Elizabeth Lamb — more about her, later — observed him washing off his clam hod, with which he had felled Mrs. Parker. He carried it about with him often, using it to convey things, and, actually, a pot of beans that had been missing from the store was found thrown in the bushes, so we assume he had brought up the beans in the hod as a gift to Mrs. Parker, as a reinforcement to whatever explanation or apology he had intended to make. Possibly if it had not been in his hand, he would have thought twice about his action, but it was all too easy to strike out with it when anger and desperation overtook him. As far as the child can recall, she saw him cleaning the hod sometime between eight and nine o'clock. There must have been traces of blood on it.

He told little Elizabeth, who knew nothing of coastal habits, that he had been digging clams for his supper, and she thought no more of it until the next day, when a chance remark of Hill's informed her that, because of the tide, this would have been impossible. She questioned Junior, who — and, Betsy, this is unbelievable of the June we thought we knew — attempted to drown her. He was thwarted by Sarah's quick thinking and by a fortunate accident to his boat.

Peyton is going to make some restitution to Miss Parker, who is being very understanding and will not prosecute him. I am afraid that it is a great temptation to the local people to steal from those who are so much more fortunate in worldly goods. I, personally, am surprised that there is a preponderance of honesty on the island.

Junior's deceit brought him thousands of dollars. He, as the leading spirit, gained more than Peyton. I supposed he felt assured that Mrs. Parker would go to her grave without ever checking her cellar, since she had not been down there since her beloved husband died. It is a fact, Peyton says, that a few cases of one wine alone, a French still red champagne — of which I had never heard and which is very scarce — went at unbelievable prices to connoisseurs in New York and London.

I should interpose that Dora suspected, from their unwonted prosperity, what her brother and Junior were doing, and gave out with veiled hints, but was either too loyal or too unsure of her facts to speak plainly. After the murder, I think she half-suspected Junior, especially since Doreen had, from the kitchen porch, observed him acting what she termed "suspicious-like," and Dora was frightened of him to the unheard-of extent of actually giving him a meal in her kitchen. She says now she was about to tell Hill of Doreen's observation, but they got into one of their customary wrangles, and so she held her tongue.

But I have even more news: Jane Lamb, Elizabeth's secretary, is in fact her daughter-in-law and the little girl, Elizabeth Lamb, is her granddaughter and my grand-niece! Jane, a charming, quiet girl, as you noticed, has been bravely supporting herself and her child for several years while Peter was attempting to recoup his fortunes in a South African diamond mine — somewhat of a bootleg one, I fear, knowing both Peter's temperament and the South African government's restrictions. He has had wonderful success, Betsy, you will be glad, I know, to hear.

Jane's father was the painter Everett Lamb and she used her maiden name professionally. She had no intention of revealing her identity to us. After first refusing the assignment to Elizabeth, she accepted it because of the large salary but more, I think, because of some curiosity about Peter's mother, who had not been welcoming at the time of the marriage. All Peter's fault; he was always too impatient and proud to explain a situation clearly. I rather think that Elizabeth knew who Jane and the little girl were, if not at first, then after they appeared at The Bungalow, but she simply smiles and shakes her head when I question her.

My letter has been long, but I wanted to explain fully. Now, Betsy, do let us hear when you are returning. Elizabeth wants to have you and Henry over again, and we can but trust that there will be no untoward incident the next time you come!

Your affectionate cousin,
Emily Elbridge

Augustus W. Halstead to Mr. Clive Bolton-Smith of St. Paul's School:

Dear Mr. Bolton-Smith,

I have almost finished the make-up English assignment you gave me. This is to explain why I will be a little late in getting it to you. It is because of a kind of upset we have had here. It sort of threw me off my feed, not literally, of course, and it resulted in my having to do a lot more work around the place. An old lady across the cove got murdered, and my cousin, who is only eight, caught the murderer. And it wasn't the butler, either; it was the caretaker. Or the gardener, as my cousin called him.

He did it because he sold the old lady's wine and kept the money, and she found out. There was some non-sparkling French red champagne in it, which, I remember from that talk we had in your apartment about vintages, you said was so rare as to be almost legendary. As my cousin keeps saying: it was all because of champagne and a gardener. (Or Gardiner! That was his name.)

I hope she'll get into SPS when they let girls in, as you think they will. She knows a lot about food and wine, like you do. As you do, I mean. You'd enjoy her. I made the family the omelet you taught us how to make. They liked it. It wasn't burned like most of them are up here. As, I mean.

Well, I must get on with the assignment. My regards to Mrs. Bolton-Smith.

       Sincerely,
       Augustus Halstead

Mrs. F. Hill Halstead to Miss Penelope Greene, Greene Country Day School:

My dear Miss Greene:

I know how very late I am in requesting this, but I am writing in the hope that you may still have a vacancy in the class for eight-year-olds for this coming autumn. The little girl I have in mind is my niece, Elizabeth Lamb Worthington, my brother Peter's daughter. My mother joins with me in the hope that

Elizabeth Lamb may be in your school in September with her cousin Persis, who is very fond of her.

Elizabeth Lamb has been educated thus far in Europe, and is a most charming and interesting child, completely unspoiled and unsophisticated although extremely well-read and knowledgeable. I am sure you could find a place for her. She is very like my mother, and I see a definite resemblance in her appearance and manner to our forbears the Elbridges and Gerrys, with whom you also are connected, I believe.

Perhaps you could send the necessary forms to me here in Maine? Elizabeth Lamb will be living with us in Dedham for some time as her parents leave shortly for South Africa to attend to the sale of their mining interests there.

Yours very truly,
Sarah Worthington Halstead

F. Hill Halstead to Mrs. Wheeler Knox, of Secretaries Unlimited:

My dear Dodie,

Naturally, there would be a telephone strike on at the moment! Dodie, listen, you have got to find me a secretary for my mother-in-law, another one, I mean. I know you'll think I'm batty and I probably am by now; this last week of trying to help Mrs. Worthington with her monographs has sent me almost 'round the bend. I'm barely able to write this. It's one in the morning and I've been up since six a.m. Besides being a secretary, I'm also caretaker, boatman, messenger, gardener, and God-knows-what-all. You name it; I do it.

I'll start from the beginning. You know that Mrs. Lamb whom you sent us last week? Well, she's gone, gone with Peter to Boston to get things for their trip to Africa. She was going to join him there anyway, but he showed up here, unexpected by all except Mrs. Worthington. Dodie, why don't you check a little more carefully into who these people are you find jobs for? Well, cross that out; we're delighted she was who she is. What I mean to say, dammit, and I'm so tired I can't see straight, is that . . . .

To the Reader:

Having already drawn the curtain over the action of our drama, we now, with a thud, drop the fire curtain over Hill's incendiary letter to Dodie, before he writes something that will inflame her forever, and leave the rest of the document to your imagination. Our imagination, having brought us all to this point, is now preparing the way for the recounting of the further adventures of Elizabeth Lamb Worthington, of which there will be, no doubt, one or two, her temperament and resources being what they are.

B.J. Morison